CHANGE OF HEART

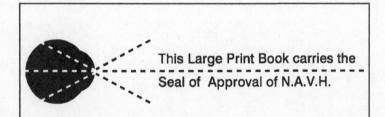

This Large Print Book carries the
Seal of Approval of N.A.V.H.

SISTERS AND FRIENDS

CHANGE OF HEART

RACHEL J. GOOD

THORNDIKE PRESS
A part of Gale, Cengage Learning

GALE
CENGAGE Learning·

Farmington Hills, Mich • San Francisco • New York • Waterville, Maine
Meriden, Conn • Mason, Ohio • Chicago

GALE
CENGAGE Learning®

LIBRARY OF CONGRESS CATALOGING-IN-PUBLICATION DATA

Names: Good, Rachel J., author.
Title: Change of heart / by Rachel J. Good.
Description: Large print edition. | Waterville, Maine : Thorndike Press, a part of
Gale, Cengage Learning, 2017. | Series: Sisters and friends ; #1 | Series:
Thorndike Press large print Christian fiction
Identifiers: LCCN 2017012259| ISBN 9781432839055 (hardcover) | ISBN 1432839055
(hardcover)
Subjects: LCSH: Women teachers—Fiction. | Sisters—Fiction | Amish—Fiction. |
Large type books. | BISAC: FICTION / Christian / Romance. | GSAFD: Christian
fiction. | Love stories.
Classification: LCC PS3607.O56285 C47 2017 | DDC 813/.6—dc23
LC record available at https://lccn.loc.gov/2017012259

Published in 2017 by arrangement with Charisma Media

Printed in Mexico
1 2 3 4 5 6 7 21 20 19 18 17

CHANGE OF HEART

CHAPTER ONE

"Please don't go out tonight," Lydia Esh begged her sixteen-year-old sister, but Emma knelt near the foot of her bed and lifted the mattress. Underneath she had concealed a makeup bag and *Englisch* clothes.

Gravel crunched in the neighboring driveway, and Lydia's stomach contracted. That must be Kyle. Emma's boyfriend always pulled in next door to avoid waking their parents.

Emma jumped to her feet, and her faceless doll, ragged and patched, tumbled to the floor. A flash of childhood sweetness crossed her face as she picked up the doll and gave it a quick hug before setting it gently on the Lone Star quilt.

Lydia missed *that* Emma, the one who still clung to her childhood toy at night, the one who once imitated everything her older sister did, the one who had bounced through the house smiling and hugging everyone. Emma had always been mischievous and exuberant — only her defiant, rebellious attitude was new.

Emma hurried to the window and waved, and the soft expression on her face disappeared. She tucked the *Englisch* clothes and makeup into a plastic bag and rushed from the bedroom. She hesitated on the landing, though, and peeked over the wooden railing to be sure their parents hadn't woken.

Lydia's sigh came from the depths of her soul. Why couldn't her sister stay home on Friday nights?

She glanced with longing at the simple wooden bed frames, hand-carved by their grandfather, sturdy enough to serve generation after generation. She wanted to curl up under the quilts that *Mamm* had lovingly pieced together of navy, slate blue, and burgundy diamonds, one for each of her daughters. The room, with its rag rug covering the gleaming wooden floors, provided a peaceful haven after the stresses of the week. Instead Lydia had to head out into a night fraught with clamor, confusion, and chaos. With a prayer for guidance, she tiptoed downstairs after Emma, past *Mamm* and *Dat*'s closed bedroom door on the first floor.

When Lydia caught up with her sister, she drew in a breath and forced out the words, "May I go with you?" Even the lye soap *Mamm* had used on her tongue when she'd lied as a youngster had never tasted as bitter as these words.

Emma whirled around. "Why?"

Because I love you and care what happens to you. Once Lydia could have said that, but this new hostile Emma took offense to any reminder of family bonds, so Lydia held her peace.

A fiery glare swiftly masked the hesitancy and uncertainty in Emma's eyes. "You're not going to make me feel guilty with those sad eyes and that hangdog expression."

Lydia forced her frown into a half-hearted smile. "I'd like to come with you." Perhaps *like* wasn't the right word. *Need* to come with you? Want to protect you? A twinge of guilt shot through Lydia. Was she lying by changing her words to cajole her sister?

With a scornful look at Lydia's sensible tie shoes, heavy wool stockings, and ankle-length dress, which were a carbon-copy of her own plain clothes, Emma grated out, "If you're so determined to come to these parties, you could at least bring some clothes to change into. Why don't you wear my pink skirt?"

9

Lydia bit back a gasp at the thought of appearing in public — or even private — in Emma's short skirt. "No, thank you. I prefer this." Lydia smoothed the triangular cape that covered the bodice of her dress.

"Suit yourself, but don't blame me if people stare at you and talk behind your back."

Better to be the subject of gossip for being too conservative than to appear half-naked in public. Although it was acceptable to dress like *Englischer*s during *Rumschpringe,* Lydia had had no desire to do so when she'd turned sixteen two years ago. The past few months since Emma reached sixteen had been the most trying days of Lydia's life. Trailing after Emma meant going to parties and dances. If only she could convince her sister that a change of heart would bring her the happiness she sought.

Emma flounced toward the door and snatched her coat from the coatrack. "Did it ever occur to you that Kyle and I might like to be alone sometimes?"

It certainly had. Why else would Lydia skip doing her lesson plans and drag her tired body downstairs to hang out in Yoder's barn, watching teenagers dance and kiss? Why subject herself to music so loud that it pounded inside her skull like a dull headache? These evenings were pure torture, but she had a duty to protect her sister.

Emma hadn't said no, so Lydia shrugged into her coat and followed her sister out the door and down the snow-dusted path to the silver sports car. The car's overhead light clicked on as Kyle leaned across the seat to open the door for Emma. Then he spied Lydia, and his face tightened.

"So you're joining us again tonight?" His tone was polite, but irritation seethed underneath. At her nod, Kyle pulled the seat forward so she could slide into the back seat.

Lydia smoothed the skirt of her deep blue dress down over her ankles and adjusted the bodice so the straight pins wouldn't prick her when she put on her seat belt. Then she slumped against the seat. All she wanted was to be home, tucked under her quilt, instead of burdened with all these worries for her sister.

Gravel spurted under the tires as Kyle zoomed out of the driveway. The car fish-tailed on a patch of ice, but he wrenched the wheel, tromped on the gas pedal, and they rocketed down the street.

Lydia clutched the armrest and mumbled prayers for everyone's safety as Kyle careened around curves at breakneck speed. Slush spurted from under the tires, and several times the car slid on patches of black ice. In the buggy Lydia enjoyed icicles glittering from trees and rooftops on these cold February days. At the buggy's leisurely pace she could immerse herself in the beauty of God's creation as twilight fell. In the car splashes of white whizzed by the window so quickly it made her dizzy.

After they whipped into a parking space at the mall and Kyle shut off the engine, Lydia exhaled slowly, trying to calm her frazzled nerves.

Emma reached for the door handle, but Kyle put a hand on her arm. "Wait a sec." He pulled his wallet from his back pocket and handed Emma some bills. "Why don't you buy yourself some killer heels for tonight?"

Instead of refusing his offer, Emma leaned over and gave him a peck on the cheek. "Thanks, babe."

Kyle and Lydia sat in uneasy silence until Emma emerged from the mall entrance a short while later. A heavy darkness settled in Lydia's chest at the sight of her sister in tight jeans, coat open to reveal a snug red top, her blonde hair falling in shimmering waves to her waist. Emma teetered across the icy parking lot in strappy high heels that exposed toenails painted to match the red of her lips.

When she opened the car door, Kyle's eyes lit up. Lydia's skin crawled as he looked her sister up and down like an ice cream cone he couldn't wait to devour.

Emma's overly pink cheeks grew even brighter. She slid into the car and pulled down the mirror. In its light she pursed her lips and angled her head to inspect her makeup.

Watching her, Lydia feared for her sister's soul. Where would Emma's indulging in *hochmut* end? This sin of pride led to so many others.

Lydia's head jerked back as Kyle barreled from the parking lot. His speeding had always worried her, but his erratic driving on the icy roads had reached a new level because one hand rested on Emma's jean-clad knee. Lydia's fear spiraled for her sister along with her anxiety for their safety. She sighed in relief when they zoomed up to Yoder's barn. Kyle slammed on the brakes, and Lydia pitched forward. The seat belt chafed her neck before she flew back against the seat. But at least they had stopped. Her relief was short-lived. Although Kyle shut off the engine, the car didn't stop shaking. Music booming from the barn rocked the car.

Emma smiled and shimmied in her seat, hands in the air, her sensuous movements reminding Lydia of a snake. A snake that brought images of forbidden fruit.

Lydia cleared her throat, making the other two jump. They'd obviously forgotten she was in the car. Emma's narrowed eyes warned Lydia not to interfere. But Lydia was determined to protect her sister. She crunched through snow, trailing behind as Kyle and Emma, hand in hand, hurried toward the barn.

Lydia settled onto one of the hay bales nearest a kerosene heater while Emma, snuggled close to Kyle, wove her way through the crowd. Their closeness, as well as the dance moves of the other couples, made Lydia blush, but she kept an eye trained on Emma.

A short, wiry teen lurched up. "Yo, babe, wanna dance?"

Tongue-tied, Lydia gazed up at the red-head, who stared at her with bleary eyes.

His gaze roved over her. "So what's with the Plain dress?" he slurred. "You here to drag someone home?" He bent closer, his beery breath hot in her face. "Come on, I'll show you a good time while you wait." Lydia leaned away, but he clutched her arm, trying to drag her to her feet.

"Excuse me," a deep bass voice said. A large hand grasped the kid's shoulder and pulled him away. "She's with me."

The kid turned, took one look at the broad shoulders and six-foot height, and backed up. He raised his hands in surrender. "Sorry, man, I" — *hic* — "didn't know." He skedaddled across the floor to another part of the room.

Lydia's rescuer gave her an apologetic look. "Hope I didn't overstep my bounds here, but it seemed as if you were in need of rescuing."

"I–I was." *Stop stammering, Lydia.* "Thank you." She gazed up at him, unable to control the rapid pitter-pattering of her heart as she took in his dark, slightly spiked hair and the mesmerizing blue eyes that pulled her into their depths. The dimple that appeared when he smiled created an attractive crease near his jawline.

He handed her his hot chocolate. "I didn't drink any of this. Maybe it'll help calm you."

Her unsteady "thank you" sent more heat rushing to her cheeks. Even the drafts of icy air wafting through the cracks in the barn walls didn't cool her burning face.

To slow her erratic pulse, Lydia clutched the Styrofoam cup he'd given her and breathed in the chocolatey aroma. She

15

wished he would leave, but that desire warred with one that wanted him to stay. Only for protection, of course.

He settled on the hay bale beside her and thrust out a hand. "Name's Caleb."

Lydia nibbled her lower lip. She'd never shaken an *Englischer*'s hand before. "I–I'm Lydia." Her voice shook as she extended her hand.

Caleb's huge, tanned hand engulfed hers. Warmth tingled up her arm. Frightened at the sensation, she pulled her hand away. She'd never felt like this with Jakob Zook, who'd been courting her for the past two years. Other courting couples held hands and kissed, but Jakob, as the bishop's son, held himself to rigid standards in everything he did. The only time he'd held her hand was when they were paired at wedding dinners.

As the music reached a crescendo, Caleb leaned closer so he could be heard. "You don't seem to be the party type. What brings you here?"

"My sister. I'm keeping an eye on her."

"Ah, so we have a lot in common then. I'm my brother's keeper. I worry about his driving after he's been partying, so I like to keep an eye on him. And his new girlfriend is a terrible influence. I wish I could convince him to stop seeing her."

Lydia found herself warming to this *En-glischer,* who obviously cared about his family. She tamped down the voice of her conscience whispering, *That's not the only reason you're drawn to him.* "I feel the same way about my sister's boyfriend. He's leading her down the wrong path."

"Let me guess. You're the oldest in your family."

In truth, Lydia often felt like the mother hen trying to keep her brood in line. "Yes, I have a younger sister and two younger brothers. What about you?"

Caleb's jaw tightened. "I'm the oldest too. And my brother's guardian."

Something in the way he said it told her that he didn't mean just for tonight, and she gave him a questioning look.

"I don't look old enough?" Deep sadness filled his eyes as he looked off into the distance. "Our parents were killed in a car accident two years ago when I was twenty-two."

"I'm so sorry." Lydia instinctively reached out a hand to comfort him but drew it back before she touched his sleeve. "That must be hard." She couldn't imagine life without her parents, let alone the responsibility of raising a sibling. Keeping up with Emma was running her ragged.

"It hasn't been easy, that's for sure. And my brother seems determined to make it even tougher. Although I blame that on his girlfriend. Before he started dating her, his life was on track, and he wasn't into this party scene. Now she's messed up every-thing."

Lydia had certainly seen that with Emma. "I know exactly what you mean. Dating the wrong person can be awful. My sister's tear-ing our family apart."

Across the room Kyle and Emma stum-bled to a stop. Then Emma started talking rapidly, gesturing to where Lydia sat. Hand in hand the couple came charging toward them.

"What's this?" Emma spat out, her eyes shooting angry sparks at Lydia. "Unite and conquer?"

Startled, Lydia stared at her irate sister. "What?"

A frown creased Caleb's brow as he glanced from Lydia to Emma and then back again. Then his deep voice broke into Lydia's confusion. "Perhaps I can explain." He drew in a sharp breath. "Lydia, meet my brother, Kyle."

CHAPTER TWO

Emma whirled and ran from the barn, Kyle at her heels. By the time Lydia reached the doorway, Kyle's car was lurching down the drive.

Beside her, Caleb shook his head. "That's what I was afraid of. Him and his reckless driving." His shoulders and jaw tense, he exhaled loudly. "At least he hasn't been drinking."

"That's a blessing."

Caleb turned to her. "I assume you came with them?" When she nodded, he said, "I'm so sorry. I've tried to teach him good manners. If you need a ride, I'd be glad to take you home."

Although she wanted to accept, Lydia was afraid to say yes. Her breathing had gone fluttery. So had her stomach.

She scanned the yard for a familiar wagon or buggy. Most of the parking lot was filled with cars, but some of the teens had driven buggies. The sea of gray boxes with their orange reflective triangles might look identical to those who hadn't grown up in Lancaster County, but small distinctive differences identified their owners. A few buggies belonged to people she knew, but were the owners in any condition to drive?

Caleb interrupted her thoughts. "Dropping you off is no trouble, if that's what's worrying you. It's on my way home."

Lydia glanced up in surprise. "You know where I live?"

Before answering, Caleb took her elbow to help her across the rutted, snowy field — as if she didn't tromp across fields every day — and she sucked in a quick breath. If not for the strange tingling in her arm and her difficulty breathing, she might have enjoyed being treated like a fragile piece of porcelain. Frigid wind sliced through the heavy wool of her coat, and she tried to convince herself that was the only reason she was shivering.

He steered her to a black truck, opened the door, and helped her in. Then he rounded the truck and opened the driver's door. "To answer your question, I made it a point to find out about the girl who was messing up Kyle's life."

Lydia let go of the seat belt she'd been

fastening, and it snapped back with a clang. "What? Emma is a good girl." At least she had been.

As Caleb climbed into the driver's seat, Lydia burst out, "Your brother is the one who —" She clamped her mouth shut, and shame filled her. What was she doing arguing with this *Englischer*? She should be setting an example of peace.

"*Who* what?"

Lydia concentrated on fastening her seat belt, not an easy task with trembling hands. "Never mind." Blaming Kyle would solve nothing.

Caleb started the engine and backed out slowly. "I'd like to hear why you think Kyle is the problem."

Lydia sighed, wishing she'd kept quiet. The Scriptures were right: the tongue set ablaze a great fire. She couldn't say Kyle was seducing Emma. Her cheeks heated at the very thought. "Kyle is encouraging Emma to, um, do things that are against our teachings."

"I wish your teachings didn't include completing school by eighth grade," Caleb muttered as he turned onto the main road.

Lydia had no idea what he was talking about. "What does that have to do with anything?"

"Plenty. Kyle's been offered a management position at a fast-food restaurant." Caleb's lip curled. "He accepted because of Emma."

"I should think you'd be glad he has steady employment in this economy." Not that Lydia knew much about the state of the economy, but several people in their community who worked for *Englisch* businesses had lost their jobs. Even *Dat*'s cabinet-making business had suffered some setbacks.

"You don't understand. He was accepted at Duke University but took a year off to work and save money for room and board. Now he plans to use that money for an apartment and has even threatened not to go to college next fall."

The irritation in Caleb's voice confused Lydia. The *Ordnung* opposed higher education because it exposed students to worldly things, so having a steady job and an apartment seemed to be a good thing.

Before she could voice her opinion, Caleb continued. "He's getting an apartment so he can move in with Emma."

Her sister was a little wild, but Emma would never go that far. "Don't worry, my sister wouldn't do that."

"She's the one who's encouraging Kyle to

rent an apartment." Caleb paused. "So they can have more privacy."

No. Please say she'd heard him wrong. Lydia leaned her head against the back of the seat and rubbed her forehead. The headache she'd had from the music increased tenfold. "You're the head of the household, right?" When he nodded, she said, "Just tell him you forbid him to do it."

"It's not that simple. We don't do things like the Amish. My authority doesn't carry the same weight it does in your community."

"That's too bad. If an older brother told me to do something, I would listen."

"The same way your younger sister is listening to you?"

The truth of his words throbbed like a toothache. "During *Rumschpringe* it's different. Teens have their 'running around years,' so they're free from community and family authority."

"Then why do you follow your sister around if she's allowed her freedom?"

"I don't want to see her hurt."

"And I don't want to see Kyle hurt, either. Not going to Duke will ruin his life the way mine . . ." Caleb swallowed hard. "Never mind."

"What do you mean?"

Caleb slowed as they approached a buggy;

23

only the orange triangle on the back made the boxy shape visible against the ebony of the star-studded night. "I dropped out of med school to care for Kyle." He heaved a sigh. "He's supposed to go to college. He graduated top in his high school class." His tone turned bitter. "And now he's giving all that up. For what? To be the manager of a fast-food restaurant?"

Lydia's heart went out to him. "I'm sorry." She understood what it felt like to have ambitions for a younger sibling who didn't live up to them.

Caleb clenched the steering wheel. "It's not your fault. And I apologize for snapping at you earlier. I'm sure your sister is a nice enough girl, but she's ruining Kyle's life."

They were back full circle to where their disagreement started.

As they pulled into the driveway of her house, Lydia tried to extend — if not an olive branch — at least an olive leaf. "We may not agree as to who is ruining whose life, but we both agree that Kyle and Emma aren't good for each other."

"That's for sure. So what can we do?"

Uh-oh. It sounded as if he wanted to work together on this. Lydia wasn't sure she could handle not breathing for hours at a time. "I–I don't know." Embarrassed by her stammering, she reached for the door handle.

Caleb put a hand on her arm. "Wait a sec."

Once again that charge — like the shock of touching metal after shuffling across a rug — shot up her arm. Lydia jerked away. "I have to go. I need to see if Emma made it home."

"I'll wait here while you check."

"No, no. That's all right." Lydia had to get out of here and away from these strange sensations. She didn't want to risk coming back out to the truck again. When she opened the door, the blast of cold air smacked her in the face, cooling her overheated face and neck.

"I insist. But, tell you what, to save yourself a trip down here, why don't you just wave to me through a window if Emma's there?"

Lydia nodded. "Thank you for the ride." She hoped he didn't notice the slight quaver in her words. "I truly appreciate it."

"You're quite welcome. And if Emma's not there, come back out, and we can drive around looking for them. I have some ideas about where we might find them." Caleb opened the console between the seats. "Just in case you don't come back down, I want to give you this." He held out a business card. "You can reach me here. I'm an intake counselor at the hospital's outpatient clinic. I usually work weekdays from six in the morning until three."

Lydia pinched a corner of the card between her thumb and forefinger to avoid touching his fingers. "Thank you," she whispered, not that she had any intention of contacting him. She needed to get away from these strange sensations. Wrenching the door handle, she slipped out of the truck.

Conscious of Caleb's gaze, she stumbled, her steps stiff and awkward until she reached the front door. Inside, she sank against the closed door and slowly released her breath. But every muscle in her body was still knotted more tightly than a tangled skein of yarn.

Lydia tiptoed upstairs to find Emma peering through a gap in the curtains. At the sight her heart and breathing returned to normal. "Thank goodness, you're home." She kept her voice low so she wouldn't disturb their younger sister, Sarah, asleep in the bed closest to the wall.

Emma jumped back from the window when Lydia turned on the battery-powered lamp. "I can't believe you did that." Her words held a bitterness that grated on

Lydia's heart.

"Did what?" Lydia plodded to the window, parted the curtains, and waved to Caleb.

Glaring, Emma reached for a jar of lotion and slathered cream onto her face. Then she spat out each word. "You contacted Kyle's brother. Now the two of you are plotting to break us up."

"It wasn't like that. I didn't contact him. I had no idea who he was."

As she patted in the cream, Emma eyed Lydia. "Are you trying to tell me that Caleb just happened to be at the party? No way. The two of you planned this."

Lydia slid the straight pins from her bodice. "I met Caleb for the first time at the dance tonight — only a short while before you came over."

"Don't lie." Emma stood, hands on her hips, fire blazing in her eyes. "And I also suppose you didn't plot to break us up?"

Lydia couldn't deny that. They had.

"I thought so." The triumph in Emma's voice made Lydia sick inside. How could she convince her sister they only wanted the best for her and Kyle?

Emma turned her back. "Knowing that you're plotting with Caleb makes my decision easier. Kyle and I are going to get an apartment. Tomorrow. That's the only way we can have some privacy. It's the only reason I came home early tonight."

"Oh, Emma, no." Lydia laid an imploring hand on her sister's forearm, but Emma shook it off and stomped to her bed.

"Please don't move out," Lydia begged. "It would break *Mamm*'s and *Dat*'s hearts." *Mine too.* "Think of the example you'd be setting for Sarah. And the boys." And what of the future? If Emma chose to marry an *Englischer, Dat* would insist they shun her even if the church didn't. Lydia couldn't bear to think of shutting her sister out of her life.

"You should have thought of that before you started trailing me everywhere. At first I felt sorry for you because you'd never had any fun during *Rumschpringe.* You were content with hymn sings, playing volleyball and baseball, letting Jakob court you . . ." Emma laughed. "I bet he's never even kissed you, has he?"

Lydia sucked in a breath. "Emma Esh, that's totally inappropriate." Her sharp tone was intended to stop her sister's words as much as it was to halt the rush of embarrassment that flooded her.

"Ha, I thought not. That's why you're so jealous of me and Kyle."

28

Jealous? How could Emma have strayed so far from what she'd been taught about right and wrong?

Emma hopped into bed and pulled the quilt over her head.

Lydia eyed the lump huddled under the covers. "Emma?"

Silence was the only answer.

Lydia had to reach her sister, make her stay. "I'll stop following you around. Please don't go."

"Too late," came the muffled reply. "No-body — not you or anyone else — is going to stop me."

With a heavy heart Lydia picked up Emma's prayer *kapp,* which had tumbled to the floor. After she hung it on a wall peg, she turned off the lamp, plunging the room into darkness, but the blackness surrounding her was no match for the deep despair in her heart. Emma's careless disregard for her *kapp* revealed her attitude toward God and the church. Even worse, her sister's leaving was all her fault.

A cloud of gloom still surrounded Lydia when she woke before dawn. Her restless sleep had been filled with dreams of a future without Emma. Lydia's mood didn't seem to be catching. Emma leaped out of bed, humming. Rather than a slow, solemn hymn from the *Ausbund,* the catchy tune reminded Lydia of the pounding music from the night before. Lydia's heart sank as Emma pulled out her bag of cosmetics and *Englisch* clothes.

"You're not leaving this morning, are you? What about chores?" Lydia winced. Her tone sounded more critical than she intended.

Emma merely laughed. "My only chore today is finding an apartment. Kyle's picking me up in an hour. And just so you know, no chaperones allowed."

"Church is at our house next Sunday. Would you leave the rest of us with your chores today?"

Emma flapped a hand. "You may as well get used to it. I won't be around to do chores anymore."

"Ever?"

With a loud sigh Emma slammed her hand onto the desk.

The crash startled fourteen-year-old Sarah awake. "Are you two fighting again? I'm so tired of your bickering." She stumbled from bed and set about dressing for the day.

"Well, lucky for you," Emma said, "you won't be hearing it again after today."

Sarah looked from one to the other as she

pinned her hair into a bun. "So you've made your peace?"

Emma tossed her head. "I've made mine. I don't know about Lydia."

Lydia squeezed her eyes shut and pressed her fingertips to her forehead. If only she were still dreaming and could fight her way out of this nightmare.

"And are you at peace with Emma, Lydia?" Sarah's soft voice struck at Lydia's heart.

Leave it to Sarah to ask a question Lydia couldn't answer. She loved Emma beyond measure. But could she be at peace with her sister's decision? "It depends on what you mean by peace. All I know is that I love Emma and don't want to lose her."

"Lose her? She's not going anywhere." Sarah turned and stared into Emma's eyes. "Are you, Emma?"

Emma's reply, when it came, carried a hint of regret. "Sorry, Sarah, but I am." She shot an irritated glance at Lydia. "I was going to wait until Kyle and I found a place and then tell everyone at the same time."

"No!" Sarah's sharp cry echoed in the room. She ran over and hugged Emma tightly. "I don't want you to go."

Emma's lower lip trembled as she embraced Sarah. "I'll miss you."

A car pulling in next door interrupted the tender moment.

Emma leaped up. "I have to go. Tell *Mamm* I don't know when I'll be back."

"Why don't you tell her yourself?" Lydia asked, knowing that Emma, for all her bravado and wildness, would never let *Mamm* know what she was doing.

Emma caught Lydia's gaze with an unspoken plea for understanding. An understanding Lydia couldn't give.

Mamm's lips tightened as she looked at Emma's empty seat at the breakfast table. Until today, even after partying until the wee hours of the morning, Emma had risen and dressed in Plain attire to do her morning chores and go to work each day. The dark circles under Emma's eyes disappeared after a day or two, only to reappear each weekend.

Mamm and *Dat* may have suspected Emma had been sneaking out, but they had yet to see Emma in her *Englisch* clothes and makeup. Lydia would prefer to keep it that way. It was one thing to have a vague idea of what was happening, but confronting it in full color was a shock she hoped her parents would never have to face.

She conveyed Emma's message about being gone for the day — more for her parents' sake than for Emma's — but didn't mention the rest of Emma's plans. Sarah caught Lydia's attention several times while they ate and raised a questioning eyebrow, but Lydia shook her head and kept silent. That would be Emma's news to tell. No point in breaking their parents' hearts until Emma made her final decision. Perhaps she'd change her mind. Lydia hoped the reality of apartment hunting would scare her sister back home.

But that night Emma's bed remained empty. Lydia hugged Emma's rag doll to her chest and, eyes wet with tears, whispered a prayer for her wayward sister.

CHAPTER THREE

Lydia slumped at her desk in the school-room on Monday morning. The warmth of the woodstove near her desk made her so drowsy she could barely keep her eyes open. Her bleary gaze took in the rows of wooden desks lined up in front of her. Some students had their heads bent over their books, reading or studying. Others sat, hands folded on their desks, watching her with eager, bright eyes. A few of the older students hunched over desks much too small for them. Two looked bored, and one sullen. Her assistant, Rebecca Zook, stood to one side of the schoolroom, waiting for the middle spelling group to file over.

One of the eleven-year-olds in Lydia's group circled his desk on the boys' side of the schoolroom.

"Samuel Stoltzfus, sit in your seat now." Lydia's voice cracked like a whip.

Samuel stopped and looked at her in

surprise. "But, Miss Esh, I was only —"

"*I said now.*" Lydia emphasized each word.

Sullen-faced, Samuel plopped into his seat, muttering under his breath.

Lydia could not tolerate that disrespect. If she lost control of one student, the others would soon follow his example, and the class would deteriorate into chaos. "Samuel, I want you to write one hundred times, 'I will respect my teacher at all times.' "

Samuel raised his hand. "I cannot in good conscience do that assignment."

Several students around the room gasped, and they all stared at Samuel. He had always been a good pupil, thoughtful and respectful. His defiance took everyone by surprise. Even Rebecca's younger students turned around to look.

Tiredness seeped through Lydia's bones. She was unprepared for such behavior, especially from Samuel. She tried to keep her tone even, but it had an edge of sharpness. "And why might that be?"

Samuel focused on the pencil clutched in his fist. He shuffled his feet. "I'd rather not say." The words came out so quietly Lydia could barely hear them.

"Perhaps then you could stay in during recess to explain yourself."

Lydia set the older students to work on

their math problems. Rebecca listened to the students who were reciting spelling words. Lydia turned her attention to the youngest students. Her mind, though, was not on the lesson but on Samuel. He had never been a discipline problem. She regretted snapping at him without finding out why he was out of his seat, but all her worries about Emma and the long weekend had drained her patience. When Emma had not returned on Saturday night, Lydia had been forced to tell her parents her sister's plans. Shame and gloom had descended on the whole family at the news.

After she'd dismissed the other children for recess, Lydia stayed behind with Samuel, who sat with head bowed and shoulders slumped. "Now, Samuel, I would like an explanation of this morning's defiance."

Samuel did not look up. "I am sorry, Miss Esh. I do not feel that I can write those words honestly. I will take any other punishment you decide to give me."

"And what is the reason that writing those words pricks at your conscience?"

Samuel's lower lip trembled. "I'd rather not say."

"If I have done something that causes you to disrespect me, I need to know what that is, so that by God's grace I can be a better

36

example to all the students."

"My mother's cousin recently bought the farm next door to Eli Yoder." Samuel's words came out so quietly could barely hear them.

Eli Yoder? "I don't understand."

Samuel *rutsched* in his seat. After wriggling first one way, then the other, he mumbled, "His barn isn't only used for sheltering animals."

Lydia's groggy mind struggled to make meaning of what Samuel was implying. *How did Eli Yoder's farming habits and barn — ? Oh no, Yoder's barn. Did he mean — ?* Heat rushed to her cheeks. Her thoughts swirled. *Surely he didn't think — ?* She couldn't tell the truth and smear her sister's reputation. "I can't explain why I've been there, but I assure you my intentions and actions have been honorable."

Samuel avoided her eyes.

He obviously didn't believe her. And she had no way to prove her innocence. A change of subject might be in order. "Perhaps you'd like to explain why you were out of your seat in the first place."

"Yes, ma'am. Lizzie Fisher's pencil fell and rolled to our side of the room. I was going to pick it up and return it to her."

Lydia rubbed her forehead. She'd disciplined him for trying to be helpful, something she had always stressed to the students that she expected. Clearly, an apology was needed, but on her part rather than Samuel's. "I am very sorry, Samuel, for keeping you in at recess. Please forgive me for misjudging you." She waved a hand toward the door. "You may go."

Samuel's quiet thank-you pointed up her earlier ungraciousness, making Lydia regret even more her hasty reprimand earlier. Worrying about Emma was taking a toll on her judgment and patience. She had trouble thinking clearly and found herself easily vexed.

Lydia had spent all day Saturday and Sunday in prayer and both nights tossing restlessly, listening for a car engine growling up the driveway. She'd come to school today exhausted and unprepared. She had to gain control of her emotions so she didn't take out her anxiety on the pupils. *Dear Lord, forgive my impatience with Samuel. Please help me to concentrate on my work and set an example for the students. And help Emma to see the error of her ways and come home to us.*

Samuel's comments added another worry to her already full load. Lydia hadn't thought about how following Emma would affect her own reputation among the students. With Yoder's barn being so far out of the district, it had never occurred to her that any of her pupils would hear of the weekend excursions. Samuel — and most likely his extended family — knew she had been attending the parties, but they had no idea she was there to protect Emma. It wasn't fair that she was suspected of misconduct. Yet how would others know that Lydia acted differently from the other party-goers? All they knew was that she went to the barn, not why.

Stay away from all appearance of evil, her conscience taunted her.

In her concern for Emma, Lydia had thought little about her own reputation, but Samuel's knowledge of the situation meant the rumors of her activities might reach the bishop. Samuel's mother was his cousin. Would the bishop come calling to discuss her behavior?

Later that afternoon, shoulders hunched against the biting wind, Lydia locked the schoolhouse while Sarah rounded up their younger brothers, Zeke and Abe, who were throwing snowballs. Lydia drew her coat more closely around her and made a quick trip to the outhouse before the four of them set off for home.

Dark clouds hung low overhead as they cut across the snowy fields, stepping between frosted cornstalk stubble or walking down rows of icy tobacco plants. Zeke and Abe raced ahead playing tag and, from time to time, skittered back to join them. From her upstairs bedroom in the *daadi haus* next door, their grandmother waved as she always did, but *Mamm,* who usually greeted them at the back door, was nowhere to seen.

Lydia found *Mamm* in the kitchen, her teeth clenched, shoulders tense, polishing windows with a vengeance. A sharp scent of vinegar surrounded her, but something other than that distinctive odor had caused her mother's face to pinch up so tightly. *Mamm* pressed so hard on the glass with the wadded-up phone book pages she used to make the windows sparkle that Lydia worried the pane might shatter.

Coming up beside *Mamm,* Lydia gave her mother a squeeze and laid her cold cheek against her mother's warm one. Rather than responding to the hug or even greeting her, *Mamm* barely nodded. She continued mumbling under her breath and scrubbed harder. That was so out of character, Lydia was shocked.

"What's wrong, *Mamm?*" Lydia asked as

she cut pieces of soda cracker pudding for her brothers, but *Mamm* only rubbed harder. Perhaps her mother was deep in prayer. Lydia would wait until her mother was done to find out what had upset her so.

"Wash up first," she warned when Zeke swooped in to snatch a coconut treat from the plate she'd set on the kitchen table. "Then get to your chores. *Mamm* will need extra help the next few days because church is at our house this Sunday." Not to mention that they'd lost Emma's helping hands.

Lydia trudged upstairs with her school supplies. She should work on lesson plans, but helping *Mamm* with chores took priority. Preparing the house for the hundred members of their church community who would attend the Sunday service took a lot of time. Usually Emma handled most of the chores, but now . . .

As Lydia walked through the door of the bedroom, something seemed different. Then it hit her. Emma's faceless doll was gone. Only one tiny change, but somehow it made the room look abandoned, forlorn.

Emma's *kapp* still hung on the wall peg. Lydia rushed to her sister's bed and lifted the mattress. She sucked in a breath.

The cosmetics and *Englisch* clothes were gone.

Emma must have come home and packed her things while they were at school. Her sister truly was gone, and she hadn't even said good-bye. No wonder *Mamm* was so upset.

Rather than setting her school supplies on the desk, Lydia dumped them onto her bed. Then she threw herself on Emma's bed, sturdy shoes hanging off the edge so as not to dirty the quilt. Hugging her sister's pillow to her chest, Lydia lay facedown, unable to release the lump that lay like unrisen dough in her chest, making it hard to breathe. *Oh, Emma . . .*

Only the thought of *Mamm* doing all the chores forced Lydia from the bed, but she moved as if struggling through a vat of molasses. As she passed the dresser, a small white rectangle caught her eye. Caleb's business card. Anger and bitterness welled up inside when she saw the name Miller. She snatched up the card, intending to toss it into the trash can. But then she stopped and uncurled her fist. Stroking a finger over the surface brought Caleb's face to mind. His kindness. The love and pride and concern that shone in his eyes when he spoke of his brother. How he had come to her aid when Kyle and Emma left without her.

42

All of those memories stopped her from crumpling the card, and an idea formed in her mind. Perhaps Caleb knew where Emma was. She studied the phone number printed at the bottom of the card. It gave an extension number for him at the clinic, which meant she could call him directly. If she had a phone.

Unlike some families, they had no phone at the end of the lane. *Dat* had one outside his cabinet-making shop, which he believed was concession enough. She rubbed her finger over the card as if to erase the memories of the weekend, but instead found her thoughts straying to the touch of his fingers against hers. Perhaps this wasn't such a good idea.

With heavy hearts the family gathered around *Dat* for the Scripture reading in the parlor the following morning. *Dat* sat rigid in the wooden rocker *Grosdaadi* had carved, while *Mamm* slumped on the upholstered chair nearby. Lydia curled up on the couch opposite their parents. Sarah and the boys took their usual places on the rag rug in front of *Dat.* Only one person was missing.

A tear trickled down *Mamm*'s cheek as she stared at the spot where Emma used to sit, her head resting against *Dat*'s knee. Lydia's eyes misted when *Dat* lifted the hand he usually set on Emma's head, glanced down, and then let it drop. Sarah scooted closer to *Dat*. Not exactly in Emma's spot, but she made the physical gap less obvious. If only the void within the family could be closed as easily. *Dat* cleared his throat twice before beginning, but his voice still came out huskier than usual.

Oh, Emma, why? Why did you do this? Don't you care about Mamm? Dat? *Sarah? The boys? Me? And what of your future? And of God?*

Lydia extinguished the flash of anger at Emma with a bucket of remorse. What could she have done differently to convince Emma to stay?

They all bowed their heads for prayer, and Lydia realized with a start that she had not heard one word of the Scripture reading. She shook off thoughts of Emma and concentrated on the words of the inner prayer she added to the end of the Lord's Prayer, begging God to keep Emma safe and bring her home again.

Guilt plagued her as she moved through her chores over the next few days. Many teens went a bit wild during *Rumschpringe*, but they eventually came back to the faith. Would Emma also return?

Without Emma, everyone in the family limped through their days. It wasn't just the extra chores that made the load heavier; Emma had flitted through her work like a bird, a song always on her lips. Her giggles had echoed through the house. On laundry day she'd cover her face with a soapsud beard and imitate a pompous neighbor. She'd hidden behind furniture and jumped out to make the boys squeal. It kept things lively. Now everyone went through their jobs by rote, and *Mamm*'s shoulders slumped as if a heavy burden had dropped on them. *Dat*'s usual stoicism sobered to grimness, and a muscle twitched in his cheek when he walked through the door and spotted the empty spot at the table.

Every time she glanced at her parents, Lydia's guilt increased, and along with it, so did her resolve. She couldn't let Emma do this to the family. For their sake, she must put aside her conflicting feelings about contacting Caleb.

Later that week Lydia lagged behind as her brothers raced ahead of her to the school-house.

Sarah slowed her steps, put a hand on Lydia's arm, and asked in a tear-choked

45

voice, "Do you think Emma will ever come back?"

"She has to," Lydia said fiercely. "It's *Rum-schpringe*. She's free to do what she wants now." Though she knew those words to be truth, something inside her railed against them. *If only* . . . "I'm sure Emma will come back to join the church." *Eventually.* Lydia hoped and prayed her sister would come to her senses soon.

Throughout the morning as Lydia greeted the students and struggled to concentrate on their recitations, her gaze kept straying to Caleb's card. Would she have the courage to call him? What would she say?

A sharp "Lydia, Lydia" interrupted her thoughts. Rebecca Zook was waving a hand in front of her face.

"I'm sorry. What did you say?"

Rebecca, who was usually the epitome of sweetness, frowned at her. "I can't find the lesson plans for the younger group. What did you want me to do with them?"

Lydia pawed through the papers covering her desk, dislodging Caleb's business card. She quickly hid it under a stack of ungraded assignments, but not before Rebecca had caught a glimpse of it, deepening the lines etched into her forehead. "I–I must have left those lesson plans at home." Had she even done them? Lydia couldn't remember. Her mind was so clouded with thoughts of Emma. "Why don't you, um, have them go over this word list?" She seized on the first age-appropriate thing she could find in the mess on her desk.

"We did those last week." Rebecca wrinkled her nose and gave Lydia a questioning glance. "Are you all right?"

Shame washed over Lydia at what Rebecca must be seeing. Lydia's clothing disheveled, her desk piled high with papers, her lesson plans missing. Worse yet, she was so distracted she could barely pay attention to the class. "I'm sorry."

Rebecca put a hand on her arm. "I will figure out something to do until you are ready for them."

"Thank you." Lydia pulled her mind from Emma and into the classroom. As if slamming shut a barn door, she closed off all other thoughts. Her pupils deserved her full attention, and she intended to give it to them. She took a deep breath and nodded to Ezra Zook. "Please recite the eight times table."

But the minute the students filed out the door for recess, Lydia fingered the card Caleb had given her. After a few moments, though, she slumped in her chair, letting

Caleb's card drift to the heap on the desktop.

All morning long the scent of *Mamm*'s potato soup bubbling on the woodstove in the corner of the room had filled the schoolhouse with warmth and love of family. Now the homey scent almost choked her. Lydia swallowed hard against the rush of tears that pressed against the backs of her eyeballs. What happened to home and family when the fabric was torn asunder?

She couldn't let Emma destroy the family this way. She had to get in touch with Caleb. But how? And even if she could reach him, would he have the information she was seeking?

Rebecca poked her head through the door. "Will you be joining us outside?" Behind her, snowflakes swirled through the air, dusting the hard, dirty ice banks surrounding the playground. "The boys were upset when I wouldn't let them chip off chunks of ice to throw, but they're hoping for a snowball battle this afternoon."

A slight smile curved Lydia's lips. A snowfall always reminded her of God's blessings falling from heaven. She murmured a prayer of thanksgiving for the freshness and beauty of the snow. Surely a God who commanded the seasons could work in Emma's heart to bring her home again. This time as Lydia once again closed the doors of her mind, shutting out thoughts of her sister, she vowed to trust God to work in Emma's life.

Lydia approached the afternoon lessons with new vigor and determined to organize both her desk and her lesson plans. God would want her to give her best to her students, and she intended to do it. She dismissed the students twenty minutes early so they could play in the new-fallen snow. She sent Rebecca outside with them while she tackled the disorganization on her desk. After she had sorted everything into tidy piles and put essays to be graded into her bag to take home, she joined them.

She smiled at the shouts of joy as students raced back and forth, sliding along the playground, and packing snow into balls for snowmen or for throwing. The heavy gray clouds overhead promised a continual snowfall throughout the evening. When the darkening sky turned the shapes of the moving children into shadows, Lydia sent the students home for their after-school chores and gathered her siblings for the trek across the snow-coated fields. Her lightheartedness at the pristine white covering the land and hiding the older, dirtier snow evaporated the closer they got to home.

Emma should be there helping *Mamm* with chores. Their mother always wanted the house to be spotless when they took their turn hosting the church service. *Mamm* saw it as a way to offer the best to God and the other church members. Without Emma to assist, *Mamm* not only needed to handle all the daily chores alone, but she also had to do the extra cleaning and food preparation. *Why, Emma, why? How could you go off and leave Mamm with all this extra work?*

Although Lydia had determined to get caught up on lesson plans and grading assignments, one look at *Mamm*'s wan face made her set that aside. She took her mother's arm and led her to the rocking chair near the woodstove. "You sit here while Sarah and I make dinner."

Mamm shook her head. "I cannot rest. So much needs doing."

Lydia placed a firm hand on her mother's shoulder, preventing her from rising. "Whatever needs doing, we'll do it. Zeke and Abe can help."

Zeke shoved the final bite of his whoopie pie into his mouth. Chocolate cake crumbs clung to his lips as he licked the last of the creamy white filling from his fingers. He narrowed his eyes. "I want to play in the snow."

"You'll have plenty of time for that tomorrow. It looks as if it may snow all night."

Zeke's lips twisted into a pout as Sarah scrubbed at his face to get rid of the remaining crumbs. Lydia gave him one of her stern schoolmarm looks, and the protest he'd started to utter died on his lips.

Mamm leaned back against the wooden headrest and closed her eyes. Her face looked almost gray. "Thank you," she whispered.

Lydia sent Zeke out to gather eggs from the hens, and then while Abe hurried to the barn to help *Dat* with milking the four cows, Lydia and Sarah cleaned and chopped vegetables for dinner. Once Lydia had the stew simmering on the stove, she and Sarah grabbed cleaning rags. They started with the living room because that's where the men's benches would go. By the time *Dat* and the boys returned from the barn, dinner was ready.

The family sat down at the table and with bowed heads gave silent thanks to God for the food. Lydia was sure her prayer wasn't the only one that also included a petition for returning Emma to them. After the meal ended, Lydia set Zeke and Abe to work on the dishes while she and Sarah prepared some of the foods for lunch following the church service. As Sarah boiled the dried apples that had been soaking overnight, Lydia rolled out several piecrusts for the snitz pie. Sarah filled the crusts, and Lydia braided strips across the top and brushed them with milk. They slid them into the oven, and soon the savory smell of cinnamon filled the air. As she moved from one chore to the next, Lydia's hand kept slipping to the card she'd secreted in her pocket. She had to find a way to contact Caleb.

CHAPTER FOUR

On Sunday morning Sarah stood in the bedroom running a comb through her hair. Tears trickled down her cheeks and dripped off her chin. "My hair's all *strubbly.*"

"Let me help." Lydia ran her fingers through the strands to loosen the knots. With swift strokes of the comb she smoothed her sister's hair. Then she spun Sarah to face her and put a finger under her sister's chin, tilting it to look into her eyes. "I've never seen you cry about messy hair before."

Sarah's gaze strayed toward the middle bed. Her face crumpled, and she gulped back a sob. "Emma's not coming back, is she? What if she never does? What if she marries the *Englischer*?"

Lydia pulled her sister into her arms. "Let us pray that she doesn't." Not given to displays of affection, she patted Sarah's back awkwardly. "Most teens who go through

53

Rumschpringe return." *If that is so, why did you spend so much time chasing Emma?*

"Why is Emma doing this?" Sarah burst out. "Doesn't she care how much we need and miss her?"

"Sometimes the pull of the world is strong. But the pull of God is stronger. We need to let her go and trust God to convict her."

"But you didn't act like this. Neither did Jakob."

"Rebellion isn't a requirement of *Rumschpringe*. Keep that in mind when it's your turn." Lydia kept her tone stern, but she softened the warning with a smile.

"I will." Sarah flung her arms around Lydia's neck and hugged. "I'm so glad you're my sister."

The words were a healing balm to Lydia's heart, but she couldn't help feeling Emma would never echo the sentiment. A tight ache squeezed Lydia's chest. She didn't want to think about that. "We'd better hurry. *Mamm* needs extra help today."

Lydia missed working with Emma in the overheated, crowded kitchen as women rushed back and forth after church, setting up the meal the congregation shared. Women loaded platters with cheese and meats or piled bread onto plates. *Mamm,*

Sarah, and other church ladies rushed in and out, carrying pickles, chow-chow, jam, apple butter, red beet eggs, and sandwich fixings. They served one group after another. Despite the bustle, the kitchen felt empty. No Emma teasing other girls about courting, surprising the older women with hugs, making faces during a long sermon to elicit muffled giggles from those around her. Although Lydia often scolded Emma for her irreverence, she couldn't help but miss her sister's antics. Emma's exuberance and boundless energy had been a trial to her parents, but she'd never intentionally hurt them the way she was doing now.

Jakob sidled over as Lydia replenished the peanut-butter-and-marshmallow church spread. "It will be nice to have you at the hymn sing tonight," he said in a low voice.

Lydia gave him a half-hearted smile. All the teens would gather here tonight, but without Emma, most of the usual fun would sputter out, the way air rushed out of an untied balloon, leaving it flat.

To distract herself from her sadness, Lydia hurried toward the kitchen to replenish yet another platter of bologna and cheese, but Jakob stopped her again.

"You look tired. Are you all right?" Jakob's quiet words touched her heart.

"I'm fine." Lydia regretted her brusqueness, but his kindness threatened to unleash the tears she'd been holding in check. She refused to break down in front of the congregation. It was hard enough heading through chattering knots of women and girls who ceased talking whenever she, Sarah, or *Mamm* passed. A few, brave enough to question them directly, made Lydia's cheeks sting with a sudden rush of blood.

"Is Emma ill?" Several of Emma's friends had leaned forward to ask Lydia before church started. More cornered her after the service. "Where's Emma?"

"She's not here." Lydia's gut twisted at telling half-truths. Sooner or later everyone would discover the truth. Better to be honest now, but she couldn't make herself say the words, *She moved out.*

Yet it seemed quite a few people already knew or at least suspected. The women were like chattering magpies when it came to passing along bad news. Most studied her with pity-filled eyes. Few pushed for more answers, but whispered gossip floated around the kitchen as she and her family scurried about the kitchen preparing the meal. Lydia only caught snatches of conversations. *"Englischer,"* "living in sin," "too much partying," "older one too." The murmuring halted whenever she was in the vicinity.

Mamm's face grew paler as the day wore on. Lydia took her elbow and steered her to an empty chair in a semi-quiet corner. "Sit here and eat something." When *Mamm* tried to stand, Lydia shook her head. "You need a rest. You're looking peaked, and I don't want you to pass out and give everyone more to gossip about."

Her mother's eyes swam with tears. "I care little what they say about me, but the things they are saying about Emma . . . and of you." She sighed. " 'Judge not, lest ye be judged.' Does that not apply in this situation?"

"It should, but human nature being what it is, everyone is curious. I'm sure we'll be the subject of many prayers." And perhaps those prayers would help to bring Emma back where she belonged.

"Prayers are sorely needed." *Mamm* smiled at Jakob's mother as Mary bustled through the door carrying empty bowls to refill, but the tired smile didn't light up her eyes the way it usually did. After Mary Zook had passed by, *Mamm* murmured, "I'm only glad *Mammi* isn't here today to hear this. It would break her heart. She always set such store by Emma."

There was no denying that *Mammi* favored Emma. The past few weeks their grandmother's aches and pains had kept her confined to bed. "I'd better get back to work before I'm missed," Lydia said. "But speaking of *Mammi,* someone needs to take her a meal. Shall I send Sarah?"

Mamm inclined her head toward the window where Sarah, cheeks and nose red from the cold, was chasing a small boy, the ends of her shawl flapping around her like blackbird wings. Several other children scattered at her approach. "Sarah is keeping the younger children occupied so their parents can eat and talk. It might be best if you went."

Lydia welcomed the chance to visit *Mammi,* not only because she'd be fleeing the gossiping crowds, but even more so because she loved being around her grandmother. After selecting her grandmother's favorite foods and heaping them on a plate, she added an extra large slice of shoofly pie and poured a glass of the creamy milk *Dat* and Abe had brought from the barn that morning. Then she slipped outside and onto the narrow wooden sidewalk that connected their side door to the *daadi haus.* Abe had shoveled the snow this morning before *Mamm* had taken breakfast to *Mammi,* but a few slippery patches remained. Lydia stepped carefully to avoid the ice.

The nip in the air and gray clouds signaled that more snow would soon be upon them. A stiff breeze billowed her shawl, so Lydia trapped the fabric under her elbows to keep it close to her body. She hunched her shoulders against the wind, which lifted the strings of her *kapp* and smacked them into her face as she hurried to the door of the *daadi haus.*

Lydia called out a cheery *gude mariye,* although it was past noon, but *Mammi* barely responded, and her faint smile ended in a grimace. Poor *Mammi.* Usually, even when her joints were swollen and stiff, she had a smile on her lips and a hearty greeting.

Lydia set down the tray and leaned over the bed to prop up her grandmother. *Mammi*'s groans tore at Lydia's heart. "Is your arthritis bothering you?"

Her grandmother's voice was so weak, Lydia had to lean over to hear. "That and other things."

Mammi never complained. She always had words of gratitude to God for His many blessings and for allowing her to enjoy another day of life. Yet this week she'd been uncharacteristically withdrawn and hadn't even mentioned Emma's absence. After *Mammi* only picked at her lunch, Lydia's uneasiness increased.

"I'll ask *Mamm* to take you to the doctor tomorrow," she said as she left the room with the plate of uneaten food.

Mammi's only response was a suppressed moan as she rolled over in bed.

By the time Lydia returned to the kitchen, the last few dishes were being dried and put away in the cupboard. Women were gathering their offspring and donning coats or shawls as the boys and men brought around their buggies. Soon the driveway was lined with square gray buggies hitched to stomping and snorting horses with white steam floating from their mouths and nostrils. Boys held the reins as men assisted their wives and children into the seats and tucked blankets around them.

Rather than taking their usual Sunday afternoon rest following the service, Lydia, Sarah, and *Mamm* headed to the kitchen to prepare for the hymn sing. In a few hours a crowd of teens would arrive, expecting to be fed. Many women had contributed the leftover desserts they'd brought for lunch. Lydia lifted the lids of the assorted wicker pie carriers covering the kitchen table to see if they had enough. She and Sarah sliced what was left of the pies and arranged them on serving platters as *Dat,* Zeke, and Abe straightened the backless benches and the tables, readying them for the evening guests. They carted the extras out to the barn to store until the church wagon came to pick them up later in the week.

As they worked, Lydia had a whispered conversation with her mother about *Mammi*'s health. *Mamm,* who looked wan and pale herself, said she'd arrange to take *Mammi* to the clinic the next day. But an hour before dinner, *Mamm* hurried from the kitchen. When she didn't return, Lydia went in search of her.

Mamm sat on the edge of her bed, groaning and clutching her stomach. Lydia laid a hand on her mother's forehead, which was burning up. *Mamm*'s teeth were chattering, and her body was shaking with chills.

"Off to bed you go," Lydia said, but *Mamm* shook her head.

"You need help. All that work to do." *Mamm*'s weak voice revealed how ill she was. "And supper still to get."

"Sarah and I will take care of everything. You get under the covers and stay warm."

After several more protests, *Mamm* allowed Lydia to help her into bed. She refused Lydia's offers of food or tea.

Lydia rushed to the kitchen to start supper, but her mind whirled. How would they get *Mammi* to the clinic tomorrow if *Mamm* had the flu? If only Emma were around. Her sister usually did these things. She took orders and did bookkeeping for *Dat*'s cabinetmaking business, so it was easier for her to take time off.

Lydia barely had time to smooth down her hair and re-pin her *kapp* after drying the dinner dishes before her friends started arriving. Her brothers helped the boys with the horses, and soon the backyard was littered with open-topped courting buggies. Some couples met in the yard, eager to see each other; even more would pair up tonight after the sing. Some of the happy couples smiling shyly at each other would marry in the fall.

Tuesdays and Thursdays in November were filled with weddings. Once the harvest had been gathered, wedding season began. If it weren't for Emma, Lydia would likely be busy planning her own marriage.

She tried to push uncharitable thoughts of her sister away, but they were replaced by a small voice reminding her that she'd taken on a responsibility that wasn't hers. Guilt stabbed at her. If she had joined the church and kept her nose out of her sister's business, would Emma have moved out?

If she started baptismal classes this spring, she and Jakob could set a wedding date this year. Lydia tried to picture Jakob with the beard all married Amish men grew, yet somehow she couldn't imagine him as anything but clean shaven.

Couples separated when they reached the long line of tables. The boys seated themselves on one side, and the girls sat opposite them. Lydia joined in the singing, but found herself mouthing the familiar words to hymns without looking at the *Ausbund,* her heart and mind not on the message. Instead she worried about *Mamm* and wished she could take *Mammi* to the clinic tomorrow so she could talk to Caleb. As much as she wanted to go, she couldn't take a day off from teaching.

When they paused for refreshments, Jakob came up behind her. "You seem so far away tonight. Are you worried about Emma?"

So he'd heard the gossip too. "Yes, and *Mammi.* Something's very wrong. She didn't even argue when I suggested going to the clinic. But I don't know who will go with her tomorrow. *Mamm*'s down with the flu."

"What about Sarah?"

Lydia shook her head. "Sarah faints at the sight of blood. She'd be useless if an emergency victim came into the clinic."

"I have an idea." Jakob beckoned to his sister, who made a face at having to end her conversation with Abner Lapp.

Abner's gaze followed Rebecca as she came and stood behind Lydia on the girls' side of the table.

Jakob smiled at his sister and then nodded toward Lydia. "Lydia needs to take her grandmother to the clinic tomorrow. Could you supervise the students while she's gone?"

Rebecca placed a hand on Lydia's shoulder. "I do hope it's nothing serious, Lydia. I'd be happy to help, but I'm not sure I can handle all the groups alone. Maybe if I had someone to assist me . . . ." She glanced around the room.

Lydia did too. Most of the older girls would gladly help, but she hesitated to ask, knowing they were needed in family businesses or had jobs working for *Englischers.* Sarah was pouring out drinks and refilling snack plates. Her sister was both helpful and responsible. "Would Sarah do?"

Rebecca nodded enthusiastically. "She's such a good student. And she's wonderful with the younger ones."

Trying not to let her excitement show, Lydia motioned to her sister, who hurried to join them.

"You need me?" Sarah asked breathlessly.

"*Jah,* we most certainly do." Jakob winked at her, and Sarah's cheeks turned crimson.

Rebecca turned to Sarah. "I'm the one who needs you. Would you like to be an assistant teacher tomorrow while Lydia takes your grandmother to the clinic?"

"Really? Me? You'd let me help?" Sarah looked from one to the other, her eyes glowing. When they nodded, she clasped her hands together in front of her. "I'd love to."

Lydia smiled at both of them. "*Danke.* You don't know how much this means to me." In more ways than one. Now she'd have to find a way to talk to Caleb. About Emma, of course. To keep her mind from straying where it shouldn't go, Lydia gave Jakob an especially wide smile and added an enthusiastic, "And thank you too for the wonderful *gut* suggestion."

After the two other girls said hasty goodbyes and skittered away, Jakob stood and returned with refreshments. When he set a slice of snitz pie in front of Lydia, he leaned closer and whispered, "I'm happy to help however I can." Sadness flitted across his face as couples paired off and headed out to their courting buggies. "I wish I could drive you home tonight."

He made it obvious he was hoping to be invited to spend the rest of the evening together, but Lydia wanted to be alone. "I would ask you to stay, but I must prepare lesson plans to send with Sarah in the morning. And I need to check on *Mamm* and *Mammi*." Guilt washed over her when Jakob's face fell.

His doleful expression increased when Rebecca, her face glowing, walked to the door with Abner. "I cannot believe it. She's too young to be courting."

"It's not easy, but you have to let go and trust . . ." Lydia's teasing remark died on her lips. She was the last person to be giving someone else advice. Look at how she'd driven Emma away.

"Don't blame yourself." Compassion in his eyes, Jakob stepped closer to her and gave her a brief hug.

It was the first time he'd touched her in that way, yet it was all Lydia could do not to pull away.

He stepped back hastily and glanced around to see if anyone had been watching. Red crept up his neck and colored his cheeks. "I'm sorry, Lydia. I–I overstepped my bounds. I wanted only to comfort you."

Lydia couldn't look him in the eye, so she lowered her head. Plenty of courting couples hugged and kissed, so they had done nothing wrong. Yet a sickish feeling swept through her, and she hid her hands behind the folds of her skirt. But her shame did not stem from his kindly gesture. Jakob deserved more from her than the comparison of another man's touch.

CHAPTER FIVE

Mammi frowned when Lydia entered the *daadi haus* the following morning. "It's Monday. You should be teaching. Where's Emma? Why isn't she taking me?"

Lydia's heart sank. "She's gone . . ."

"Speak up," *Mammi* snapped. "I can't hear you if you mumble."

Her grandmother's querulous tone shocked Lydia. *Mammi* must be in a lot of pain to be so snappish this morning. She'd never seen her grandmother this crotchety.

Lydia spoke loudly and clearly. "Emma is no longer at home."

Mammi stared at Lydia as if she were a *dummkopf.* "Of course not. It's half past nine. She should be at the cabinet shop for two hours by now."

"Well, she, um . . ."

Mammi's moan interrupted Lydia's explanation.

Poor Mammi. "Never mind about Emma

right now. The car just pulled up outside. Let's get you to the clinic."

Dat had gone to his shop earlier than usual to call Andy Lopez, one of the *Englischers* who drove people in the Amish community to appointments. Andy had driven his black four-door car as close to the *daadi haus* door as he could, and Lydia, grasping *Mammi*'s waist, assisted her grandmother past snow drifts and around icy patches. Shivering, she settled her grandmother in the front seat, buckled her in, and shut the door. Then she slid into the back seat and greeted Andy.

Mammi's head slumped against the side window, and Lydia wished she'd thought to bring a pillow.

Andy drove slowly down the winding back roads toward the clinic, passing buggies when there was room on the two-lane road. They passed clotheslines dipping under the weight of damp wash or garments frozen stiff with icicles hanging from them, and a spurt of resentment flashed through Lydia. Emma should have been home this morning helping them with the wash. *Mamm* was still in bed with the flu.

Lydia and Sarah had risen at four, and together they'd run the dirty laundry through the wringer washer and toted the heavy baskets of wet clothes out to the line. Normally they helped *Mamm* and Emma before they left for school. But Sarah had barely pinned up two pairs of her brothers' black trousers before she had to go. Lydia struggled through the rest on her own, her toes stinging as she stood in the snow, yanking on the icy clothesline to slide it through the pulley. Her frozen fingers fumbled with laundry that had stiffened in the cold.

Concerned that the undergarments wouldn't dry fast enough in the frigid weather, Lydia hung some of them in the basement. Her thawing toes and fingers tingled as she clipped each piece of laundry onto the clothespin ring hanging from the ceiling. A deep well of sadness filled her, and she murmured prayers for Emma's return.

But now *Mammi*'s pinched face, slumped shoulders, and soft moans brought Lydia's worries circling back to her grandmother.

Andy clicked on his turn signal and turned into the clinic parking lot. He drove slowly over patches of ice and drew up under the portico. Hunched against the biting wind, Lydia supported her grandmother the short distance to the doors. She hit the metal handicap opener with her elbow so she didn't have to loosen her grip on *Mammi*'s waist. Inside, her grandmother tottered to a chair, and Lydia rushed to the admissions window.

The girl behind the counter glanced at Lydia's Plain dress. "Have a seat, and one of our intake counselors will be with you shortly. Would you prefer one who speaks some Pennsylvania Dutch?"

"That would be nice," Lydia replied. *Mammi* was more comfortable speaking German, and Lydia wouldn't have to translate unfamiliar words.

The phone rang, and the receptionist held up a hand. While the girl talked, Lydia reconsidered. If they went with a non-German speaker, perhaps she might get Caleb. How likely was that? After all, it was a busy hospital.

The girl hung up the phone. "Have a seat. Either Leah or Caleb will be with you shortly."

Lydia's heart erupted into a patter that seemed louder than a gas generator. But Caleb was a common name. Some of the younger Amish men in their community worked as hospital aides. No doubt, this German-speaking Caleb would turn out to be Amish or Old Order Mennonite. Lydia tried to relax as she sank into a metal-armed chair beside her grandmother. She worried about Rebecca and Sarah handling the schoolroom, *Mammi*'s health, *Mamm* alone at home, and Emma, but nothing could distract her from the odd symptoms she'd experienced on hearing the name Caleb.

Ten minutes later a Mennonite girl in a blue-flowered dress, her bun tucked under a small prayer covering, stood in the doorway holding a clipboard. "Esther Esh."

Lydia sighed as she assisted *Mammi* to her feet. They'd gotten Leah. Now she wouldn't find out if the other intake counselor was the Caleb she'd hoped to see.

Leah led them down a hallway lined with chairs facing plastic-windowed cubicles. Lydia glanced in each window they passed, but didn't see Caleb. After indicating two green-cushioned seats with metal arms and legs, Leah entered the cubicle and sat on the other side of the window. She waited while Lydia settled *Mammi* into a chair. Lydia had just taken a seat when a deep voice spoke from farther down the hall.

"Lydia?"

She turned to see Caleb striding toward her. Her heart sped up. He was here.

"Are you ill?" he asked.

Mammi's eyes snapped open. She glanced sharply from one to the other, her brow creased.

72

Lydia's mouth went dry at the sight of him in a blue lab coat. "I–I . . ." She shook her head and gestured toward her grandmother. *Think, Lydia. Say something.* But no words came. She should introduce him, but she couldn't even remember her grandmother's name, let alone get coherent words out.

Caleb tapped a finger on his clipboard. "I have to register a patient now, but maybe I'll see you later?" He set a hand on her shoulder, squeezed it lightly, and telegraphed something with his eyes, but Lydia was too flustered to decipher it.

Did he mean he wanted her to stay, to talk? She may have nodded, but she wasn't sure. What was it about him that set her nerves *rutsching* worse than a wriggly schoolboy? He was halfway down the hall before her brain engaged enough to form words. Had she made a fool of herself? And how would she explain that intimate touch to *Mammi*? To an *Englischer* that might be only a casual gesture of support, but *Mammi* would think otherwise.

Her grandmother's quiet voice startled Lydia. "He seems to be a nice young man."

What? Had *Mammi* not seen the touch? Lydia turned an astonished gaze in her grandmother's direction, praying that her flaming cheeks would not give her away. "Y–

Yes, he is."

Pain lines were etched deep into *Mammi*'s face, and her mouth worked for a few moments before she managed to say, "Take care with your heart."

How had *Mammi* jumped to such a conclusion? Lydia hastened to reassure her grandmother. "I will, *Mammi*. I promise."

Her grandmother's words came out slowly. "You have not yet joined the church, so you are still free to do as you wish. But use your freedom wisely. And remember your students and sisters may be following your example."

Lydia drew in a sharp breath. She had no intention of doing anything that went against the *Ordnung*.

Mammi patted Lydia's hand, which was clenched around the metal chair arm. The gesture brought tears to Lydia's eyes. *Mammi* had never been affectionate. It wasn't their way.

Leah smiled at them from the other side of the window. *"Gude mariye. Wie gehts?"*

Lydia responded with an automatic *good morning,* but as to how she was? Flustered, startled. More so as Caleb brushed past heading the opposite direction, followed by a young woman in Plain dress holding a baby. But Lydia couldn't say that. Then she realized Leah's question was directed toward *Mammi,* who was hunched over, her hands crossed over her abdomen.

"My grandmother is in a great deal of pain," Lydia said to Leah. "Can she see a doctor now?"

Leah's face scrunched in concern. "I'm so sorry. As soon as we fill out the paperwork, someone can see her. What seems to be the matter?"

Between quick indrawn breaths, *Mammi* described her symptoms in German, and Leah noted them on her clipboard.

After they signed various forms, Leah stood. "I'll make copies of these, and a doctor will be with you shortly. Have a seat in the waiting room."

Lydia took her grandmother's arm to assist her. Groaning, *Mammi* shuffled down the hall, leaning heavily against Lydia. When she sank into a waiting room chair, she slumped back and closed her eyes. The pallor of her grandmother's skin worried Lydia. Hoping the wait would be brief, she kept her gaze on the doorway that led to the cubicles. Nurses came out to announce patient names. But Lydia wasn't only listening for *Mammi's* name. Caleb might come through there too.

After drawing in several deep breaths,

Mammi opened her eyes and glanced in the direction of Lydia's gaze. "Sometimes the heart leads you astray in spite of all the warnings of your conscience," *Mammi* said.

Lydia started. Had her grandmother read her mind?

Mammi had a faraway look in her eyes. "I speak from experience."

Experience? "What do you mean?"

Mammi waved a hand in a never-mind gesture.

Lydia was too curious to let this drop. "Please, *Mammi,* tell me."

Between groans, *Mammi* choked out, "I once loved an *Englischer.*"

Lydia's mouth flew open. *Mammi?* Surely she'd heard her wrong.

Still bent over, with her hands across her abdomen, *Mammi* said, "Don't look so surprised. I was young once." She rubbed a hand crabbed with arthritis over the papery skin of her cheek. "I went through my own *Rumschpringe.* Myron Landis. He works for the Mennonite Central Relief Committee, and he and his brothers own Landis Grocery."

So *Mammi* saw her old boyfriend whenever they held the annual Amish-Mennonite fund-raiser? Her grandmother supervised the charity quilts for the event.

Mammi sucked in a pain-filled breath and squeezed her eyes shut. But when Lydia leaned toward her, *Mammi* waved her away. After a tiny gasp, she continued her story. "It was years ago. We each married someone of our own faith. But the pain of breaking off the relationship still lingers. *Daadi* was a good man, and we were happy. I never regretted joining the church or marrying him. And God blessed us with many children and grandchildren. My only regret . . ." *Mammi*'s voice trailed off, and she clutched her abdomen again.

"Oh, *Mammi*." Lydia's heart ached for her grandmother.

"My only regret is that I gave away my heart too soon. I wish I had saved all of my love for your grandfather." A tear trickled down her cheek. "He never knew that my heart wasn't whole when I married him. And I spent years filled with guilt."

She fixed a fierce gaze on Lydia. One that made Lydia squirm. One that showed she could see into Lydia's heart. One that pierced Lydia's soul. "School your heart now before your emotions take control. It is easier to stop a horse with firm control over the reins from the start rather than trying to rein in a runaway cart."

Lydia had only recently met Caleb, but

had her horse already careened out of control?

CHAPTER SIX

Ten minutes after they'd taken *Mammi* back to the examination room, Caleb stood in the waiting room entrance, glancing around. When his gaze lit on Lydia, he smiled and approached. "Hi, Lydia. How's your, um — ?" He motioned to the empty seat beside her.

To keep her pulse under control, Lydia stared at the plastic name tag pinned to his jacket rather than meeting his eyes. "My grandmother. They just took her back." *Mammi* had insisted on seeing the doctor alone.

Caleb sank into the chair next to her. "I'm on break now. Would you have time to get a quick snack in the cafeteria?"

With his face only a short distance from hers, a sudden dryness in Lydia's mouth made it difficult to answer. "I–I don't know. My grandmother . . ."

Caleb glanced around the room. "Most

likely she'll be a while. They're understaffed today, but I'll let them know where you are. They can page you."

After getting *Mammi*'s name, he left a message at the desk, took Lydia's elbow, and steered her down a corridor to the right. Warmth flooded her body at his gentle touch. Her grandmother's warning came back, and Lydia slipped her arm from his grasp. She steeled herself against his nearness, but despite all her conscience's warnings, her pattering heart took on the cadence of hoofbeats. Perhaps she shouldn't have agreed to this. She could have asked about Emma in the waiting room.

Lydia stopped so abruptly that a nurse hurrying along behind them bumped into her. After apologizing profusely, Lydia turned back to Caleb and blurted out, "Where are Emma and Kyle?"

Caleb eyes appeared haunted. "I hoped you'd know."

If Caleb had no idea where they were, how would she ever find Emma?

He reached for her elbow again. "We should move. We're blocking the hallway."

The floral paintings lining the dimly lit corridor blurred into a murky puddle of colors. Lydia longed to flee — from Caleb's pull on her senses, from the faint hospital smells that seemed to soak into her skin, from the flickering lights that sputtered and flashed like her emotions. Was there any point in accompanying Caleb to the cafeteria? He had no information, and she was only endangering her heart.

People scurried around them, brushed by them, bumped into them, glared at them.

Caleb gestured toward the cafeteria. "Can we talk in there so we're out of everyone's way?" He glanced at his watch. "I only have ten minutes left."

Only ten minutes. Surely she could handle being with him that long.

When they entered the glassed-in room, Lydia blinked in the sudden shock of sunlight. The scrape of chair legs on the floor, the chattering groups, and the clatter of silverware assaulted her ears from all sides. Over it all hung the heavy, steamy smell of overcooked food, almost smothering her, the way Caleb's nearness kept crowding her thoughts, her emotions, and her senses.

Although he motioned for her to go first, she followed him and imitated him as he slid a blue melamine tray along the metal bars. She selected her silverware and napkin from the holder, but ended up taking only a packet of potato chips.

Caleb grabbed a Styrofoam cup of macaroni and cheese. "This'll have to hold me until later this afternoon. We have so many staff out with the flu, I won't get my usual lunch break." He led the way to the nearest vacant spot at the crowded tables, stood aside so she could slide in, and then squeezed in beside her.

Lydia scooted over on the bench until she almost touched shoulders with the heavyset nurse on her left. She left the chips on her tray and kept her elbows tucked against her side so she wouldn't bump Caleb or her other neighbor. Their closeness pressing in on her made her claustrophobic. She wrung her hands in her lap, wishing she'd never agreed to accompany Caleb.

Between bites, he filled her in on his brother. "Kyle moved all his things out of the house while I was working overtime last Saturday. I stopped by the restaurant where he works several times, but he refused to speak to me, and he won't answer his cell. I even tried following him home one night" — Caleb looked sheepish — "but I couldn't keep up with him on the icy roads."

Lydia's shoulders slumped. Caleb had been her only hope.

He finished his last bite and stood. "I'm sorry to rush you, but I need to get back."

Lydia trailed him to the disposal area,

clutching her bag of chips. When Caleb rejoined her, Lydia forced her hands to stop crinkling the foil.

Caleb rubbed his jaw. "I've been thinking we should try Yoder's barn on Friday night. Maybe Kyle and Emma will be there."

Not *we*. Lydia took a step back. "Um, maybe it would be better if you went alone."

"Kyle's not talking to me." Caleb motioned for her to precede him out the door. "I was thinking you'd have better luck talking to Emma."

After Emma's accusations the other night, Lydia doubted her sister would even speak to her. "I don't think . . ."

As they walked down the hallway, Caleb turned imploring eyes in her direction. "Please? Kyle has only a few weeks to sign and return the financial aid form." His voice sounded desperate. "If you can convince your sister to leave him, I'm sure Kyle will get back on track for college. I can swing by and pick you up around six on Friday night."

Caleb's plea was hard to resist. She was playing with fire, but Lydia nodded.

As the afternoon stretched on, thoughts of meeting Caleb next weekend started her stomach churning. And worry over *Mammi* increased it. The longer she waited, the tighter her nerves stretched.

When a nurse called her name, Lydia hurried to the desk.

"They're taking Esther Esh into surgery now for an emergency appendectomy," the nurse informed her.

Lydia stared at the nurse, trying to make sense of the words. *Mammi* needed an operation? "Will she be all right?"

The nurse gave her a *calm-down-it'll-be-fine* smile. "It's routine surgery."

Maybe for someone who worked in a hospital every day, but not for *Mammi*. "Where is she? Can I see her? I should be with her."

The nurse shook her head. "She's being prepped for surgery. You can wait in the surgical waiting room. A doctor will speak with you after the appendectomy." She pointed to the elevator. "Second floor on the left."

Lydia crossed the lobby and almost bumped into Caleb, who was shrugging his broad shoulders into a down jacket. Faint stubble darkened his jaw. Tired lines bracketed his mouth, but his lips still curved up at the sight of her, and surprise registered in his eyes. "You're still here? Any word on your grandmother?"

"She's —" Lydia struggled to keep her voice from wavering. "They said it was her appendix."

His dimple appeared as he flashed her a reassuring smile. "That's routine surgery. Don't worry. She'll be fine."

Caleb's soothing words calmed Lydia. She hoped he was right. When he reached out to comfort her, Lydia stiffened, willed her erratic pulse to calm. She stepped back before he could touch her.

He let his hand fall to his side. "Is your family here?"

When Lydia shook her head, he held out his cell phone. "Would you like to call anyone?"

Lydia left a message on *Dat*'s shop phone. *Dat* ignored the phone during the day while he was working, but he'd check his messages for new orders before he went home. She couldn't ask a neighbor to go out in all this snow to give *Mamm* a message. Her mother would be worried, but she'd fret even more if she knew *Mammi* was in the operating room.

"Why don't I stay with you until your father arrives? It's hard to wait alone when someone you love is in surgery."

It sounded as if he had some experience with that. Had he done it after his parents' accident? Lydia hesitated to ask. And she didn't want to keep him here when he appeared so exhausted. "I'm sure you have plenty to do."

"Not more important than this."

A surge of gratitude flooded through Lydia. Having company while she waited would be comforting.

Caleb escorted her to the packed waiting room, where a television blared in one corner. Lydia seated herself with her back toward the moving pictures and kept her eyes averted from the covers of the racy magazines tossed carelessly on nearby tables. But with so many people paging through magazines, it was hard to avoid the pictures of half-dressed women and men, their arms, legs, and most of their chests exposed.

Caleb didn't seem to notice. His friendly chatter soothed her nerves and blocked the squawking television.

Concern for her grandmother sped up Lydia's pulse, and she tried to convince herself that the shivers running through her limbs when Caleb leaned close were worry for *Mammi,* not a reaction to his nearness.

Each time a surgeon entered the room, the murmurs stopped, and all eyes turned expectantly toward the green-garbed figure.

Lydia let out a soft *whoosh* of disappointment whenever they called someone else's name. Finally, after what seemed like endless hours, a doctor emerged and called her grandmother's name.

Caleb set a hand over hers and gave it a light squeeze. "I hope all went well."

Lydia had to clutch the chair arms even more tightly to rise on shaky legs. *Concentrate, Lydia. Breathe.* One foot in front of the other, she managed to cross the room.

At the surgeon's grim expression, her heart plummeted.

The doctor glanced at her, then down at his clipboard. "The operation itself went smoothly; however, the infection was extensive. We won't close the incision for a few days." The doctor tapped his pen on the clipboard. "Your grandmother is now in recovery. She should be in her room within an hour."

Lydia stood, stunned, staring after the surgeon as he pivoted and exited.

Caleb appeared at her elbow. "Is everything all right?"

Her mind still reeling from the doctor's report, Lydia said, "I'm not sure. He said the operation went well, but —" She repeated the surgeon's words.

"That happens sometimes in the case of

bad infections," Caleb assured her. "She'll be in the hospital for a few extra days, but it's nothing to worry about."

His matter-of-fact tone calmed her a little. He had medical training, so he would know these things.

Caleb checked with the desk for *Mammi*'s room number and accompanied Lydia to the sixth floor. When they reached Room 312, Lydia bid him good-bye and sat in the orange vinyl chair near the window. The partially drawn curtains blocked the dying sunlight. Late afternoon shadows striped the linoleum floor and the empty bed across the room. Carts filled with food trays clattered along the hall.

Lydia fidgeted for what seemed like hours until the squeak of wheels announced her grandmother's arrival. *Mammi* seemed groggy as two men rolled her bed into place. She lay deathly still until the attendants left. Then she surveyed the room from under half-lidded eyes. Her eyes opened slightly when they rested on Lydia. "Go home." Her voice sounded faraway and slightly slurred.

Mammi had never liked people fussing over her when she was ill, but she'd just had a major operation. Surely this was different.

But her grandmother repeated, "I said

go."

After one last glance at *Mammi*'s stern face, which was almost as bleached out as the sheets covering her frail body, Lydia bit her lip and headed for the door.

Caleb was hovering by the nurse's station when she emerged. "It's getting dark. Do you need a ride home?"

Bless him. He was so thoughtful. What would she have done without him today? Despite her jumpy pulse, being around Caleb had eased her fears and given her needed support. She had no idea if *Dat* had gotten her message yet or what time he'd arrive if he did. She could call Andy, but that could take a while, and *Mamm* might be worried. With a tremulous smile, she accepted Caleb's offer, grateful for his kindness.

The whole way home Caleb explained more about *Mammi*'s operation and what to expect over the next few weeks. Lydia was grateful for the information and glad that it kept her mind from straying too much to Caleb's nearness.

When they turned in at her house, the truck's headlights picked out a buggy in the driveway. Jakob's courting buggy. What was Jakob doing here on a Monday night?

The front door to the house flew open,

and Jakob emerged, followed by Sarah, who looked bewildered when Lydia emerged from the black truck.

Sarah rushed toward them. "Where's *Mammi*? Did Andy have car trouble? Why didn't he drive you home?" She fell silent and eyed Caleb, who had climbed from the cab. As soon as Lydia moved into the brightness of the headlights, Sarah's woodpecker-like barrage of questions started up again. "Oh, Lydia, what's wrong? Is *Mammi* in the truck?"

Lydia waved a hand in the air to slow her sister's questions. "They admitted *Mammi* to the hospital."

"The hospital? What happened? What's wrong? Will she be all right?"

Caleb's deep voice interrupted. "The appendix operation went well. I'm sure your grandmother will be fine."

Jakob's eyes narrowed into a *how-do-you-know-that?* glower.

Sarah glanced from one to the other. "Are you sure?"

Lydia hastened to reassure her. "I talked to *Mammi* when she came out of the recovery room. She seemed almost her usual self." Except for her sharpness, but she'd just had an operation.

"But why did you come home in that" —

90

Sarah gestured toward the truck — "instead of with Andy?"

Her usually reticent sister had suddenly turned garrulous. Was it concern for *Mammi*? Or was it being around Jakob? His presence often brought out Sarah's talkative side.

"I wasn't sure when *Dat* would get to the hospital, and Caleb kindly offered so . . ." Lydia shrugged.

Although curiosity brimmed in Sarah's eyes, she only said, "*Dat* came home early. He has the flu now too."

"Oh, no." Lydia longed to hurry into the house to check on her parents, but a quick glance from Caleb to Jakob showed she'd need to defuse the tension here first. "Could you run in and tell them about *Mammi* if they're not sleeping?"

"Of course, but have you eaten?" When Lydia shook her head, Sarah said, "I saved you some dinner. Jakob said you need to hurry, so I'll run in and get you a plate." With a shy glance at Jakob, she said, "I can fix you one too."

"Thanks, but I've already eaten."

Sarah turned to Caleb. "Would you like some dinner?"

"That's kind of you, but my brother will be waiting." Caleb shot Sarah his dazzling

91

smile, the one that sent Lydia's insides somersaulting.

Sarah blinked, then turned her gaze back to Jakob and Lydia. "I'll be right back. And don't worry, Lyddie. I'll tell *Mamm* and *Dat* about *Mammi.*" She caught her lower lip between her teeth for a moment before saying, "I do hope she's all right."

"*Mammi* will be fine, Sarah." Lydia said automatically, her mind still on Sarah's comment about needing to hurry. As soon as Sarah rushed toward the house, she turned questioning eyes toward Jakob.

Caleb stepped closer to Lydia. "I'll be going so you can spend time with your family. But if you need a ride to or from the hospital again, just let me know."

Jakob crunched through the crusted snow into the circle of light, his chest puffed out like a banty rooster. "I can drive Lydia to the hospital if she needs transportation." In contrast to his usual friendly demeanor, Jakob's tone matched his aggressive stance.

Caleb held up his hands as if in surrender. "Hey, I didn't mean to cause any trouble. I only offered to help because I work at the hospital."

Red crept up Jakob's neck and flamed his cheeks. "I apologize. It's just that Lydia and I, we're, well" — he glanced at Lydia, and

the crimson in his cheeks deepened —
"friends."

Lydia stood, fists clenched at her side.
She'd seen roosters circling to fight, and
Jakob still looked ready to peck. She hoped
he'd control his temper.

Caleb relaxed his stance and shoved his
hands into his pockets. "I see."

Now it was Lydia's turn to blush. No, he
didn't see. His tone implied a lot more than
the innocent relationship she and Jakob
shared. He didn't think she was like Emma,
did he?

Jakob shuffled in the dirt, or maybe pawed
was more like it. A bull preparing to charge?
Lydia caught his attention and shook her
head almost imperceptibly. Jakob blew out
a breath.

Caleb smiled at both of them — a neutral
smile, impartial, grouping them together.
"Well, I'll be seeing you —"

Lydia threw him a warning glance, so he
wouldn't mention Friday night, although
the secretiveness bothered her conscience.

Caleb stopped mid-sentence. "Hope your
grandmother gets better quickly," he finished.

"*Danke.*" Lydia answered automatically.

"*U bent welkom.*"

He spoke German? Lydia started. He

must be the German-speaking Caleb the nurse had mentioned. Unless he only knew a few pleasantries like "you're welcome." That might be the case working in a hospital in this area.

Eyes narrowed, Jakob studied Caleb as he returned to the truck. Jakob didn't speak until the vehicle shot off down the road. "You were alone in that truck with a man."

Although Jakob's accusation added to her guilt about the feelings tumbling around inside whenever she was around Caleb, Lydia defended herself. "I've ridden alone with Andy before." Not often. But twice in emergencies. And she would have come home alone with him tonight if —

Jakob's jaw was set. "Andy's different."

"Different how?" Lydia couldn't keep the defensiveness from her tone.

He shrugged. "I know you are pure in heart, but others have doubts . . ." He scuffed the gravel under his feet. Keeping his gaze on his shoes, he mumbled, his words crowding and bumping each other in his haste to get them out, "My father sent me to get you. The school board is waiting for you at our house. But with your grandmother in the hospital, I can tell my *dat* —"

Still reeling from the day's events and from being alone with Caleb, Lydia struggled to make sense of what Jakob had just said. Ordinarily the bishop came calling when someone in the community had fallen into sin. But to be called to meet with the bishop and the school board? Lydia twisted her hands together under her cloak. That sounded ominous. And Jakob's nervousness added to her fear. What had she done to warrant this summons? "No . . . if they're waiting, I should go."

CHAPTER SEVEN

Sarah rushed out the door and thrust a plate in Lydia's hands. After hurriedly asking her sister to tell *Mamm* and *Dat* where she was going, Lydia climbed into the buggy beside Jakob. She huddled into her coat and wrapped the blankets tightly around her legs, but it didn't stop the chills that shook her body. Maybe she should have let Jakob tell the school board about *Mammi* and reschedule the meeting, but that would only postpone the inevitable.

Except for asking after *Mammi*'s health, Jakob was withdrawn on the ride to his family's farm. Lydia, her thoughts swirling, was grateful when the conversation stuttered to a stop. She hurried through the meal Sarah had prepared, but her nerves made swallowing hard.

After they arrived, Jakob ushered her into the kitchen, briefly greeted the men gathered around the scarred wooden table, and then cleared his throat. "Um, *Dat,* Lydia's gr—"

Lydia shot him a warning glance, and the words died on his lips. Then, with a sympathetic glance at her, he hurried back outside to care for the horses. His mother bustled about finishing the last of the dinner dishes, and Lydia turned to face the three school board members — Jake Fisher, Elmer King, and Elam Petersheim. The knots twisting and tangling in her stomach tightened.

Hiram Zook motioned for her to sit on the bench opposite them. Then he took a seat beside the other men. Stony faces met her quick glance. Lowering her eyes, she slipped into the seat Bishop Zook had indicated. All she could see were two long black beards and Bishop Zook's gray one, black galluses, and blue shirt fronts. But the three pairs of clasped hands, one resting on a stack of papers, filled her with dread.

In unison all four men bowed their heads and closed their eyes. Lydia did the same, and after silently reciting the Lord's Prayer, she added a petition that she would be open to hearing their counsel.

When they raised their heads, the other men looked toward Bishop Zook. He cleared his throat and began. "Lydia Esh, you agreed as a schoolteacher to set a good example for our students."

Hands clenched in her lap, Lydia nodded and kept her eyes fixed on the table, head bowed to show respect, but inside she squirmed.

Bishop Zook cast a disapproving glance her way. "We have received a complaint about you attending parties in Yoder's barn. We understand that alcohol, drugs, dancing, and other unacceptable activities take place at these gatherings. Your presence at such a place does not set a good example for the pupils."

Lydia's dinner clotted in her stomach like curdled milk. She wanted to defend herself, but that would be considered *hochmut,* and pride was a greater sin than these accusations.

The bishop adjusted his glasses and read from the paper in front of him. "We are charging you to do the following. First, you will never again attend a party at Yoder's barn. Second, you will confess in front of the church about attending these parties and about any indulgences you have engaged in there. Do you agree?"

Lydia's stomach clenched. How could she make these promises when she'd already made plans to go with Caleb to Yoder's barn this weekend? The silence stretched as Lydia fought an internal battle.

Bishop Zook cleared his throat.

Lydia stared at her hands clenched in her lap. "I agree," she choked out.

Following another silent prayer, the men dismissed her. The bench scraped across the wooden floor as she rose, head still bowed. Though the school board may have taken her lowered head as a sign of repentance, Lydia squirmed inside, knowing her real purpose was to prevent them from seeing her guilty face.

She stumbled from the kitchen and bumped into Rebecca. How much had her assistant heard? Lydia swallowed hard and tried not to let her distress show. "Jakob, is he around?"

Rebecca's tense frown relaxed into a smile. "I will find him for you. Although I am surprised he was not sitting where he could gaze at your beauty." She giggled when Lydia gasped. "Oh, don't pretend you don't know he's besotted with you. The two of you have been courting. Surely he's told you how beautiful you are."

Bemused, Lydia shook her head. "Surely he hasn't." That wouldn't be proper. Compliments such as that led to *hochmut,* the last thing she needed right now.

Rebecca chuckled. "I'll have to give him

some courting advice. Abner tells me —"
She stopped abruptly. "Never mind. I'm
sure Jakob will be overjoyed to have time
alone with you. He was complaining" — she
clapped a hand across her mouth — "I
mean, wishing, you two could spend more
time together." She dashed upstairs.

A few moments later Jakob came downstairs. "Rebecca says you are ready to go.
Would you like some hot water bottles for
the ride? *Mamm* has water heating on the
stove."

With the guilt and shame swirling through
her mind, Lydia was humbled by Mary
Zook's thoughtfulness. "That would be
lovely. Please thank your mother for thinking of me."

Jakob smiled. "I believe she has an ulterior
motive."

Ah, yes, keeping her future daughter-in-
law warm and on her good side. Not that
Jakob had directly mentioned marriage, but
as she was the only girl he'd ever courted,
Lydia assumed a proposal would come
sometime in the near future. Once they had
both joined the church.

When they reached his courting buggy,
Jakob set the hot water bottles around her
feet without touching her and handed her a
blanket. Some men took the opportunity to

tuck blankets around their dates, but Jakob always behaved with propriety. He took his role as the bishop's son seriously and did all he could to keep his reputation spotless. Which was more than she could say for herself lately.

As the horse clomped toward her house, Lydia gazed at the stars that spangled the sky. Each point of brightness illuminated only a tiny spot in the vast blackness. Yet together they created a pattern of beauty, much like the star quilts *Mamm* had sewn for their beds. Much like she and her fellow Plain brethren were to be lights in the darkness of the world.

Lydia wanted to share that thought with Jakob, but he was a practical man, given to discussing that which he could see and touch, that which he could affect by action. Though he had a strong faith, he saw God more as a list of rules and regulations set down in the *Ordnung*. As long as he set his feet on the right path, he would plod forward, doing what was expected of him. Although part of her longed for someone who would talk about stars and appreciate their beauty, she reminded herself that Jakob was a good man and had all the qualities a woman needed in a husband. She should be grateful he would be her lot in life.

Jakob kept one wheel of the buggy off the side of the road as was the usual custom, although with the snow, Lydia worried the wheels might slide on hidden patches of ice. The snow lay deeper on the road's shoulder, and at times the steel wheels seemed to stick. The snowbanks muffled the clip-clop of the horse's hooves, and as the buggy swayed from side to side, she grew drowsy. She had gotten so little sleep the past few nights.

A sudden jerk jolted her awake. "Wha—?"

"I apologize for waking you. A car fishtailed through the intersection up ahead. I did not want to risk getting closer."

"Are they all right?"

"*Jah,* they straightened themselves out and kept driving. They would do better to go slower in this weather. The roads are slippery."

"I'm glad they weren't hurt. And thank you for your safe driving."

Jakob's cheeks, already ruddy from the cold, grew a shade redder in the moonlight, and a faint smile curved his lips. He quickly erased it and said, "*Ach,* it was nothing. Anyone would have done the same."

Lydia's cheeks warmed too. Perhaps she shouldn't have praised him. She did not want pride to cause him to stumble.

After Jakob pulled into her driveway, he held the reins loosely in his hands, waiting for an invitation. Once again, she used lesson plans and her parents' illness as an excuse, but Jakob's melancholy face haunted her long after he pulled away.

Perhaps she should have asked him in. Who knew how long it would be before she could again ride in his courting buggy? Especially once the church community discovered she'd disobeyed the bishop.

CHAPTER EIGHT

With the school board's ultimatum and *Mammi*'s earlier warning ringing in her ears, Lydia's conscience tormented her. Was God trying to warn her not to go to the barn with Caleb?

Questions and guilt tumbled around in her mind as she prepared the lesson plans the board had demanded. Hour after hour, until gray dawn lightened the horizon, she labored. She sat back with a sigh and twisted her body first one way, then the other to stretch her sore muscles. She longed to curl up under the quilt, but instead she dragged herself downstairs. With *Dat* ill, she needed to stoke the woodstove, gather eggs, and feed and milk all four cows. She started breakfast, then trudged back upstairs to wake Zeke and Abe. They'd all have to share the work so they could get to school on time.

Zeke moaned and clutched his stomach

when she shook him. She laid a hand on his forehead. He was burning with fever. Sarah would have another patient. Poor Sarah. She'd slept downstairs on the sofa to nurse *Mamm* and *Dat* through the night.

After Lydia sent Sarah up to care for Zeke, she and Abe rushed through the morning chores but left the dishes undone. Lydia had no wish to add tardiness to her list of failures.

She managed to keep her mind on the lessons and have the correct plans ready for Rebecca throughout the morning. After lunch, when Rebecca and the students tromped into the snow to enjoy recess, Lydia laid her head on the desk a moment to rest her eyes.

The school door banging open jolted her awake, dizzy and disoriented.

"Oh, Lydia," Rebecca said, helping the younger children out of their coats, "you look so tired. Are you coming down with the flu?"

Lydia shook her head. "Just exhausted."

For the rest of the afternoon Rebecca hovered over her until Lydia waved her away. "I'll be fine. Don't worry."

Rebecca laid a gentle hand on Lydia's shoulder. "You have so much on your mind. Your parents ill. Your *Mammi* in the hospital.

And Emma . . . Jakob and I both begged *Dat* not to listen to idle chatter."

"About Emma?"

The way Rebecca studied the laces of her sturdy brown shoes told Lydia that Emma hadn't been the only subject of gossip. She longed to find out what Rebecca had heard, but she couldn't ask her to repeat it.

Rebecca's hand tightened on Lydia's shoulder. "Have no fear. Jakob has great faith in your innocence. As do I."

The word *innocence* echoed in Lydia's brain after she dismissed the students and followed Abe across the snowy fields. Going with Caleb to Yoder's barn would stir even more talk. Worse, she'd be going against the bishop's instructions.

As she completed her father's chores, fixed dinner, and grabbed the horses' harnesses, Lydia's conscience warred within her. *Dat* was too sick to forbid her to take the buggy. Normally he did not allow her to drive on icy roads, but she had little choice. Someone had to visit *Mammi* in the hospital. Lydia was struggling to harness the horses when Bishop Zook drove in. Her heart lurched. Had he discerned her guilt? Come to give her another lecture? Or had God laid on his heart a stronger warning?

"Good evening, Lydia. When Jakob returned last night, he told me of your grandmother's surgery. I am very sorry to hear that Esther is in the hospital. I wish I had known that last evening. We would have postponed the meeting."

Lydia stood, tongue-tied, clenching the harness.

The bishop said gently, "You do understand that we all love you and care what happens to you."

Lydia hung her head. "Yes, I know." Guilt tightened her vocal cords, making her voice gravelly. After the bishop's kindness and forgiveness, how could she go behind his back and disobey?

"Rebecca says she has all your lesson plans for this week. She can handle the classroom." He waited until Lydia nodded and then continued, "That will free you to spend your days with your grandmother. She should not be left alone in the hospital."

Lydia could not look him in the eye, but she managed to choke out, "Thank you for your thoughtfulness. And Rebecca's as well. I appreciate her willingness to substitute."

Bishop Zook cleared his throat and then said, "Yes, well, she must learn to handle the schoolroom on her own. Is that not so? I expect she will take over when you marry."

Lydia sucked in a quick breath. Many

couples kept their wedding plans secret until shortly before they married in November. But it seemed Jakob had spoken to his family of his future plans. A subject he had never discussed with her. But they'd been courting for almost two years; of course their parents assumed they would marry. All the other couples had paired off, so it was only natural for people to expect Jakob and her to have a future together.

The bishop studied her face. "Perhaps I spoke out of turn. If so, I apologize. Oh, and when they are ready to discharge your grandmother, please let Aaron Stoltzfus know so he can handle the payment from the fund."

"Thank you so much." Lydia's eyes stung. The community banded together to help its own. With the downturn in *Dat*'s business recently, they could use the assistance.

Behind them, horses' hooves crunched on gravel.

The bishop peered down the driveway. "Ah, there's Jakob now. I know your father has forbidden you to drive in the snow and ice." A frown creased his brow as his glance returned to the harness she twisted in her hands.

Lydia's cheeks burned. She longed to hide the harness behind her back, but that would not conceal her guilt. Disobeying *Dat* wasn't the only sin she'd been considering. If the bishop knew about her weekend plans, the disappointment in his gaze would turn to condemnation.

Jakob pulled up nearby, climbed from the buggy, and approached them. The bishop laid a hand on Jakob's shoulder. "My son has offered to take you to the hospital each day and bring you home. He is worried about your safety."

Unspoken words hung between them. The bishop's inflection implied that Jakob had an additional motive. To stake his claim? To protect her reputation? Or to keep her from further sin?

By offering to transport her, Jakob would keep her from temptation. It would allow him to keep a closer eye on her and prevent her from talking to Caleb, so perhaps it was for the best.

Though Lydia was grateful for Jakob's kindness, she could think of little to say on the way to the hospital once they'd finished discussing her family's health. And no matter how hard she tried to forget, thoughts of her conversations with Caleb crowded her mind. Lydia breathed a sigh of relief after Jakob pulled up in front of the hospital and let her out. She hurried inside and waited for Jakob to park the buggy and join her.

When they reached *Mammi*'s hospital room, Lydia bent to kiss her grandmother's cheek. "How are you feeling? I'm sorry you were alone all day."

A sly smile crossed *Mammi*'s face. "I wasn't. I had company. That nice young man stopped in to see me. He even spoke to me in *Deutsch.* Quite kind of him."

Nice young man? Caleb?

Jakob's scowl caused Lydia's words to come out more sharply than she'd intended. "You mean Caleb? He's a hospital worker. It's his job to care for patients." Although she doubted that his responsibilities included checking on patients in their hospital rooms.

Mammi's long, drawn-out *ahhh* left doubt hanging in the air.

Jakob bristled. "He works on this floor?"

Lydia sighed. Jealousy was so unlike the Jakob she'd always known. The one who always thought the best of others and acted meek, patient, and humble. She tried to keep her tone neutral. "Caleb works in the clinic admissions department."

"And he considered it his duty to check on your grandmother's health? And to drive you home last night?"

Mammi pinned Lydia with a probing stare.

110

How was Lydia going to explain this to Jakob's satisfaction? And her grandmother's? "Caleb is the older brother of the *Englischer* Emma has been" — *how could she put this delicately?* — "seeing."

Jakob crossed his arms and frowned, and her grandmother's brow furrowed.

Lydia plowed on trying to ignore their stares. "Caleb is as unhappy as we are that Emma is dating his brother. So we've talked about ways to break them up."

Jakob interrupted. "And that is the reason he drove you home?"

Grateful that Jakob couldn't peek into her thoughts, Lydia made her statement as casual as she could. "He passes our house on the way home." She had to change the subject before Jakob questioned her about that. "Maybe I should visit with *Mammi* since we can't stay long."

Crimson swept up Jakob's cheeks at her rebuke. He hung his head. "Forgive me," he said, his voice stiff and formal. "I did not mean to keep you from spending time with your grandmother."

Now she had offended him. Lydia sucked back the sigh that rose to her lips. "I did not mean to imply that you were at fault. Only that our time here is limited."

Jakob's head bobbed in what might have

111

been acknowledgment or possibly irritation. He motioned to the chair closest to her grandmother's bed. "Have a seat. Please. I will sit over here out of the way." He dragged one of the chairs to the farthest corner of *Mammi*'s half of the room.

"You're welcome to be part of the conversation."

Jakob waved his hand. "I have no wish to intrude."

Was it her imagination, or was he acting like a petulant child?

Mammi looked from one to the other, an amused smile playing about her lips.

Too tired to argue, Lydia sank into the chair. A pin from her dress dug into her side, its sharp prick like the jab of her conscience. Lydia had shared some surface facts about Emma and Kyle with Jakob and *Mammi,* but she had not delved into the deeper underlying truths. She also had withheld the truth from the school board. By the time the next church Sunday arrived, she would have a long list of sins to confess.

CHAPTER NINE

Lydia rose long before dawn. She stoked the woodstove and finished the milking and ironing before sending Abe off to school. Then she helped Sarah change the sheets on Zeke's bed as her younger brother sat shivering, huddled in a quilt, on Abe's bed.

Lydia fluffed the pillow, and Sarah helped Zeke back into bed and tucked the quilt around him. Then she smiled at her sister. "You're so good at caring for people. Perhaps you would like to go with Jakob to spend the day with *Mammi*."

Sarah drew in a quick breath. "Oh, no. I couldn't." She fumbled with the end of the quilt she was tucking in, pulled it out, and tried again. "I–I don't do well in hospitals. And I'm not sure I can bear to see *Mammi* there."

"But you're caring for three patients here. It might be a break for you after being up much of the night."

Sarah put her hands on her hips. "And how would you know that?"

"I checked on Zeke a few times." The truth was Lydia had lain awake most of the night, her thoughts racing in circles like a cat chasing its tail, until she'd made her decision. She couldn't go to Yoder's barn. But how could she slip away from Jakob's watchful eye to let Caleb know?

As Sarah picked up the glass beside Zeke's bed, someone knocked at the front door. "You'd better go. You don't want to keep Jakob waiting."

When Lydia opened the door, Jakob studied her. "Are you feeling well?"

Lydia did her best to look perky. "I'm fine." Except for the heavy load of guilt she was carrying around like a week's worth of unwashed laundry.

But her answer didn't satisfy Jakob. "Are you sure? You look peaked. You're not coming down with the flu, I hope?"

"No, I'm just a bit tired." *And hiding a multitude of sins.*

Jakob reached for the doorknob. "Perhaps you should stay home and rest this morning. I could let your grandmother know."

"I said I was fine." The harshness of her tone made Lydia cringe. Jakob shouldn't bear the brunt of her tiredness and irritability. To make amends, she said hastily, "I have water heating on the stove for the water bottles. Please let me warm yours."

"No need." Jakob's words were abrupt, his jaw tense.

She'd offended him again.

She hadn't meant to. What was wrong with her? Ever since she'd met Caleb, her patience had worn so thin it was almost threadbare. Acting out of character, telling half-truths, allowing her thoughts to stray — all that and more had piled on layers of guilt. Guilt she was now taking out on an innocent party.

"I'm so sorry. Please forgive me for being so grouchy."

"Of course." Jakob followed Lydia to the kitchen and waited while she filled hot water bottles. "I know you're under stress with all that is happening in your family."

"That's so." And with other things Jakob couldn't know or even imagine.

Although he tried one last time to convince her to stay home, Lydia shook her head. "Please, let's go." The sooner she got to the hospital, the more likely she could find some way to communicate with Caleb. And take at least one blot off her conscience.

■ ■ ■ ■

Jakob shadowed Lydia throughout the day, so she had no opportunity to speak to Caleb. His hovering increased after Caleb popped his head into the room at lunchtime.

Caleb gave *Mammi* a quick wave. "I see you have plenty of company, Mrs. Esh, so I'll go grab a bite. Nice to see you again, Lydia. And you too, um . . ."

Jakob growled his name and stepped closer to Lydia.

Caleb's smile was a cross between apologetic and friendly. "Right. Jakob." He gave another flick of his hand that may have been a wave, then turned and headed for the elevator.

"He met me the other night," Jakob groused. "Didn't even remember my name."

Had she introduced them? Lydia couldn't remember. All that stuck in her mind was a memory of the tension between them.

"So handsome he is, that boy." *Mammi* tapped a finger on her chin. "Reminds me of someone. Wish I could bring to mind who."

The doctor's arrival provided a welcome change of subject. To give *Mammi* her privacy, Lydia and Jakob retreated to the lounge. When they returned to the room, *Mammi* lay with her eyes closed, but the rapid rise and fall of her chest indicated she wasn't sleeping.

"*Mammi?*"

Her grandmother cracked one eye open.

"What did the doctor say?"

"The infection is draining. More slowly than he'd like, but I am old." *Mammi* wheezed to a stop like a generator running out of gas. "So it's only to be expected."

"You're not old," Lydia protested. "Did he say when you can go home?"

Mammi turned her head away, and her eyelids fluttered shut. "Please go now. I need my sleep." She waved a weak hand in the air as if shooing flies. "Shouldn't you be at school, Lydia? And, Jakob, doesn't your father need you?"

"Yes, Mrs. Esh, he does. This is a very busy time for him."

Mammi harrumphed. "I thought so. And the school needs Lydia. So I suggest you both go to work where you belong."

Lydia stepped closer to *Mammi*'s bed. "I don't want to leave you alone. Rebecca is doing a fine job of substituting."

"I have no doubt she is, but you should do your duty. If I were sick in bed at home, you would not miss school to sit beside me.

Please do not shirk your responsibilities on my account."

Jakob, who had been pacing the floor since her grandmother spoke, turned to Lydia. "*Dat* has two rush orders that need to go out today. Without my help, he may not meet the deadline."

"Please do not feel you have to stay if your father needs you," Lydia said. *Besides, I need to speak to Caleb.*

Myriad emotions flashed across Jakob's face — worry, disquiet, foreboding, hesitation. He glanced at the open doorway to the hospital room with pursed lips and furrowed brow. Like the patriarch in the Bible, this Jakob too wrestled unseen forces. Jealousy warred with responsibility.

Lydia had to convince him to go. "I don't feel right keeping you if your father needs you." A prickle of unease skimmed along her spine. Never had she been so deceitful.

Jakob was nothing if not responsible. And in the end, duty won. "I will go home to help him. If you are sure you don't need us, Mrs. Esh."

"Quite sure."

Relief spread across Jakob's face. "Thank you for reminding me of my duties." He inclined his head toward *Mammi* and then picked up Lydia's bag of school assignments. "Come, Lydia. We will leave your grandmother to her rest and prayers."

Lydia set her jaw. "I am not leaving." She strode toward the orange vinyl chair beside the bed and plopped into it, ignoring the pinpoints scratching her skin.

Mammi raised her weary gaze to Lydia's. "Go with Jakob. I need time alone."

"Fine. Then I will not speak. I will sit here and do my lesson plans." Lydia had never talked back to her grandmother before. And though she should be ashamed of her defiance, part of her took pleasure in her boldness. Was this what Emma felt when she disobeyed the *Ordnung*?

Jakob was staring at Lydia as if she had turned into a strange beast. *Mammi*'s gray eyebrows arched upward.

To soften her strident words, Lydia said meekly, "The bishop made these arrangements. Would you have me go against his wishes?"

Mammi shook her head. Jakob looked chagrined.

Lydia held out her hand. "May I have my bag please?"

Jakob nodded, a new respect in his eyes, along with a touch of wariness.

Lydia's smile stretched even the normally unused muscles of her face, so great was her relief. Surely she'd be able to speak to Caleb and explain why she couldn't go on Friday.

She jolted back to the present to see Jakob staring at her, mesmerized. He obviously thought the smile was for him. His hands hung by his side, his grip on her bag so slack that it could easily drop.

"Ahem."

Mammi's throat clearing made him jump. Lydia's bag tumbled from his hand, and papers spilled across the floor. Jakob scrambled to retrieve them.

Lydia waved a hand to stop him. "Don't worry about it. I have plenty of time to collect them. You should hurry home." Preferably before it dawned on him that she might meet Caleb.

With a lingering glance over his shoulder, Jakob walked from the room. The weight that lifted as he disappeared into the elevator made Lydia giddy. Now all she needed was an excuse to leave her grandmother's side.

By the time Lydia had gotten all the papers in order, *Mammi*'s eyes were closed, but her lips were moving rapidly. Lydia didn't want to disturb her grandmother's prayers, so after a quick prayer of her own, she set to work on her lesson plans.

A short while later a light snoring signaled that *Mammi* had drifted off to sleep. Now was her chance. How wonderful it would be to have the worry about Yoder's barn off her conscience. And perhaps if Caleb talked to Emma at the dance, he'd be kind enough to tell her about *Mammi.*

Lydia tiptoed from the room, and although the rapid movement made her stomach queasy, she breathed a huge sigh of relief as the elevator descended.

Crowds filled the waiting room, and intake counselors hurried back and forth, escorting patients to their windows. No sign of Caleb. Should she wait for him to emerge? But he would be working, so she couldn't talk to him. Perhaps she could catch his eye, and he could meet her on his break. She had no idea how long *Mammi* would sleep. She didn't want her grandmother to wake and discover her gone. She could only imagine the questions that would provoke.

But as the hands of the clock swept past the quarter hour, then the half hour, Lydia grew nervous. Maybe she should leave a message. She waited for a lull in the crowd and then approached the desk.

"I wondered if it might be possible to speak to Caleb Miller. When he's free, of course."

The woman frowned. "He wasn't feeling well and went home early."

Now what? "May I leave a message for him? For when he returns?" She only hoped he'd come back in before Friday.

The woman nodded, but Lydia's brain filled with fog. What could she say? If she wrote *I can't go with you on Friday night,* people might think they had a date. What if he had a girlfriend? She didn't want to give the wrong impression. Or upset his girl-friend, if he had one.

"Hey, girlie," a loud voice said near her ear. "Some of us got emergencies."

Lydia jumped. "I'm so sorry."

The man pushed past her and up to the window. The woman gave Lydia a sympathetic glance, and Lydia backed up even farther.

Her cheeks flamed. "Maybe I'll just wait until he returns." She turned and scurried toward the elevator. How could she let Caleb know?

CHAPTER TEN

On Friday Caleb was still out sick. Lydia breathed easier knowing they wouldn't be going to Yoder's barn. After the rest of the family went to bed that evening, she and Sarah started the weekend baking. Lydia peeled apples for strudel, while Sarah rolled out the dough. Wisps of hair escaped from their *kapps* and stuck to their damp foreheads. A fine coating of flour filmed their heavy skirts.

When a knock sounded at the door, they glanced at each other.

"You go," Lydia insisted. "You don't look half as bad as I do."

Sarah held out dough-covered hands. "No, I look worse. Please, Lyddie?"

Lydia sighed. She wiped her flour-coated hands on the dish towel and went to answer the door. "Caleb?" She breathed in a cleansing breath to slow the rapid patter of her heart. Rather than opening the door, she left it ajar only a crack and hid as much of herself as she could behind it. A light flurry of snow drifted from the overcast sky.

A nearby streetlight illuminated his smile. "Hi. Are you ready to go?"

Lydia blinked. The glow on his face matched the glow in her heart, but she wasn't prepared for company. Especially not Caleb's. Bending over the stove had already heated her cheeks, but now they flamed. "I — no. I tried to leave a message for you. I can't go."

Caleb shivered in his winter coat, making Lydia ashamed of not inviting him in. His brow furrowed. "I don't understand. You're not ill, are you?"

Lydia thought for a moment of saying that she was. It might explain her flushed cheeks and refusal to open the door. But her conscience wouldn't let her. "No, I'm not sick. But I've been forbidden to go. By the bishop. And the school board."

The creases between his brows deepened. "Even to see your sister? It's not like you're doing anything wrong."

"You don't understand."

"I'd like to try," Caleb said through chattering teeth.

Untidy appearance or not, Lydia couldn't leave him outside in the snow. She pulled the door open. "Come in. I'm so sorry for letting you freeze. And you've been sick. Are you well now?"

Caleb dusted the powder off his coat and stomped the snow from his boots before stepping into the foyer. "I'm over the flu. Still a bit tired and achy, so I stayed home from work. But I didn't want to let you down."

On the street behind Caleb, Amos Schrock's buggy crawled along. Lydia hoped Amos's gaze was fixed on the slippery road. But no such luck. Amos waved. Had he seen Caleb? Even if he hadn't, the black truck parked in the driveway would give it away. Amos lived next door to Jakob. No doubt he'd mention it. Lydia's heart sank.

Caleb followed her into the parlor, and Lydia resisted the urge to brush the wayward strands of hair from her face and shake off her flour-dusted skirt. She wouldn't want him to get the wrong idea. After Caleb settled in the rocker, she sat on the couch across from him.

Worry creasing her brow, Sarah peeked into the living room. "Is everything all right, Lyddie?"

"It's fine, Sarah. Caleb is here because he may help us find Emma."

"That would be wonderful." Sarah

beamed, glanced at Caleb, and then ducked her head in greeting before disappearing from the doorway. "I'll take care of the strudel so you can talk."

"Sarah's rather shy around strangers," Lydia explained as her sister scurried down the hall.

"She looks like you," Caleb said with a smile. "But about Yoder's barn . . . you've been forbidden to go?"

Lydia found it easier to speak if she didn't look at him, so she kept her gaze fixed on her lap. "I'm a teacher. The school board believes going there sets a bad example for students."

Caleb leaned forward, his hands gripping the rocker arms. "But didn't you tell them what you planned to do?"

His question surprised Lydia. "I couldn't contradict my elders."

Caleb looked puzzled. "Not contradict, just provide additional information so they could make an informed decision."

Ordinary principles that were so simple to Lydia didn't seem to translate well to the *Englisch* world. How could she help Caleb understand their ways? She tried again. "But that would be defending myself."

"Exactly." Evidently sensing by her silence that he'd said something wrong, Caleb asked in a hesitant tone, "Is that something you can't do either?"

Lydia forced herself to study her knotted fists. It was easier on her pulse. "To defend yourself is *hochmut*. I mean *pride*." To control her rapid heartbeat she reminded herself of Jakob, who would understand all these concepts naturally. But even though her mind gave her logical reasons for keeping her distance from Caleb, her heart and body refused to listen.

Looking as pleased as a struggling student who'd gotten his recitation correct, Caleb grinned. "I know what *hochmut* is. I do speak some German."

Lydia flushed. "Oh, that's right."

But a frown rapidly chased away his look of triumph. "I still don't get it. You mean it's pride to explain your motives?"

Lydia used her patient schoolteacher voice. "Yes, and you don't contradict the bishop."

Caleb rocked so far forward Lydia worried he'd pitch face first onto the rag rug. "What if he's mistaken?"

She breathed a sigh of relief when he tilted the chair upright. "It is God's job to set him straight."

"I see." Caleb slid to the edge of the chair. "So I guess that means you won't be going." He waited for Lydia's nod to confirm it before getting to his feet. "I suppose there isn't any use in me going then."

Lydia glanced up, and then wished she hadn't. She tried to tell herself that looking at Caleb was like admiring the beauty of God's creation, but staring at beautiful landscapes didn't set her pulse thrumming this way. "But how will we find out where they're living?"

"I don't know, but I do know Kyle won't speak to me. I was counting on you getting the information from your sister."

"Ask Emma. She'll respond. She was raised to be polite." Although Emma was also raised to be many other things that she had forgotten.

Caleb's deep sigh revealed the weight of his worry. "So was Kyle. But I think all bets are off."

Lydia gave him a puzzled look.

"I mean that neither of them is following the rules they learned at home."

How true. This conversation had clearly shown her that she and Caleb spoke different languages. Though she appreciated his chivalry at Yoder's barn, his kindness to *Mammi,* and his willingness to look for Emma, the two of them inhabited separate worlds. The only thing they had in common

128

was their concern for their siblings. Somehow she'd lost sight of that purpose. She walked Caleb to the door. "If you go and they're there, could you please tell Emma about our grandmother being in the hospital?"

"Will do." Caleb gave her his dazzling smile before heading out to his truck.

Her thoughts churning, Lydia watched until his tail lights disappeared into the blackness of the night.

Two hours later, a sharp knock resounded through the downstairs. Who would come calling this hour? Perhaps the gravity of Caleb's message had brought Emma home.

Lydia flung open the door. "Caleb?" At least she'd had time to tidy up. "Come in, come in." The snow swirling down was piling up into drifts. Excited as she was to see him, she had to remind herself of why he was here. "Did you talk to Kyle or Emma?"

"No, but . . ." Caleb stepped onto the rag rug and bent to remove his boots.

Lydia's shoulders drooped. Why had he come then if he had no news?

Caleb padded into the parlor in stocking feet and sat in the rocker he'd used earlier. He ran his hands over the satiny wood finish. "I noticed this earlier. It's gorgeous."

"My grandfather's handiwork." Lydia gestured around the room. "He made most of the furniture in the house."

Caleb studied the rest of the pieces one at a time. "He's very talented."

"Was." Lydia still had a hard time believing *Grosdaadi* wasn't still around. So many times when she opened the door to the *daadi haus,* she expected to hear *Daadi*'s hearty laugh, to hear him teasing *Mammi.* "He died three years ago. We all still miss him, *Mammi* especially."

A wistful look crossed Caleb's face. "I know how hard it is to lose someone you love. And I never had any grandparents. You were lucky to have yours. Your grandmother's a great woman. Easy to talk to, and very wise."

Yes, *Mammi* was definitely wise. "That reminds me. *Mammi* said she'd like to see you again. When you have time, of course. I know you're busy."

"I'll look forward to it, but the reason I'm here is that I have some news." Caleb reached into his pocket and drew out a scrap of paper. "Emma and Kyle weren't at the barn, but I ran into one of Kyle's friends. And he told me where they're living." He held out the paper, but loud rapping interrupted them.

Lydia jumped to her feet and hurried to the door before the noise disturbed *Mamm* and *Dat.* She yanked open the door.

"Jakob? What are you doing here this time of night?" Her tone sounded less than welcoming. She pulled the door wider. "Come in out of the snow." She willed her heart to stop pounding so hard. This time its rapid drumming was from the fright he'd given her. "Nothing's wrong, is it?"

Jakob studied her intently. "I don't know. Is it?"

Lydia stepped back at the accusatory note in his voice. Although she had done nothing wrong, heat crept up her neck and splashed onto her cheeks as Jakob shook off the snow and stepped inside, his gaze darting around the foyer and into the rooms beyond. In the rocker in the corner, Caleb wasn't visible, but his truck was parked outside.

"So why are you here?" Lydia tried to infuse warmth into her words to cover her alarm.

Jakob held out a wicker pie carrier. "*Mamm* sent this peach cobbler."

Lydia had been so nervous, she hadn't even noticed it on his arm. Peach cobbler at this time of night when everyone was in bed? Somehow it didn't seem like something Mary Zook would do. "How kind of her.

Please come into the kitchen." She disliked leaving Caleb alone, but she didn't relish seeing Jakob's reaction if he actually saw the visitor relaxing in the rocker in stocking feet.

Jakob craned his neck as they passed the parlor, but Caleb sat beyond his line of sight. Jakob followed so closely on her heels that Lydia worried he might step on her hem.

When they reached the kitchen, he set the pie carrier on the table. Then he cleared his throat. "I'd hoped to spend time with you. We've had little chance to be alone."

Lydia busied herself with removing the cobbler, which was still warm, and setting it on the wide windowsill to cool. "Be sure to thank your mother for us. I know we'll all enjoy it. She's such a wonderful cook."

When she turned, Jakob looked as sad as a puppy whose favorite bone had been stolen. He pulled out the bench as if to settle in for a talk.

Lydia needed to get rid of him, while still assuring him that she cared about him. "It's rather late. Why not come calling tomorrow? We can have most of the day together."

He sat down and indicated the space next to him. "I'll come then, but wouldn't you like to sit and talk for a while now?"

Lydia swallowed hard. "I would, but I have a guest."

Jakob's shoulders slumped. "So he is here. Calling on you?"

Lydia bristled at his implication that she was having a relationship with an *Englischer,* although his barb hadn't fallen far from the mark. Her response was crisp, almost cutting. "No, he's here to give me information about Emma. We've been trying to find out where she's living."

Jakob's eyes held deep pools of sadness. "And that is more important than spending time with me." He didn't look at her but kept his gaze on the thumb worrying his forefinger.

"It's not a question of who I'd rather spend time with. I need Emma's address. Caleb has that information."

"And he couldn't have told you at the hospital? He seems to have plenty of time for visiting your grandmother."

"Jakob." Lydia infused his name with enough sharpness to indicate he'd overstepped his bounds.

"I'm sorry. Please forgive me." Jakob's plea held a note of humbleness that touched Lydia's heart.

He had a right to be hurt and possibly even jealous. Although Lydia had never

133

considered marrying anyone but Jakob, he did not have that knowledge or reassurance. They had never spoken of what was in their hearts, nor had they made a commitment. If Jakob were spending time with an *Englisch* girl, she too might worry.

"Caleb just found out the news tonight. At least I hope he did. He didn't have time to say before you arrived."

"I'm sorry I interrupted you."

Lydia blew out an exasperated sigh. "You did not interrupt. Caleb arrived only a short while before you did. I had just ushered him into the parlor when you knocked."

"If that is so, why did Amos see the truck here hours ago?" Jakob pressed his hand to his lips and looked as if he wished he could bite off his tongue.

Ah, so Amos had tattletaled. She'd expected as much. "Caleb stopped by earlier to see if I wanted to go to Yoder's barn."

"And why would he issue an invitation such as that?" The suspicion in Jakob's eyes overrode the distress. "I have been defending your reputation and yet —"

"Jakob." The word conveyed the depth of Lydia's hurt that he would believe the rumors about her. Though even she had to admit this put her in a bad light.

Pride made her want to hold her tongue.

And it had been ingrained into her not to defend herself against accusations, even false accusations. But she couldn't let Jakob go on believing something that was not true. Something that would hurt him. Something that would eat away at him. "Caleb wanted me to speak to Emma. He was afraid his brother wouldn't talk to him. He was here for only a few minutes when Amos saw him earlier."

"But he's here now?"

"Yes. He returned from Yoder's barn with Emma's address."

"Then where is he?" Jakob glanced around the kitchen as if he expected Caleb to be hidden behind the stove or to pop out of the pantry.

"I left him in the parlor when I went to answer the door."

"The parlor?" Jakob's gaze skimmed the simple wooden benches and scarred walnut tabletop.

Lydia could read his thoughts. When Jakob called, they always sat in the kitchen. She hastened to assure him. "Yes, we always take visitors and strangers into the parlor. Family and good friends we entertain in the kitchen. The heart of our home."

Jakob looked somewhat mollified, but a challenge still lingered in his eyes.

Lydia issued a challenge of her own. "If you would like, you may accompany me to the parlor so you can hear the rest of our interchange."

Jakob's cheeks turned ruddy. "There's no need. I trust you, Lydia. Forgive my — my —"

Lydia's heart melted at his distress. "There's nothing to forgive."

He stood and headed toward the hall. At the door he turned and gazed at her with a new, underlying sorrow in his eyes. Then he hung his head and studied his boots. "I am sorry I rushed over here. And the peach cobbler wasn't *Mamm*'s idea. I asked her to make one so I could —"

Lydia held up a hand to stop the rush of words. "It is all right. I understand. If I were in your place, I might have done the same."

"Thank you for understanding." A touch of formality colored Jakob's words. "I will see you tomorrow."

"Drive carefully," she said softly.

As soon as the door closed behind him, Lydia rushed to the parlor. "I'm so sorry to keep you waiting."

Caleb's understanding smile warmed her insides. No — melted them like marshmallow puddling over slow heat. "I hope my being here didn't cause trouble. I don't want to come between you and your intended."

"He's not my intended. I mean —"

Caleb held up a hand. "Your Jakob made it quite clear the other night that he was staking his claim. So I'll just give you this and be on my way."

Lydia's hand shook when she took the slip of paper Caleb extended. "I can't thank you enough. You don't know what this means to me."

"I needed it as well, so I was glad to do it." Caleb stood and headed toward the door. "Would you like me to pick you up tomorrow afternoon and take you there?"

Lydia hesitated. She would, but she'd better not. "I'll see if Jakob can take me."

Caleb gave her another heart-stopping smile. "Well, you know where to reach me if you need me."

Lydia hoped her unsteadiness didn't show in her voice. "Yes, yes, I do."

"Maybe I'll see you at the hospital then. And I'll stop by to visit your grandmother."

"She'll enjoy that. Thank you for that. And for this." Lydia held up the slip of paper with Emma's address. "I hope I can talk some sense into Emma."

"I do too." With that he was gone, leaving

behind a coldness in the room that made Lydia shiver.

CHAPTER ELEVEN

Jakob arrived after lunch the next day, and Lydia invited him into the kitchen while she dried the dishes.

His face brightened. "At last I'm alone with you. For the first time in a long while."

Lydia hated to burst his joy, but she wanted to talk to Emma. "I wondered if you might be willing to go for a drive."

"In this weather?" He gestured out the window. "The sun may be shining, but it is frigid. And the roads were icy when I drove over."

"Please? I have Emma's address. She doesn't know about *Mammi.*"

Jakob heaved a sigh. "So we will not have the afternoon together?"

"We'll be together on the ride there and back. And you're welcome to visit with Emma too." Lydia disliked the pleading note in her voice, but she had to tell Emma about *Mammi* and hope that family ties would be stronger than the lure of the world.

Although he agreed to take her, Jakob moped until they pulled up outside the squat three-story apartment building with its unadorned yellow brick exterior, and he insisted Lydia go inside alone.

"Are you sure? It's cold out here."

Jakob waved his hand. "*Ach,* don't worry about me. Take as long as you need."

"Thank you so much for doing this."

"I would do this and much more for you." Jakob's wind-chapped cheeks grew even more ruddy. "I mean —"

"I understand." Lydia cut him off. She wasn't ready for that. Not here. Not now. Not yet.

She hurried into the building, more to escape Jakob's words than to seek shelter from the biting wind.

As she mounted the narrow cement steps to the third floor, Lydia prayed that Emma would be receptive to what she had to say. When she reached the scratched metal door of apartment 3G, she drew off her gloves and blew on her hands to warm her tingling fingers. Then, swallowing the lump of fear blocking her throat, she knocked. The hollow rapping filled the dingy hallway and echoed in the cavern of her heart. How could Emma stand to live in a cheerless building of metal and concrete?

The door opened a crack. Emma peeked out from behind the chain. Her face tightened when she caught sight of Lydia.

"*Mammi*'s in the hospital. I thought you'd want to know. May I come in?"

Emma sighed, unlatched the chain, and opened the door. "If you promise not to lecture me or bug me about coming home." She gestured toward the living room, but the motion came out so stiff and forced, it appeared ungracious. After she shut the door, she waved toward the sofa and the mismatched chairs. "Have a seat."

Heart sinking, Lydia settled in the bile green one. After Emma curled up on the brown plaid couch across from her, Lydia recounted *Mammi*'s bout with appendicitis, then ended with, "Jakob's outside. Will you come with us to see her?" When Emma frowned, Lydia hastened to add, "I'm not trying lecture or get you to come home." She pinched her lips together for a moment to hold back the words, *Although I wish you would.* "I'm sure *Mammi* would love to see you. We all would. We care about you."

Emma snorted. "This isn't just about *Mammi.* All you really care about is your reputation. One I'll never match." Emma's voice took on a high mocking tone. "Ooh,

141

isn't Lydia such a wonderful *gut* example for the young ones? Such a help to her parents. But that Emma, *ach,* her poor parents, they have their hands full dealing with that one."

"Oh, Emma, that isn't so."

"You don't know what it's like." The fierceness of Emma's tone belied the sheen of moisture in her eyes. "You sat motionless for hours during the sermon; I wriggled and *rutsched.* You helped *Mamm;* I teased the boys. You think before you speak; I blurt out whatever comes to mind and must always ask for forgiveness."

"You're just more lively."

Emma glared at her. "Even during your *Rumschpringe,* you did nothing wrong. But when I started mine, you followed me around in Plain dress, showing how pious you were and how wrong I was."

Was that how it appeared to Emma? That had never been Lydia's intention. She tried to explain that she'd only wanted to help Emma, not make her feel guilty, but her protest only upset her sister more.

Emma clenched her fists in her lap, and bitterness dripped from her words. "Why would you need to *help* me?" Her voice rose. "Doesn't helping imply that you're better than someone else?"

Lydia twisted her hands in her lap. It was true. She had been guilty of judging Emma.

Emma leaned closer, almost in Lydia's face. "I may have ignored the *Ordnung,* but what of you?"

Inside Lydia cringed. In God's eyes her behavior had been far from exemplary, particularly lately. "I've tried hard to follow the rules, but I often fall short." *In the ways you just pointed out and many more. Many, many more.*

"That at least is truthful. You act humble, but inside you're filled with pride. You compare yourself to me to make yourself feel better."

Lydia sat in stunned silence as her sister's words hit her, each blow stinging worse than the one before. "Emma," she choked out. "You're right. I am often guilty of *hochmut.* But I do love you. And I don't want to see you hurt."

"If you really cared, you'd leave me alone. Can't you see how happy I am?" Emma said with such fierceness that Lydia cringed. Yet under that declaration, Lydia detected a quaver of loneliness and uncertainty.

Emma stood and strode to the huge gilt-edged mirror. She fluffed her hair, which had been cut short to feather around her face, and blew a kiss to her image.

Oh, Emma, how you have changed. So arrogant and prideful. A small voice in Lydia's head chided her. *Pointing out your sister's faults does not excuse your own.*

Then Emma turned to Lydia. "Kyle will be home from work soon, and I don't want you here when he arrives. Whenever I spend time around family, Kyle and I always fight. I love him too much to subject him to that."

Lydia stood and smoothed down her skirt. She wanted to say that perhaps spending time with her family caused Emma's conscience to war with her rebelliousness. But she held her tongue. She walked over and hugged her sister, the silkiness of the low-cut blouse so alien to her touch. Emma stood stiff in the embrace and did not return the gesture. Lydia blinked back the tears that stung her eyes.

Emma didn't shoo her out with her hands, but her eyes conveyed the message that she wanted Lydia gone. Now.

After the door closed behind her, Lydia leaned her head against the cold metal. Had she done more harm than good? Would Emma ever speak to her again? *Dear God, please show me what You would have me to do. And forgive me for any and all truth in Emma's accusations.*

From inside the apartment, faint sounds

of weeping reached Lydia's ears. Was Emma crying? A tiny sprout of hope pushed its way through the parched ground of Lydia's heart. Maybe her sister's hard shell was only an act. *Thank You, Lord,* she whispered. *I will keep coming back and trust You to touch her heart.*

Some of the heaviness in Lydia's heart lifted. Perhaps in spite of her belligerence Emma still cared about her family and her faith. Lydia hurried down the steps, pushed open the door, and strode out. Straight into a muscled chest. Hands reached out to steady her, and Lydia stared up into the blue depths of Caleb's eyes.

The chiseled lines of his chin softened into a smile. "Fancy meeting you here."

"Um . . . yes." What was it about this man that made her so tongue-tied? The nearness of his body, the woodsy scent of his after-shave, his hands warm on her forearms made her insides career like an out-of-control buggy. *Think Lydia. Say something.* "Kyle's not there yet."

"I know. I wanted to talk to Emma."

"Oh." An unreasonable twinge of jealousy shot through her. Surely she didn't wish that he were coming to see her? It dawned on Lydia that Caleb still held her arms. She shook free of his grasp, ashamed of the part of her that didn't want him to let go.

Caleb gaze caught and held hers. "You have a beautiful smile, you know."

Lydia ducked her head to hide the heat in her cheeks. "Thank you," she whispered. She almost preened inside, then caught herself. That little worm of pride snaking its way through her threatened to turn into a huge rattlesnake that would come back to bite her. Emma had been right. She did have a problem with *hochmut*. "I–I have to go. Jakob's waiting."

Caleb glanced toward the buggy where Jakob sat staring down the sidewalk, jaw set.

Had he seen her interchange with Caleb? Lydia cringed inside.

"You're lucky to have a man who waits for you like that."

Lydia couldn't tell if he was mocking Jakob for waiting or indicating that she wasn't worth waiting for. Either way, it stirred her ire. And inside she knew luck had nothing to do with it. "And I'm very grateful."

"Then why don't you put the poor man out of his misery? Anyone can see he's crazy about you. And you're leading him on a merry chase. Keeping him by your side so you have transportation when you need it. It's not fair to use him that way."

146

Lydia planted her hands on her hips. "What do you know about my feelings for Jakob?"

"I don't. Or I should say I didn't. I took a stab in the dark. And you proved me right." A thoughtful look crossed his face. "I notice you didn't protest that you loved him."

Ooh. Lydia itched to slap his face. No one had ever roused her to this much anger — or was it anger? "How I feel about Jakob is none of your business." She struggled to keep her words civil. "I'd better go." She couldn't force the words *it was nice seeing you* from her lips, but she had to maintain some semblance of politeness. "I wish you a good day," she said finally.

"And I wish you the same." Caleb dipped his head in a mocking bow.

The nerve of him. Lydia's hands curled into fists as she stalked past him to the buggy.

Jakob stared at the buggy floor when she climbed onto the seat beside him. Rather than flipping the reins to start the horses into motion, he cradled them lightly in one hand, while the fingers of his other twisted the leather ends draped across his knee. The tilt of his hat brim shadowed his eyes.

"You know I care about you, don't you, Lydia?" Redness crept up Jakob's neck and

147

splashed across his cheekbones. He didn't wait for her to answer as he plunged on. "I—I've decided to join the church when classes start in a few weeks. I wish you'd join when I do."

Was he trying to imply that he wanted to marry her? "I want to do that so much, but Emma —"

"Let Emma get this out of her system. It's time to think about yourself." He cleared his throat. "And us," he added softly.

"I can't, not right now. How can I stop caring for my sister?"

"Be sensible, Lydia. What have you done so far to convince her to return?"

Jakob's words were like a knife stabbing her in the heart. All her inadequacies, failures, discouragements piled on her heart like heavy logs on a woodpile. She had failed. But she couldn't let Emma drift away from the faith.

Around them traffic whizzed by, throwing slush from swiftly moving wheels. The horses edged away from the flying wetness and stamped impatiently, but instead of giving them a signal to move, Jakob sat motionless, pinning her with his gaze. "Have you ever thought that by following her around, perhaps you're driving her farther away?"

Lydia's eyes and cheeks burned. Jakob was

rarely critical, so this stung.

He cleared his throat. "I have no right to tell you what to do." The wistfulness of his words convinced Lydia that he wished he did. "But it seems that you are taking on a responsibility that is not yours."

Lydia hung her head. She had convinced herself she had a duty to watch over Emma, but had it only been self-righteousness and vanity?

Jakob's voice held kindness and understanding. "I care about Emma as I do Rebecca, but you need to allow your sister to have her running-around time." The sympathy in his tone hardened into resolve. "After this, I won't be taking you to Emma's apartment again."

Remembering Emma's sobs, Lydia insisted, "Please, Jakob. I think she's close to coming home."

But Jakob only pursed his lips and watched for an opening in traffic, then flicked the reins to start the horses. After the buggy moved away from the curb and into the flow of traffic, Jakob turned to her. "I'm sorry, but I cannot do this anymore. I've made my decision. Now I hope you'll make yours."

They sat in silence as the horses clomped down the road. Jakob pulled over every few miles to let traffic speed by. Lydia wanted to beg him to reconsider, but Jakob — who took a long time to come to decisions — always abided by them once he did.

She did have one question, though. "Did your father have anything to do with this?"

"My father is a wise man." His clipped answer showed she had offended him. "He has concerns about some of your actions, your reputation. He agreed to trust my judgment. But today I came to my own conclusion."

"But why today?" When, for the first time, Emma had shown signs of changing her mind.

"I have my reasons." A quiver of hurt underlay his answer.

So he had seen the interchange with Caleb. Jakob had nothing to be jealous of. Lydia would never have a relationship with an *Englischer*. She wasn't like Emma. The very idea of it churned her stomach. *But you are attracted to him,* her conscience taunted. Lydia shook the thought away. Of course she wasn't. She'd been momentarily distracted.

Yes, Caleb was handsome, but she often stopped to admire the delicate petals of a rose, and her spirit soared when a ruby-throated hummingbird fluttered around the bird feeder. She had only been gazing at God's magnificent handiwork, lost in the beauty of — Lydia could hear Emma's voice quite distinctly, *Yeah, right.*

"I worry about you, Lydia." Jakob's solemn voice interrupted her internal debate. "Spending so much time around *Englischers* seems to be changing you. You have no time for hymn sings. You used to cringe at the sound of rock music, but now you don't even notice when it blasts from passing cars. And you don't seem to mind when *Englischers* paw you."

"What? How can you say such a thing?"

A heavy sigh escaped Jakob's lips. "I saw you, Lydia. I wasn't spying. I always watch the entrance to be sure you're safe when you come out. I kept glancing in the side mirror, and when you appeared, I kept an eye on you until . . . until I couldn't bear to watch anymore."

Imagining how the encounter with Caleb must have appeared to Jakob, Lydia blushed.

"He touched you in ways I have never done. Never considered doing. I've always respected you." Jakob pulled over to let cars pass. He skewered her with his gaze. "I wanted you to respect me. Should I have done differently?"

"No, no." Lydia tucked her hands under the folds of her skirt. "I didn't welcome his touch. I–I was only startled and a bit dazed after running into him so suddenly."

"I see." He sounded far from persuaded.

How could she convince him when she couldn't even convince herself?

CHAPTER TWELVE

A biting wind blew bits of snow from the drifts piled in the front yard, making Lydia grateful it was an off-Sunday. She wouldn't want to be riding in the buggy in this weather. Stinging pellets smacked her in the face as she stepped out of *Mammi*'s front door after checking that everything was ready for her grandmother's homecoming tomorrow. Lydia ducked her head against the onslaught and stepped carefully around the patches of ice. She had almost reached the front door when horse's hooves clomped up the driveway.

Bishop Zook? Lydia's stomach knotted. Had she done something *else* she needed to be reprimanded for? Or maybe God had laid it on his heart to speak to her about her conduct around a certain *Englischer.*

One hand clamping his hat to his head, the bishop strode toward her. "*Gut-n-Owed,* Lydia."

"*Gut-n-Owed,* Bishop Zook," Lydia choked out. She reached the front door and pulled it open. "Won't you come in?"

The bishop grasped the edge of the door to keep it from blowing shut. Then he motioned for Lydia to precede him. Inside, they stamped the snow from their boots, and Lydia offered to take his coat, but the bishop declined.

"I won't be staying long. I have come to apologize about Yoder's barn. I had a visit from a young man who vouched for your conduct. Although he is an *Englischer,* I did not discount his story. And I did some investigating."

Caleb? She couldn't believe he had gone to the bishop.

"I owe you an apology. I should not have acted in such haste. Will you forgive me?"

"I . . . there's no need to apologize." Lydia shifted from one foot to the other. How did one accept an apology from the bishop? "I too must apologize for going there in the first place. I should have thought of how it would look to others."

"Nevertheless, I was wrong. I should have had all the facts first." The bishop's bushy brows drew together. "That does not mean, however, that you are free to go there again."

"I have no intention of going again." Tears

welled in Lydia's eyes. There was no need now. She lowered her head so the bishop could not see the moisture in her eyes.

The bishop cleared his throat. "Well, then, shall we put this matter behind us? I have spoken to the school board, and they also wish to ask for forgiveness."

Lydia nodded, too choked up to speak.

Bishop Zook set a hand on her shoulder. "I'm sorry this happened, and we are all keeping Emma in our prayers."

"Thank you." Lydia's tear-choked voice was barely a whisper.

Bishop Zook fumbled for the doorknob but stopped. "Oh, I almost forgot. Our niece just had a baby and needs Rebecca's help for a few days while her husband is out of town. I know it's a lot to ask, but could Sarah handle the class alone? I know Esther is being discharged, and she'll need you."

Snow swirled through the door as the bishop exited. Absentmindedly Lydia wiped up the floor. Caleb had gone to the bishop to set things right. She needed to thank him before *Mammi* was discharged tomorrow. Because after that, she'd never see him again.

She tried to ignore the pang that thought brought by heading into the kitchen, where she was greeted by the savory aroma of garlic, onion, and peppers in *Mamm*'s tomato sauce. She grasped the handle of the wooden spoon to stir the red sauce bubbling on the stove.

Sarah hurried into the kitchen. "I'm so sorry. I lay down for a minute and fell asleep." The half-moons under Sarah's eyes stood out like dark bruises against her pale skin.

Lydia had been so busy visiting *Mammi* and worrying about Caleb that she hadn't paid attention to Sarah. Her sister set one dinner plate on the table and then collapsed on the bench, her head in her hands. When Lydia placed the back of her hand on Sarah's forehead, she could feel that her sister was burning up. She gave Sarah two aspirin and tucked her into bed with a cool cloth on her head. Then she hurried downstairs to feed her brothers and *Dat.* After taking *Mamm* some tea and toast, Lydia finished the dishes and sank onto a chair.

Sarah was too sick to teach tomorrow, *Mamm* was still in bed, and *Dat* hadn't been able to shake the deep cough that rattled in his chest, so he'd headed to bed as soon as he and the boys had finished their chores. If she took Sarah's place at school, someone else would have to pick up *Mammi* tomorrow and care for her over the next few days.

If only Emma were here.

Would her sister help if she knew *Mammi* needed her? There was only one way to find out.

With *Dat* sick, Lydia had no choice but to hitch up the horse herself. She was grateful the roads had been salted, but car tires splashed slush across the asphalt. Those patches would freeze over later as the temperatures fell. She'd need to be extra careful coming home. She sighed in relief when she pulled in front of the dingy yellow brick apartment building. Emma wouldn't welcome another visit, especially so soon after the previous one, but surely her sister's heart hadn't hardened so much that she wouldn't agree to care for *Mammi* for a few days.

When Lydia knocked, Emma unlocked the door and flung it open, beaming. "You got my message —" The smile died on her lips, and her brows pinched together. She took a step back and started to close the door. "I thought I made it clear you weren't welcome here."

"You did. Very clear. But *Mammi*'s coming home —"

Emma put a hand on her hip. "And you came all the way over here to tell me that?"

Lydia wished Emma would let her in

rather than talking to her through the crack in the door, but she explained that *Mammi* was being discharged from the hospital tomorrow. Before she could get to her request, Emma interrupted.

"Yeah, right. So why are you here?"

Her sister's sarcastic tone hurt, but Lydia needed to convince Emma to come home, so she kept her words even. "Please, Emma, we need you to take care of *Mammi* for a few days." Lydia rushed through her message before her sister could slam the door in her face. She had to impress on her how much they needed her. "You've always been *Mammi*'s favorite, so I thought . . ."

Emma studied Lydia, her eyes narrowed. "*Mamm* and Sarah can handle it."

Maybe she'd underestimated Emma's resentment. Lydia kept her voice calm, even. "They both have the flu, and I need to teach."

Emma opened the door only wide enough for Lydia to squeeze through. "This doesn't mean I'm agreeing to do it." She slammed the door and turned to face Lydia. "How is *Mammi*?"

"She's very weak. The infection was bad, but the doctors expect her to recover." Lydia studied her sister's pale face. "Is everything all right?" Emma's mumbled *yes* sounded far from convincing, so Lydia persisted, "Are you sure?"

"I–I just need to talk to Kyle." Emma didn't meet Lydia's eyes, but then her voice hardened. "It's none of your concern."

"If things aren't going well, you can always move home."

"Everything's fine between Kyle and me." Emma's defensive tone made Lydia wonder if her sister was telling the truth.

Emma had a scarf thrown casually around the neck of her emerald green sweater. With her black trousers tucked into calf-high leather boots, she looked as if she could grace the pages of the fashion magazines scattered across the coffee table. Her cheeks pinkened as she bent over and stacked the handful of glossy magazines. Then she opened an end table drawer and shoved them in.

Maybe Emma wasn't as brazen as she acted. Lydia's heart lifted a little.

Her sister kicked off her boots to reveal striped socks that matched her sweater and scarf. Then she curled up on the couch, her feet tucked under her.

Lydia drew in a breath. "*Mammi*'s recovery has been slower than expected. I stayed with her every day at the hospital, and she was in pain, but after the second day, she refused the painkillers."

"*You* stayed with her? What about teaching?"

"I haven't been teaching since *Mammi* had her operation. Someone needed to be with her in the hospital."

Lydia hadn't said the *someone* should have been Emma, but her sister, who had been twisting the ends of her scarf, stilled. She nibbled at her lower lip and didn't meet Lydia's gaze. "Why didn't *Mamm* or Sarah do it? And who took over at school?"

"You know Sarah and hospitals. And *Mamm*'s been ill the whole time. Rebecca and Sarah substituted for me, but neither of them can teach tomorrow. Even *Dat*'s been sick. He still has a horrible cough, but being *Dat,* he manages to drag himself to work and milk the cows twice a day. So we need your help."

"You don't know what you're asking. I want to see *Mammi* . . . be with her . . ." Emma's voice trembled. "But I can't. I don't want her to know . . ."

"She was young once, and it is your *Rumschpringe,* after all." Emma might be surprised at how much *Mammi* understood. Lydia held her tongue about *Mammi*'s attraction to an *Englischer.* That was her grandmother's story to tell — if she chose to tell it.

"I–I didn't mean that. I meant —" The cell phone shrilled and Emma jumped up. "That must be Kyle. I have to take it." She paced over to the kitchen island, where she murmured into the phone.

Lydia couldn't help but overhear Emma's final statements before she hung up.

"I went to —" Emma glanced over her shoulder at Lydia. "I can't tell you now. Just hurry home as soon as you can." After she hung up, she crossed the room, and without meeting Lydia's eyes, she said fiercely, "I'll care for *Mammi* even if it means . . ." She sucked in a breath. "I'll have Kyle bring me after he gets off work tonight."

"*Mamm* and *Dat* will be so happy to see you."

"Don't be so sure." Emma's words were grim. "But I have to do it. But only until *Mammi*'s better."

In spite of Emma's insistence her homecoming would be temporary, a smile tugged at Lydia's lips as she descended the steps. If anyone could convince Emma to stay home, it would be *Mammi.*

Lydia opened the door of the apartment building cautiously this time. But no one stood outside. She silently scolded herself for wishing she could repeat her run-in with

Caleb. She tried to shake off the memory of his hands on her arms and her head resting against his chest. But the wish to be enfolded in his arms was so compelling, so real, it stayed with her as the horse picked his way carefully along the icy roads. Lydia also regretted that she'd never had a chance to thank Caleb. And now she never would. Emma would bring *Mammi* home from the hospital tomorrow. Perhaps that was just as well. In spite of *Mammi*'s warnings, Lydia realized she had fallen for an *Englischer*.

As the evening wore on, Lydia's worry increased. A puddle of moonlight falling through the window illuminated Emma's empty bed. Maybe Kyle had talked her out of returning. Lydia knelt beside her bed, the chill of the bedroom floor penetrating her bedclothes, and prayed that God would bring Emma home as well as control her own wayward thoughts about Caleb.

Ambulances shrilled in the distance as Lydia rose and removed her *kapp*. Automatically she did what she always did when sirens sounded and whispered a silent prayer for those who had been hurt. She was about to unpin her hair when someone knocked on the front door. She rushed downstairs before the noise awakened her

162

sleeping family.

Bishop Zook stood at the door. Lydia's heart lurched. Why was Jakob's father here so late at night? Had something happened to Jakob?

Dat hurried from the bedroom to stand behind her. He'd dressed so hurriedly that his galluses were twisted. "Come in. Come in," he said to Hiram. "Lydia, don't keep Bishop Zook waiting on the porch."

Lydia came out of her daze. "Sorry, *Dat*. Sorry —"

Hiram brushed past her to grasp her father's arms. "Reuben, I'm so sorry to be the one to bring this news. There's been an accident. A bad car accident across from our pasture." He choked up and swiped at the moisture in his eyes with one sleeve. "It's . . . it's Emma. She's —"

"Emma? No, it couldn't be. Why would she be on this road so late at night?"

Sickness filled Lydia's heart. *Because she was coming home, Dat. Because I begged her to care for Mammi.*

Dat shook his head. "It can't be Emma. What makes you think — ?"

"I saw her," Hiram said dully. "I recognized her despite . . ." He dabbed at his eyes, this time with a handkerchief. "But they'll need you . . ."

163

Dat's face went ashen. Every muscle sagged, making him look older than *Mammi*. "No, no, it can't be."

Yes, please let it be a mistake. Lydia clenched and unclenched the folds of her skirt as they waited for the bishop's response.

Hiram squeezed his eyes shut. "The police are on their way, but I wanted to come first. We'll be praying," he choked out.

A siren cut through the air. The bishop hurried outside to his buggy, led the horse sideways onto the grass, and held the reins while a squad car cruised up the driveway. The siren died, but red lights pulsed across the barn and lawn.

Two officers emerged from the vehicle. When they reached the porch, the male officer took off his hat, practically crushing it as he clenched it in front of him, shuffled his feet, and cleared his throat.

The female officer took the lead. "Mr. Esh?" After *Dat* nodded, she said in a low, gentle tone, "There's been an accident."

Dat reached for his hat on the peg near the door. He jammed it on his head, shrugged into his jacket, and stepped onto the porch. "I only hope this is a mistake on Hiram's part." His strained tones made Lydia's heart clench.

She started to follow, but *Dat* stopped her with a sharp command. "Go back inside, Lydia."

"But Emma? I want to go too." *I need to go.*

Dat shut the door on her protest. Lydia slumped onto the couch in the parlor. No, no, it couldn't be Emma. It was dark outside, and Hiram's eyes weren't what they used to be. Maybe he'd been mistaken.

Her mother stumbled from the bedroom. Strands escaped from her bun, and she'd pinned her *kapp* crookedly. "Did I hear voices? What's wrong?"

Words wouldn't come. If she didn't say them, maybe they wouldn't be real. Eyes brimming with tears, Lydia could barely force out the words. "*Dat* went with the police to the hospital. Emma was in an accident by Zook's farm."

Mamm pulled her close. "Don't cry, Lyddie. Emma had no reason to be near Zook's."

"Yes, she did."

Mamm held her at arm's length, a frown creasing her brow.

Lydia gulped back tears. "She was coming home, *Mamm*."

Her mother's frown deepened. "What are you saying, Lydia?" After Lydia explained about visiting Emma and about Emma's promise to come home to care for *Mammi,* her mother's words came out sharp, biting. "Emma wouldn't have been returning this late at night." Then her voice wavered. "Would she?"

Lydia had no answer. She'd expected Emma hours ago. Perhaps the bishop had been mistaken.

They sat in silence as minutes ticked slowly into hours, each one dragging out longer than the rest. When *Dat* finally walked through the door, his shoulders hunched, grief etched into every line of his face, he didn't have to say a word. There was no doubt it was Emma.

CHAPTER THIRTEEN

In spite of the flu, the whole family gathered for the Scripture reading the following morning. *Mamm,* wrapped in an afghan, slumped in the rocker. Sarah huddled on the couch, her face flushed with fever, her eyes glassy and red-rimmed. Mary Zook had volunteered to substitute until Rebecca returned, so Lydia sat on the floor with an arm around each of her brothers. They wouldn't be going to school today either; it was more important for all of them to be together.

Before, the Emma-shaped hole in the family gathering had caused sadness, but they'd held out hope she would one day fill the space. Now she might never bounce through the door. She might never play another joke or make them laugh. She might never —

Lydia should be rejoicing that Emma was alive, but the specialists had warned she might never regain her mental capacities. To stop the brain swelling and keep Emma still enough to heal, the doctors had put her in a drug-induced coma.

The family bowed their heads for a silent recitation of the Lord's Prayer, but the words, *Thy will be done,* opened a chasm of grief rather than quiet acceptance. *Why, God?* So many unanswered questions tumbled through Lydia's mind. The familiar routine of the prayer, performed in unison several times a day, left everyone with tears shining in their eyes or glistening on their cheeks.

Dat cleared his throat and opened the Bible. His voice hoarse, he read Job 1:21: "The Lord giveth, and the Lord taketh away; blessed be the name of the Lord." The Bible fell into his lap. He rested his elbows on his knees and dropped his head into his hands. A sob escaped him.

Tears streaming down her face, *Mamm* pushed herself to her feet and hobbled to his side. She laid a hand on his shoulder, and he reached up to squeeze it. Abe and Zeke gulped back tears, while Sarah sat, eyes squeezed shut as if in pain.

Lydia herded the younger children from the room to give her parents some privacy. She set the boys to doing their chores while she tucked Sarah into bed. Zeke, who usually complained or gave things a lick and a promise, went to work with vigor. Abe moped through his chores, leaving spilled water behind that Lydia silently mopped up.

When the morning chores were done, Lydia approached *Dat*. "Could Andy pick us up earlier so I can visit Emma before I bring *Mammi* home?"

"Emma will not know you are there." *Dat*'s voice held a sharp edge that showed he was fighting back tears.

"Please, *Dat*, I want to see her."

Dat shook his head. "You do not know what you are asking." He covered his face with his hands and massaged his forehead. "I see no point." His Adam's apple moved up and down convulsively, and he pinched his lips together until they disappeared from view. He turned and walked away, saying gruffly, "You will get your *mammi* as planned. And forget the foolish notion of . . ." His voice trailed off.

Lydia stood stock-still for a few moments. "You aren't going along?"

"They will bring your *mammi* to the door. Andy has agreed to help you from there." *Dat* continued walking down the hall, his back to her.

Lydia trailed behind him, her mind racing

169

with unanswered questions. "But—but why aren't you — ?"

His voice thick, *Dat* snapped out, "I do not want to enter that building again." He reached the bedroom, yanked open the door, and as soon as he was inside, slammed it.

Lydia stood outside the closed door, tense and trembling. Emma's accident had distressed all of them, but to see *Dat,* who rarely lost his temper or showed emotion, act so out of character shocked her to her core.

Worry for *Dat* filled her thoughts as Andy drove her to the hospital. She had only a few minutes to peek into Emma's room before she headed to get *Mammi.* Her sister lay motionless, but except for a bruised cheek and tubes snaking into her body, she could have been sleeping.

"Oh, Emma, I'm so, so sorry," she whispered past the lump in her throat. "I have to get *Mammi,* but I'll be back to visit as soon as I can." If *Dat* would let her, that was. Lydia hurried from the room, tears stinging her eyes. If she hadn't asked Emma to come home —

"Lydia?" Caleb's voice stopped her. He headed toward her from the elevator, his eyes brimming with compassion. "How is

Emma?"

"She–she's —" She shrugged helplessly.

Caleb wrapped his arms around her and hugged her.

The warmth and comfort of his embrace mitigated the shock of his touch. Lydia yearned to linger in his arms, to accept the strength and caring radiating from him, but *Mammi* would be waiting, no doubt impatiently. "I–I need to go. *Mammi . . .*" She forced herself to step back.

Caleb's brow wrinkled in concern as he glanced into the room behind her. He swallowed hard. "I'm sorry this happened. I wish . . ." He glanced off into the distance, his eyes deep pools of sadness that made Lydia long to comfort him as he had done for her. Then he shook his head as if to dislodge the thoughts and turned to her. "I'd be happy to help you with your grandmother."

As much as she'd enjoy his company, it would be better to go alone. When she declined his offer, Caleb offered to sit with Emma until his break ended. Her sister would have no idea Caleb was there, but having someone in the room with Emma eased Lydia's mind about not staying, and she thanked him profusely before scurrying to the elevator.

As she'd expected, *Mammi* was impatient to leave. She pointed to the wall clock. "Discharge was at ten, not five after."

Lydia apologized for her lateness, then took a deep breath and explained about Emma's accident. She ended with the bad news. "The doctor says that if — when — she wakes, she may be brain damaged."

Mammi bristled. "Doctors don't know everything." She looked around. "So that's why your *dat*'s not with you? He's with Emma?"

Lydia shook her head. "He sees no point in going when Emma can't respond."

"Humph. How does he know that? Where is she? I want to see her for myself."

Lydia spent the next few minutes arguing with *Mammi* that visiting Emma wouldn't be good for her. A nurse, who entered pushing the wheelchair, echoed Lydia's response. "The only place you're going, Mrs. Esh, is out to the car, um, buggy?" She turned questioning eyes to Lydia.

"We have a car to pick her up." Lydia assured her. "*Dat* thought it would be more comfortable."

"Good, good. Now let's get you into this wheelchair, ma'am." The nurse bent to help *Mammi,* who shook off her assistance and insisted she was capable of walking. The nurse sighed, and in a weary voice that showed she'd argued with many patients, explained the hospital rules: on discharge *Mammi* had to be pushed downstairs and out the door in the wheelchair.

"And those rules won't allow me to visit my granddaughter?" *Mammi* didn't pause for an answer. "Fine, then, push me out of here, but I'll just turn around and come back in. I don't need this contraption. Haven't you all been making me walk up and down the halls several times a day?"

The nurse glanced at *Mammi*'s set jaw, questioned Lydia about Emma, and hurried from the room. When she returned, she had obtained permission for *Mammi* to visit Emma, but with the caution that, in her weakened condition, she was not to stay longer than twenty minutes. Lydia hurried downstairs to check with Andy about the delay, and by the time she returned, *Mammi* was settled in the wheelchair with her few possessions in her lap.

Mammi's victory grin changed to grimness as the nurse wheeled her into Emma's room. To Lydia's disappointment, Caleb was gone, so his break must have ended. Perhaps it was for the best. *Mammi* would be sure to question his presence. Once again Lydia's heart caught at the sight of Emma lying deathly still, her skin pale, her shoulder-length blonde hair spread loose across the pillow, making her look even more fragile.

"What did they do to her hair?" *Mammi* demanded. "Why did they cut it like that? And where's her *kapp*?"

Lydia pressed a knuckle against her lips. Should she explain that Emma had done that to herself?

Mammi directed the nurse to maneuver the wheelchair as close to the bed as possible. Then she motioned to the other chair. "Drag that chair closer, Lydia, and hold your sister's other hand." *Mammi* reached over and set a weathered hand over Emma's limp white one.

Oh, Emma. Lydia's heart ached with a heaviness too great for words. She picked up Emma's hand and stroked the veins showing through the almost-translucent skin. *Would this have happened if I hadn't begged you to come home?*

Mammi's voice jolted Lydia back to the present. "Emma's still in there. We just need to talk to her. Ease her back to us."

Lydia swallowed the lump blocking her throat. "Emma, *Mammi* and I are here with you." Her words came out thickly. "We're praying for you. That you'll get well."

"Not like that, Lydia. Talk some sense into her." *Mammi* turned to Emma. "We can't have you lying around in this bed, girl. Your *mamm* needs you. There are chores to be done."

At the sound of *Mammi*'s voice, Emma let out a slight moan.

Lydia studied Emma's prone figure. Had she twitched? "I think she's responding to you, *Mammi.*"

"Of course, she is. She knows I mean business. Tell her what you'll be doing in school. And tell her what you expect her to get done."

Lydia complied, with frequent interruptions from *Mammi,* but Emma made no more sounds or movements. The whole time Lydia frequently eyed the clock and her grandmother's face, and just before the twenty minutes was up, she went out to the nurse's station to have them call someone to transport *Mammi* downstairs.

When the aide arrived, *Mammi* tottered to the bed and leaned down to kiss Emma's forehead. "You have to get better, girl. I may need you to take care of me." Exhaustion and pain written in every line in her face, *Mammi* hobbled the few steps back to the wheelchair and lowered herself into it.

In the elevator Lydia chided her grandmother. "You should be home in bed." She was worried because *Mammi*'s lips were pressed together so tightly that a network of fine lines encircled her mouth and most of the color had drained from her face.

"There's no need to worry. Save your concern for someone who needs it. Your sister and I don't. Our lives are in God's hands."

Lydia had no trouble convincing *Mammi* to go straight to bed when they arrived home, but *Mammi* chafed at staying in bed for the week that the doctor had recommended, although much of the time she was still in pain. Lydia stayed home from school to help care for her, and the rest of the family — now largely recovered from the flu — struggled through their daily routine with worry over Emma clouding every action. *Dat* refused to go to the hospital or to permit anyone else to visit. But on Saturday afternoon *Mammi* insisted that she was well enough to visit Emma, and nothing Lydia or *Dat* said could dissuade her. Finally *Dat* relented, allowing Lydia to go with *Mammi* by car rather than buggy to prevent too much jostling. In the car *Mammi* winced when they hit bumps, even small ones.

Andy must have noticed, because he drove more slowly than usual. The whole trip

Mammi's lips formed the silent words, *Hurry, hurry,* but when Lydia helped *Mammi* along the walkway, her grandmother's steps slowed. The wind whipped their capes and iced Lydia's nose, and she longed to urge *Mammi* to walk faster. Instead *Mammi* stumbled to a halt in front of the doors. A look of fear flitted across her face to be swiftly replaced by determination.

Lydia hadn't thought about how hard it might be for *Mammi* to return to the hospital. The last time they walked through those doors, *Mammi* had been whisked off for an operation. She squeezed her grandmother's elbow. "It'll be all right," she whispered.

Mammi flashed her an irritated look. "Of course it will be. Why would you think otherwise?"

Lydia shook her head and reached for the door handle. The warmth of the lobby stung her chilled hands, feet, and cheeks. A different heat rose inside as she glanced toward the passageway where Caleb usually worked, but she quickly doused it. He wouldn't be here on a Saturday, would he?

Mammi's curious glance flustered Lydia. It was as if *Mammi* could read her mind. Eager to get away from the probing stare, Lydia pretended to study the picture hanging on the lobby wall. She managed to compose herself, but when they entered Emma's room, Lydia's heart stutter-stepped.

Caleb sat beside the bed, holding Emma's hand and talking to her. For a moment joy filled her. A joy that fizzled when she glanced at Emma's still body and pale face.

Caleb let go of Emma's hand and stood, motioning for Lydia to take his seat. "I hope you don't mind my being here. I thought no one would visit today." He repeated it in German with an extra apology to *Mammi.*

Seeing him had Lydia so tongue-tied she couldn't form words, but *Mammi* smiled. "The doctor wanted me to stay in bed a full week, but I didn't listen."

In a voice so low only Lydia could hear, Caleb said in English, "Now why doesn't that surprise me?" After a conspiratorial wink at Lydia, he turned to *Mammi* and spoke in German. "I'm glad you're feeling well enough to come today."

"I couldn't stay away from my Emmie any longer. She needs her family." *Mammi* settled into the chair on the opposite side of the bed. "It was wonderful kind of you to visit when we couldn't."

Caleb inclined his head in a slight bow. "Glad to do it, ma'am." He continued the conversation in perfect German. Lydia was amazed at his fluency.

Mammi let out a small humph of satisfaction. "And how is your brother?"

"My brother's injuries are minor compared to —" Caleb gestured toward the bed and swallowed hard. "I'm so sorry."

"You weren't driving, were you?"

Caleb squirmed under *Mammi*'s piercing gaze. "No, but I share the blame. My brother's my responsibility."

"Take responsibility only for your own mistakes and sins. It should keep you busy enough without taking on the guilt of others."

Caleb looked taken aback. "That's true," he muttered.

Lydia shot him a sympathetic look. Caleb's answering smile accelerated Lydia's pulse so much that she was grateful she wasn't hooked up to a heart monitor.

Mammi frowned at Lydia. "Are you going to sit there gawking or visit with your sister?"

Cheeks burning, Lydia tore her gaze from Caleb.

Mammi inclined her head in Caleb's direction. "Why don't you pull over a chair and join us?" She waited until Caleb had settled in a chair to ask again, "So how is your brother?"

179

Caleb looked down and rubbed his forehead before replying, "He'll be fine. He had a concussion, stitches in several places, and a broken arm. He came home Tuesday." He glanced at Emma. Then he looked from *Mammi* to Lydia with apologetic eyes, and his voice came out husky. "I'm so sorry this happened. He's struggling under a load of guilt. All the cards, letters of forgiveness, and flowers have been overwhelming. I can't believe the way your people care and forgive."

"That is what God commands," *Mammi* responded. "He forgives us and we forgive others. That's part of our daily prayer."

Caleb nodded, seeming a bit uncomfortable with the subject of God. He glanced at Emma. "Have the doctors said anything about her prognosis?"

Lydia cleared her throat. So far she'd been sitting here like an unresponsive lump, her heart heavy as she studied her sister's still form. "The only thing we heard was right after the accident. *Dat* has been, well . . ." Lydia had no words to describe *Dat*'s strange behavior. "Anyway, the doctors won't know for sure until she's out of the coma, but they said she may have brain damage."

Caleb's expression turned grave. "I'm so sorry."

Mammi interrupted. "Doctors don't know everything. And you shouldn't say things like that in front of Emma." She turned and picked up Emma's hand. "Don't listen to that nonsense, Emmie. They don't know what they're talking about. You're going to be fine. And so am I. We'll show those doctors a thing or two."

Caleb chuckled. "I'll just bet you will. And with you by her side, I'm sure Emma will have no choice but to get well." He sobered. "What you're doing, talking to her, encouraging her, is the best thing you can do. Miracles do happen. Even doctors have to admit that."

"You're a sharp one, Caleb — Caleb, what?"

"Miller."

"Caleb Miller, eh?" *Mammi* studied him for a few seconds. "Miller, Miller." She stared off into the distance. "Ever since I set eyes on you, I've been trying to recollect who you remind me of. Wish this old brain of mine were sharper. A fuzzy picture keeps forming on the edges." She shook her head. "It will come to me."

"I'll be happy to hear it when it does, but I really must go." Caleb stood and gave another slight bow in *Mammi*'s direction. "It was nice seeing both of you again." Then he turned toward the bed. "It was good to see you again too, Emma. Be sure to listen to your grandmother. She's very wise. I'm sure she'll have you up and out of bed in no time."

"I certainly will," *Mammi* muttered, "God willing." Then as Caleb waved and exited the room, she followed up with, "Wise, eh? I knew there was a reason I liked that boy so much."

Lydia stared after him until *Mammi* snapped, "Why don't you pay attention to Emma? We've been here all this time, chattering and ignoring her."

Again, under *Mammi*'s direction, Lydia told Emma all the family news. But *Mammi* seemed distracted. Every once in a while, she'd glance off into space and repeat, "Miller? Miller?"

When Lydia raised an eyebrow, she shrugged. "I know the answer's in there somewhere. If I could just remember. And he speaks such good German."

A few days later, after work, Lydia accompanied *Dat* in the buggy when he went to pick up *Mammi,* who had spent the day with Emma at the hospital.

"I wish your grandmother would stay home in bed," *Dat* grumbled as he navigated the icy roads at an even slower pace than usual. "There's no use in her going to the hospital when Emma doesn't even know she's there. She'll only wear herself out."

"I don't think you need to worry about her, *Dat*. She seems to have more energy than she did before. When she's taking care of Emma, *Mammi* forgets her own pain."

Dat harrumphed, and the set of his jaw and stiffness of his back revealed his annoyance. "I don't like you going to the hospital either, Lydia. All this foolishness. And traveling back and forth in this weather is dangerous. One of you could have another accident." He gestured toward a car that had just slid through a stop sign. "The *Englischers* have no control of their vehicles. Not like a horse that you can pull to stop and who instinctively knows where to step when it's icy."

Usually her *dat* was a man of few words, so Lydia was surprised by his garrulousness this evening. Ever since Emma's accident he'd been out of sorts. That was understandable, as they were all worried about Emma, but *Dat*'s worry — *was it anger?* — seemed to run deeper than fear for Emma.

When they got the hospital, *Dat* waited in

the buggy. Lydia couldn't convince him to come inside to see Emma. "Bah, a waste of time it is. Talking to one who is not awake. Who might never wake . . ." *Dat*'s voice broke.

Lydia longed to reach out and hug him, but *Dat* had never been affectionate. She had no idea how he'd react. Probably push her away and tell her not to be sentimental. Squashing the urge to comfort him, Lydia climbed out and hurried from the buggy. "I'll bring *Mammi* down as quickly as I can. I don't want you sitting out here in the cold for long."

"But you didn't mind bringing me all this way in the cold," *Dat* muttered.

It was not like *Dat* to grumble and grouse. Was worry over Emma making him so *grexy*?

When Lydia arrived at the room, she opened the door and stopped. Caleb was sitting there, chatting with *Mammi*.

Her grandmother turned a huge smile on Lydia. "After Caleb got off work, he offered to keep me company until you arrived. Wasn't that kind of him?"

It certainly was. "But what about your brother?"

Caleb gave her a welcoming smile that set her pulses racing before explaining, "One of

184

our neighbors is a retired nurse. She's caring for him. She has trouble making ends meet with only her Social Security payments, but she's too proud to accept help. This way she can earn some extra money."

"Social Security?" *Mammi* huffed. "She doesn't have any family to care for her?"

"If she does, I've never met them. Not like you. You have a wonderful family to care for you."

Lydia gasped. "Oh, speaking of family, *Dat*'s sitting outside waiting. We need to hurry."

Caleb stood. "I can accompany your grandmother out to the parking lot so you can spend more time with your sister." He assisted *Mammi* from her chair and took her arm.

The two of them walked toward the door, chatting as if they were old friends. Lydia marveled at how much livelier *Mammi* seemed in the past few days. Her pain was evident in the tightness around her mouth and her sudden winces, but her eyes sparkled, and her voice held an underlying joy that had been missing for a while.

If any good had come of Emma's accident, it was that it had given *Mammi* new energy and purpose. Lydia turned toward the bed, where Emma lay hooked up to the machines keeping her alive. But was *Mammi*'s newfound vigor worth the accident that had hurt her beloved sister?

"Oh, Emma," Lydia whispered. "Please come back to us."

She'd barely had time to say a few words to her sister before Caleb returned, his face troubled. "Your father is waiting, but I wanted to let you know how sorry I am about the accident." He gestured toward Emma. "And your sister."

Lydia was confused. "It wasn't your fault."

Caleb turned haunted eyes toward her. "I deserve some of the blame. I knew my brother was reckless driver. I should have tried to calm him down, forced him to take defensive driving lessons . . . done something. I'm also sorry that he's not here at Emma's side."

"But he's hurt."

"Not so hurt he couldn't be here." Caleb's voice held a note of censure. "I don't know what's gotten into Kyle."

Beside them, Emma's heart monitor increased. Alarmed, Lydia turned to stare at the jagged movement. "Should we call a nurse?"

Caleb studied the monitor. "It seems to be in the normal range, and they're keeping an eye on things." He smiled. "Her reaction to our conversation could be a good sign." But he leaned closer and whispered, "If she's listening, perhaps we should talk in the hallway. Or maybe I could walk you to the car so you don't keep your father waiting?"

Caleb's concern, coupled with his nearness, set Lydia's pulse thrumming. Though she wanted to edge closer, she forced herself to put more distance between them when they reached the hallway. At the elevator Caleb motioned for her to go first, and then he stood aside to let others enter. By the time he squeezed in, he and Lydia were so far apart they couldn't speak, giving her time to calm her racing heart. After he exited the elevator, Caleb stood aside until she emerged, and her pulse skyrocketed as he moved closer.

His face was troubled as they walked to the exit. "Kyle doesn't even seem to acknowledge his part in the accident. And" — shame filled his voice — "he went into a rage and demanded that I never mention Emma's name again."

"Maybe he's blaming himself for her injuries." Lydia had blamed herself many times for Emma being on the road that night. She could only imagine how Kyle must feel as the driver. And if she were honest, sometimes she blamed him too. He and his reckless driving had almost killed Emma. Though the Lord's Prayer said she needed to forgive to be forgiven, she hadn't yet reached the point where she could send a letter assuring him of her forgiveness.

Beside her, Caleb looked thoughtful. "I'm not sure. It seems like something deeper. It's more than the anger he's showing on the surface." Heavy lines on his face showed the weight of responsibility he bore in his role as guardian.

Lydia could sympathize, but Caleb carried a much greater burden than she had with Emma. She couldn't imagine having to be a parent as well as a sibling. Especially in a situation like this.

"Ever since he turned fifteen, we've been butting heads. He doesn't want to listen to what I have to say. I understand. I'm not really old enough to be a father figure, and he's almost as tall as I am. He wants to be treated as an equal. Except that sometimes I need to restrict him for his own good." The sadness in Caleb's voice tugged at Lydia's heart. "I've been afraid to correct him, though, because once he knows something bothers me, he does it on purpose. So I started giving him less and less direction. And look where that led."

"It sounds as if you made the right decision not to correct him. If he was rebellious, he may have gotten into a lot more trouble."

"More trouble than he already is?"

Lydia didn't have an answer for that. She stayed silent, but tried to convey her sympathy and understanding with her expression.

"Most people in the Amish community have dropped off cards or notes to Kyle, encouraging him, letting him know they don't blame him for what happened, offering him forgiveness, support, and help. Each letter makes him angrier than the next. When I came in yesterday, he was crumpling them into balls and hurling them across the room with his good arm."

"I'm sorry the letters aren't comforting, but maybe in time . . ." Maybe in time he'd forgive himself. Maybe she would too. But Caleb shouldn't be blaming himself for his brother's actions.

They had reached the glass doors, but Lydia stopped. She couldn't leave when Caleb was so upset. She wished she could think of something to lighten his worries.

"You'd think that the letters would ease his guilt. Instead they make him more furious." Caleb shook his head.

"Maybe he feels as if he got off too easy, while Emma paid the price. Guilt can often

189

lead to anger." She paused as another idea struck her. "Or perhaps he's upset because Emma wanted to come home."

Understanding dawned in Caleb's eyes. "She was leaving him?"

"Not permanently. She only planned to stay and help *Mammi* until she was better. But I was hoping *Mammi* could convince her to come home for good." Lydia glanced out at the parking lot. She couldn't keep *Dat* waiting much longer.

Caleb followed her gaze. "I'd better let you go." But he put a hand on her arm and, with a heartfelt apology in his eyes, looked deeply into hers. "If I'd known the cost," he choked out the words, "for Emma, for you, for your family, I'd never have hoped for an end to their relationship. Not like this."

As Lydia walked out into the dusk, the warmth of Caleb's touch lingered on her arm. And his words lingered in her mind. She wasn't sure she'd made it clear they didn't hold him responsible for Emma's accident. Caleb had such a heavy burden caring for a younger sibling; he didn't need the added guilt he'd laid on himself.

Dat's anger, when she reached the buggy, was palpable. Lydia's apology for making him wait did little to cool his temper. He drove as cautiously as usual, but the tension in his shoulders and jawline, along with the way he clenched the reins, made his displeasure clear. Since the night of Emma's accident, he had been jumpy and irritable. With the exception of picking *Mammi* up tonight, he'd refused to go to the hospital and had forbidden *Mamm* to visit. In his current mood Lydia feared he might forbid her to visit Emma. And then she'd never see Caleb again.

Why did that thought cause her heart to sink?

CHAPTER FOURTEEN

Lydia had been right to worry. The following evening *Dat* insisted that she stop visiting the hospital, but *Mammi* intervened, claiming she needed Lydia to look after her. When *Dat* suggested *Mammi* should also stop going, she stared at him, long and steady, until he hung his head. He dealt the final blow in the argument, though, by refusing to pay Andy and forbidding Lydia to use the buggy. They couldn't get to the hospital unless Jakob was available to drive them. Jakob had difficulty getting away from his father's business and Lydia had gone back to teaching, so they could only visit on occasional evenings or weekends.

Because Caleb worked weekdays, Lydia never saw him anymore. She told herself it was for the best, but felt bereft and kept glancing at the doorway throughout their visits, hoping he'd walk through. But he never did.

Then one Friday afternoon a few weeks later, Lydia hurried down the hall to Emma's door with Jakob trailing behind her. *Mammi* had stayed in bed for a rest, but Lydia suspected her grandmother had been trying to give her and Jakob time together. She hadn't had any time alone with Jakob since Emma's accident. Although Jakob had hinted he'd like to do something else together today, Lydia had insisted on being at Emma's side.

When she reached the doorway, she stopped so abruptly that Jakob plowed into her back. She hadn't expected to run into Caleb.

He looked as startled to see them as they were to see him. When he saw Jakob, he dropped Emma's hand and stood. "I was just leaving."

"Oh." Lydia hoped the disappointment in her voice wasn't obvious.

Caleb nodded briefly in Jakob's direction, but gave Lydia a huge smile. "I stopped by to congratulate Emma."

Lydia tried to gather her wits about her and put together a coherent sentence. With Jakob glowering from one to the other, she couldn't think straight, let alone speak. Or was it Caleb's presence that held her tongue-tied?

"Isn't that terrific that they'll be weaning her off the vent?" Caleb's smile brought an answering one of her own.

Jakob, though, looked as puzzled she felt.

Caleb looked from one to the other, a question in his eyes. "Oh, no. Perhaps your grandmother wanted to surprise you, and I've spoiled it."

Jakob spoke up. "You've spoiled nothing, because Lydia and I have no idea what language you're speaking. Wean? Vent? We wean calves, but with Emma not being a bovine, you make no sense."

Lydia hastened to make amends. "I think what Jakob means is: Could you please explain what you said?"

Caleb pointed to the machinery by Emma's bed. "Since the accident, the ventilator has been breathing for her."

"So that's the vent?" Jakob muttered.

"Yes, that's the vent. Anyway, they've been weaning her off it. I'm guessing it's the way you wean calves? She's using it less and less. They're even talking about taking her off it completely, possibly as soon as next week." Caleb beamed at Emma and then turned his high-wattage smile on Lydia again.

"Oh, Caleb, that's wonderful!" Lydia gazed into his shining eyes.

Eyes that revealed that he was as thrilled

as she was. Eyes that held a deeper message Lydia couldn't quite decipher.

Jakob's cough broke the connection.

Lydia turned toward him. "Jakob, that's so exciting, isn't it?"

He nodded but shot a look at Caleb that was anything but friendly.

Caleb smiled at both of them. "I'd better be going." He clapped Jakob on the shoulder as he passed. "Nice to see you again, man." He waved to Lydia. "Take care, Lydia. Bye, Emma."

Once Caleb left the room, Jakob demanded, "How often does he stop in to see Emma?"

"What? Who?" Lydia was still staring at Caleb's retreating figure.

"That *Englischer.*"

"You mean *Caleb*?"

"I mean the *Englischer* who never remembers my name."

Lydia turned to face Jakob. "The way you don't remember his?"

Jakob had the grace to blush. "Yes, that one. Is he here often?"

"I have no idea how often he visits Emma." Lydia maneuvered around the bed and sat beside Emma. She didn't point out that Jakob usually accompanied her, so he'd know how often she'd seen Caleb recently.

She'd seen Caleb so little that her heart ached as he left the room. But she tried to douse the fire of Jakob's jealousy. "He obviously hasn't been here the times we've been here."

"So how does he know so much about Emma's condition?"

"Perhaps because he works here?"

"Don't doctors have to keep patient information confidential?"

"Do they?" Lydia didn't know enough about hospitals to answer that, but it sounded as if it would be the proper policy. She picked up her sister's hand. "Emmie, I'm so proud of you. If you keep this up, you'll soon be coming home."

"Lydia, are you avoiding my questions?"

She frowned. "What exactly is it you want to know? How often *Mammi* and Emma see Caleb? Or how often *I* see him?"

Jakob stared at the floor and shuffled his feet. "I'm sorry, Lydia. I'm letting jealousy get the better of me. It's just that I —" He glanced at Emma. "We can discuss this tomorrow night. That is, if you'll see me?"

Lydia agreed, but her insides knotted up. What was wrong with her? Though they had never discussed it, Jakob was her intended, but she seemed to be doing everything she could to avoid being alone with him. She needed to get her mind off the *Englischer* and concentrate on the man she would marry. She reminded herself of *Mammi*'s talk. If *Mammi* could get over Myron Landis, then she could get over Caleb, given time. She would do the right thing and marry Jakob, and trust God to erase all thoughts of Caleb from her mind and heart.

Monday evening Lydia was in the middle of making a salad for dinner when someone knocked on the door. She hadn't expected Jakob to show up this early.

She pulled the door open, but sun glinting off the snow blinded her. "I'm not ready yet, Jak —" But it wasn't Jakob. *Caleb?* No, not Caleb either. Someone who looked very much like him. "Kyle?"

Kyle stood on the porch, bouncing from one leg to another. One arm was in a cast. In his other hand he clutched two plastic trash bags.

When Lydia opened the door wider and invited him in, the frigid March air raised goose bumps along her arms.

Kyle shook his head and thrust the bags at her. "Thought you might want this stuff."

The second she grasped the bags, Kyle turned and rushed down the steps, but not before Lydia saw moisture glistening in his eyes.

"Kyle?" she called after him. "What is this?"

He kept his back to her. "It's Emma's." His gruffness was edged with pain. "I gave up the apartment. I need to save money for college."

The lump that blocked Lydia's throat made it impossible to swallow. Caleb had gotten his wish. Kyle was going to college. And Lydia had gotten her wish too. Emma was no longer with Kyle. Except Lydia had never imagined her sister would be locked in the silent world of a coma.

"Oh, and tell people to stop sending me cards and letters." Kyle's voice cracked as he yanked open the car door. "I don't deserve it."

He rocketed out of the driveway without a backward glance.

Lydia stood on the porch, shivering, weighted down with trash bags and guilt. Would all this have happened if she'd allowed her sister to experience *Rumschpringe* without interference?

"Lydia?" *Mamm*'s sharp voice echoed down the stairwell. "Is everything all right?"

"Everything's fine, *Mamm*." Or as fine as it could be when she was holding bags filled with Emma's possessions. "Kyle stopped by to drop something off."

Mamm's ragged *oh* tore at Lydia's heart. Lydia glanced at the bags in her hands. From the looks of them, they were *Englischer* clothes. Seeing them would drive her mother deeper into despair. As much as she wished she could donate them to charity, it must be Emma's choice. If Emma was ever well enough to make it.

Lydia dragged the bags upstairs to the bedroom. Going through the door, one bag tipped, spilling out the green sweater and scarf Emma had been wearing during that last visit. Lydia's eyes grew misty. She stuffed the green sweater back inside the bag. The dull edges of a headache began at her temples as she knelt and twisted the tie more securely to close the bag. *Oh, Emma, please come back to us.*

Lydia dragged the bags up the steep steps to the attic. She was heading down the stairs when Sarah called everyone for dinner. Rushing into the bathroom, Lydia ran water over her wrists and splashed some on her face. She massaged her cheeks to bring some color into them, but she feared *Mammi*'s eagle eyes would notice her distress. Trying to calm her breathing and act natural, she headed for the kitchen.

She had barely slipped onto the bench at the table when *Dat* cleared his throat. Deep lines bracketed his mouth as he waited for everyone's attention. "*Mammi* told me that they will be taking Emma off that machine on Tuesday. I have informed the doctors that whether or not she breathes, I will not have her hooked back up again."

A collective gasp sounded around the table.

Lydia's fork clattered to her plate.

Milk sloshed from Sarah's glass, and her hand shook as she set it on the table.

Both boys gaped.

Mamm's face was ashen as she lowered her fork and laid it beside her half-eaten meat loaf. "Reuben, you can't mean that."

Zeke's chin trembled. "But if she doesn't breathe by herself, she'll die."

Dat frowned down at his plate as if the congealing gravy contained an important message, one he was determined to read. "She's already as good as dead. And I don't abide by all these machines keeping her alive." His voice was thick with tears. "It's not like she'll ever recover."

"She might." The words rushed from Lydia's lips. "She's been improving every day."

Dat's hand slammed down onto the table,

making the dishes chatter against the wood. "Is having a machine pumping air into you the same as breathing? No, it is not. Emma is gone. Gone. Do you hear me?" A sob burst from his throat, and he shoved back his chair, stood, and turned his back, but his shoulders were heaving.

"So you want to kill our daughter?" *Mamm*'s voice was shrill.

"I am not killing her. She's already dead."

Everyone sat in stunned silence as *Dat* stumbled from the kitchen.

Surely he couldn't be serious. He'd change his mind. He had to.

As soon as the dishes were done, Lydia went in search of *Dat.* He sat in the rocker in the parlor. He had *The Budget* open but was gazing out the window. When she appeared in the doorway, he pretended to be engrossed in the paper. As soon as she called his name, he rattled the paper as if annoyed at being disturbed.

But this was too important to be scared away by his irritation. She tried again. This time he looked up with such a fierce glare that Lydia took a step back, uncertain around this stranger who used to be her steady, dependable father.

Her mouth dry, she plunged into what she needed to say. "Emma's been improving so

201

much she's in the step-down unit now. Can't you give her more time to recover if she's not ready tomorrow?"

Dat stared as if mesmerized by the articles, but his jaw tensed and his hands tightened, shaking the paper. He turned his head away, but not before Lydia caught what looked like a glimmer of tears. "I have already informed the bishop of my intentions, and he agrees that it is the wisest course of action."

"Could we at least talk to the doctors?"

Dat spoke through clenched teeth. "The doctors held out little hope when they admitted her. It seems they were right. Can Emma talk, eat, breathe? Can she carry on a conversation?"

"No, but —"

"This discussion is closed. I will not have my authority challenged in this matter, nor in any other."

But Lydia couldn't let the discussion end. "*Dat*? Please, don't let her die."

Her father shot to his feet. "Not another word, Lydia," he thundered.

A vivid picture of Emma, helpless, struggling for breath, swam before her eyes, but the way her father loomed over her, a vulture swooping down on helpless prey, kept her silent. *Dat* had always been strict, but he had never spoken to her this harshly. Now it seemed the only tone he used. She hung her head and forced herself to say, "I'm sorry." Anything to calm *Dat*'s wrath.

Then she backed slowly out of the room, hugging her arms around her chest. But nothing could stop the chills running through her. She might not only lose her sister, but it seemed she'd also lost her *dat*.

By the time she reached the doorway, the air had deflated from *Dat*'s chest. He sank into the chair and buried his head in his hands. He mumbled something, but Lydia could not make out the words. She turned and fled up the stairs.

When she opened the door to her room, Sarah sat on the edge of the bed dressed in her nightgown. "Did you talk to *Dat*?" Hope edged her voice, but the eager light in her eyes died when she studied Lydia's face. "I can't bear to think of losing our Emma. I thought . . ."

Her voice broke on a sob. She flung her arms around Lydia's neck. They clung together until Sarah's tears were spent. Lydia's remained in a hard lump in her chest.

After the light was out, Lydia said softly, "Sarah, are you still awake? I want to tell you something." At Sarah's murmur, Lydia described her last visit to Emma's apartment.

"So Emma was coming home? Oh, Lyddie, thank you for sharing that. I'd been so worried about her, but if she cared enough to return . . ."

"At least enough to come and be with *Mammi,* but —" Lydia buried her face into the pillow.

"You blame yourself for the accident? Don't, Lyddie. It wasn't your fault."

"She wouldn't be in a coma if I hadn't begged her to come home."

"It's God's will. We have to trust Him. He had a purpose for it, though I'm not sure why." The tenderness in Sarah's words soothed Lydia's heart like a healing balm. "You need to forgive yourself."

But guilt over Emma was only one blot on her conscience.

"I'm not sure I can." Lydia whispered the words into the dark, too softly for Sarah to hear.

CHAPTER FIFTEEN

The family filed into the hospital room. Sarah stood by the window, shivering, clasping Zeke's and Abe's hands. *Mamm* clung to *Dat*'s sleeve, studying Emma's face as if imprinting it in her memory. *Dat* fixed his gaze on the floor by his feet. Despite his reluctance, he had given permission for everyone in the family to see Emma one last time.

As Lydia and *Mammi* moved to their usual places on either side of the bed, Bishop Zook entered, followed by Jakob. The bishop moved to *Dat*'s side and laid a hand on his shoulder.

Jakob gave Lydia such a sympathetic glance that tears formed in her eyes. He took a step toward her but hesitated, as if reluctant to intrude on her time with Emma. Then he looked around at her family, and his mouth pinched together so tightly his lips formed a white line.

205

Only one person was missing. Caleb wasn't family, but he'd spent so much time with Emma that his absence left a gap. Lydia wished for his calming presence; she'd come to depend on his support, his quiet words of wisdom, his kindness.

A movement in the hallway caught her eye. Caleb had come after all! He'd positioned himself so he could see her, *Mammi,* and Emma, but the doorjamb blocked him from Jakob's view. *Mammi* made a motion as if to invite him to join them, but instead settled for a brief nod. She too evidently appreciated his thoughtfulness and tact. Lydia hoped he could read the gratitude in her eyes.

When the medical team entered, Lydia turned her attention back to Emma and to the prayers she'd been murmuring all morning. *Please, God, help Emma to breathe on her own.*

As they were setting up, *Mammi* announced, "I want to talk to Emma first."

When the doctor nodded, *Mammi* turned to Emma and picked up her hand. "They're going to turn off the machines, Em, but you don't need them to stay alive. Now you need to stop all this nonsense and get better. Your *mamm* needs help with the chores." She stopped. "Humph, that probably won't bring you around, will it?"

She swallowed hard. "We need you, Emmie girl." Her voice came out thick and clogged. "Please don't leave us."

Lydia took Emma's other hand. "*Mammi*'s right, Emma; we need you." Her throat hurt from the effort of keeping her tone light, normal.

Mammi cleared her throat, and this time her words were stern. "You know how to breathe, young lady. In and out. In and out. And that's what I expect you to do." She bowed her head, eyes closed, and lips moving. Then she looked up at the doctor. "She's ready."

Lydia closed her eyes and whispered a desperate prayer. When the swishing sound ceased, Lydia turned a fearful gaze toward Emma.

Her sister's chest did not move.

"Emma Esh!" *Mammi*'s voice cracked like a buggy whip. "You remember how to breathe. In and out."

Emma twitched.

"She moved, *Mammi*." Lydia squeezed Emma's hand.

"Of course she did. God knows Emma's needed here."

Emma's chest fluttered, a barely perceptible up-and-down movement.

The doctor leaned over to examine her. "She's breathing."

"Keep going, Em. You can do it." Lydia let go of her sister's hand and moved her chair back so the medical staff could surround Emma.

"Time to leave." *Dat* issued the gruff command.

"But . . ." Lydia's protest died when she saw *Dat*'s clenched jaw and damp eyes. *Mamm* stood beside him, handkerchief to her eyes.

In the hallway Caleb sent her a quick thumbs-up before he slipped into the elevator.

Sarah's terror of hospitals showed in her wide, wet eyes. Zeke and Abe shot curious glances at the drama around Emma's bed. They dragged their feet as Sarah shepherded them toward the door.

"Now." *Dat*'s imperious tone stopped their lollygagging.

Jakob gave Lydia a sympathetic smile as she reluctantly followed.

Mammi pulled herself to her feet and took a final glance at Emma. "I told everyone that she didn't need those stupid machines." Then she leaned close to Emma and whispered, "You did wonderful *gut,* girl. You just keep breathing like that, and it won't be long until we take you home. And now that I'm better, I'll be here every day until we do."

A week later when Lydia arrived at the hospital after school, *Mammi* pulled her into the hallway. "Something's wrong with Emma. I overheard the doctors say she should have come out of her coma by now. They're scheduling more tests. Ones with alphabet letters. Like EQ or something."

"Perhaps Caleb will know."

"Will know what?"

Lydia jumped when Jakob's voice sounded behind her. She breathed deeply to calm her rapid heartbeat. Had Jakob sneaked up on them on purpose?

"Is something wrong?" Jakob glanced from one to the other with worry creasing his brow.

"The doctors want to do more tests on Emma. She isn't coming out of the coma."

Mammi motioned toward the door. "I thought Lydia could ask Caleb what's happening."

Jakob frowned. "Why must you ask him? Won't the doctors or nurses tell you?"

Mammi patted Jakob's cheek. "What a smart young man. Of course, they'd tell me."

"Worry for Emma must have clouded your thinking." He studied Lydia. "Yours too, I assume?"

Was he being sarcastic or sympathetic? Lydia had enough to worry about without reading innuendos into Jakob's comments.

"*Ach,* that is so," *Mammi* agreed. "This has been quite stressful for all of us. Isn't that so, Lydia?"

Lydia nodded, but her brain remained stuck in a game without rules. First *Mammi* warned her away from *Englischers,* then she encouraged a friendship with Caleb, next she championed Jakob's cause, now she seemed to be allying with Lydia against Jakob.

Perhaps if her body hadn't been so tired and her mind so filled with worry about Emma, Lydia might have puzzled it out. But all she wanted was some rest from the swirling thoughts and roller-coaster emotions of the past weeks. And now after Emma had been doing so well, Lydia was unprepared for another setback. When would this nightmare end?

Evidently not now. Caleb was striding out of the elevator toward them.

"*Gut* day, Mrs. Esh. Lydia. And . . ."

"Jakob," came the low, territorial growl.

"Yes, of course. *Gut* day to you, Jakob."

Caleb peeked around the door frame. "And a good morning to you too, Emma."

Mammi exchanged greetings with Caleb and then asked her earlier questions in hushed tones so Emma wouldn't overhear.

Caleb looked thoughtful. "I wouldn't worry too much about it. It's only a precaution to be sure there's no lingering damage from the accident. I'm guessing she's coming out of the coma more slowly than expected. Doctors always err on the side of caution."

Mammi didn't look convinced. "But they sounded worried."

"Of course. They have to consider lawsuits and such. They don't want to take any chances that they've made a mistake."

"We don't believe in suing people," *Mammi* said.

Caleb smiled. "I know. But the doctors may not. And in any case, they wouldn't want to make a wrong diagnosis." Ignoring Jakob's glare, he gestured toward the room. "Were you planning to visit? Or were you just leaving?"

"We had planned to visit." Jakob made it sound as if their plans had changed now that Caleb arrived.

Caleb smiled at each of them in turn before leaning past the door frame and calling a cheery farewell to Emma.

After Caleb left, Jakob muttered, "He treats her as if she's awake."

"We all do," Lydia said. "She can hear us. She's been responding to commands. Yesterday she squeezed my hand several times when I asked her to. And she moved her foot for the doctor."

Mammi sat in the chair beside Emma's bed. "Let's hope Caleb's right and the tests are to be sure the doctors have made the right diagnosis." She picked up Emma's hand. "It's *Mammi,* Em. Can you squeeze my hand?" *Mammi* winced. "Not such a good idea with my arthritis." She patted Emma's hand. "Good girl."

Lydia smiled. With the way Emma was responding, she had no doubt Caleb was correct. Emma was on her way to recovery. She should be thrilled, but once her sister left the hospital, would she ever see Caleb again?

CHAPTER SIXTEEN

The following week the family sat in a consultation room at the hospital, waiting for the doctor to appear. The boys and Sarah had joined them this time. Lydia wondered why the doctor had insisted on the whole family being present. She scanned the bare green walls, which held only a large clock over the doorway, indicating the doctor was already eight minutes late.

Just then Dr. Burton, Emma's doctor, entered the room followed by a man with a gray goatee. Dr. Burton sat across from them and introduced her colleague, Dr. Ralph Pearson, as a psychiatrist. *Dat* made a noise of disgust deep in his throat. *Mamm* reached out and touched his arm, but *Dat* moved away. He did not believe in psychiatrists or in expressing emotion.

Lydia hoped he wouldn't make his distaste any more evident. She wasn't sure she trusted psychiatrists much either, but if this one could help Emma, she was willing to listen.

Dr. Burton lifted the file in her lap and paged through it. When she looked up, she addressed her comments to *Dat.* "As you know, we've successfully weaned Emma from the ventilator. She is doing fine breathing on her own. And all of the neuro-imaging tests indicate that her brain is functioning properly. Truly a miracle considering the original prognosis. She is also responding to commands, such as to squeeze a hand or to move her foot."

Mamm's sigh of relief echoed Lydia's internal one. And *Mammi* caught Lydia's eye and smiled. They had already experienced that.

Dr. Burton continued. "The drugs we had given her are completely out of her system. So that leads us to the question as to why Emma remains in a coma when we can find no damage or lingering effects of the accident. I've asked Dr. Pearson to join us today to discuss some of the emotional aspects of comas. I'll leave you in his capable hands." She stood, nodded toward *Dat,* and exited.

After the door closed behind her, Dr. Pearson cleared his throat and slid his glasses higher on his nose. He too addressed his comments to *Dat*. "As Dr. Burton explained, there is no medical reason for your daughter" — he fumbled with his clipboard of papers — "um, Emma, to remain in a coma. In cases like this the patient has often suffered an emotional trauma."

Dat started forward in his chair as if to jump to his feet. Only *Mamm*'s gentle hand on his coat sleeve seemed to anchor him in place. But his eyes flicked toward the door as if longing to escape.

Lydia's stomach clenched. How *Dat* hated emotion of any kind. And he didn't set much store by psychiatrists. Quacks, he always called them.

"I realize this may be difficult, but I'd like you to think of reasons why Emma might not want to return to reality, what she may be avoiding facing."

Dat's body tensed, and his Adam's apple bobbed up and down. Lydia worried he might explode and spew out his opinions about psychology messing around with people's minds. Would he stop them from hearing what this doctor had to say?

Dr. Pearson leaned forward and gazed at each of them intently. *Dat* squirmed in his chair and refused to meet the psychiatrist's eyes. When the doctor stared into Lydia's eyes, it was as if he were probing her deepest secrets. The silence in the room grew strained.

Mamm opened her mouth as if to speak, but at *Dat*'s frown, she slumped back in her seat.

Dr. Pearson leaned back in his chair and studied the ceiling.

Lydia picked at a hangnail on her thumb. *Dat*'s look at *Mamm* made it clear he did not want any family matters divulged. To him discussing private family business — especially with an *Englischer* — was tantamount to appearing in public in your underwear. The shame, the humiliation of exposing themselves kept his jaw set and his fists clenched.

Dr. Pearson sat forward so suddenly that Sarah gasped. The green plastic cushions whooshed as the boys *rutsched.*

"Even if you aren't sure of the reason, discussing some of the problems Emma was facing recently, anything at all that might be bothering her, could lead to an answer."

Lydia wriggled in her chair trying to find a spot that would ease her conscience. Words crowded behind her clenched teeth, but a glance at *Dat,* who was now gripping the chair arms so tightly the veins in his hands were throbbing, made her choke them back.

The psychiatrist's gaze swept the room, resting on each one in turn. "Sometimes siblings know things their parents don't."

His probing stare swung toward Lydia.

"Emma . . ." Lydia's throat muscles convulsed, so the word came out as a squeak. In her peripheral vision *Dat*'s arm moved as if signaling her to stop, but Lydia kept her gaze locked on Dr. Pearson. Swallowing hard, Lydia tried to loosen the muscles strangling her words. She wet the inside of her mouth, which had gone dry at the thought of defying *Dat*. "I saw Emma the day of her accident."

Then the words tumbled out — describing Emma's initial anger and defiance, her hesitance about coming home, her decision to care for *Mammi*. As Lydia spoke, the poison of guilt drained from some of the deep wounds in her soul. "Emma was worried *Mamm* and *Dat* would be upset."

"About what?" The psychiatrist's quiet question stemmed Lydia's frantic flow of words.

Lydia stopped and considered. "I don't know for sure. I thought it was because she'd moved in with an *Englischer*." At the psychiatrist's raised brow, she explained, "Someone who isn't Amish."

"And that wasn't acceptable in the eyes of your family?"

"Of course not," Lydia replied. What an odd question. Would anyone consider something like that acceptable?

"And this young man, is he the one who was driving the car at the time of the accident?" At Lydia's nod, his face tightened. "I'd hoped to meet with him today as well, but he refused."

"He prob'ly thought we'd be mad at him," Zeke said.

"Oh, I hope not," Sarah's words were barely a whisper. "We sent him a card to let him to know we forgive him."

Abe bristled. "I signed it, but sometimes I want to punch him. He hurt our sister."

Sarah's sharp intake of breath was the only sound in the room. When all eyes turned toward her, her cheeks reddened. She clapped a hand over her mouth and shrank back in her seat. "Sorry," she mumbled and shot an apologetic glance at *Dat.*

Dr. Pearson smiled at Abe and then included the rest of the family in his glance. "It's natural to feel anger in a situation like this."

"Oh, but we shouldn't." Sarah's words were shaky, and she was trembling, fear written in every line of her body at contradicting an adult. "We must forgive others so God will forgive us."

"I see." Dr. Pearson's frown and tight lips made it clear that he didn't understand or approve. "So all of you believe this?" He scanned each face one by one. After everyone nodded, he shook his head almost imperceptibly. "And you've all forgiven this young man?"

At the touch of incredulousness in his voice, *Mammi* straightened. "Of course," she snapped. "It's our duty. What happened to Emma was God's will."

The doctor locked eyes with *Mammi* as if testing the truth of her statement. *Mammi* stared back equally as intently.

Lydia released the breath she'd been holding, relieved Dr. Pearson wasn't looking at her. If he looked her way, his probing gaze might see deep inside her and discover she not only blamed herself, she still had flashes of anger over Kyle's irresponsible driving.

Sarah, with her gentle nature, forgave quickly and easily. *Mamm*'s pursed lips, though, revealed her own inner struggle. And *Dat* had slumped forward, head in hands, his face hidden.

A triumphant grin flashed across *Mammi*'s face when the psychiatrist was the first to look away. He cleared his throat and turned toward Lydia. "So back to the issue of your sister and this young man. Were they having any problems that you know of?"

Lydia hesitated, remembering Emma crying. And the blip on the heart monitor. Had hearing Kyle's name caused fear or excitement? She said slowly, "Emma said she was happy."

"But you're not sure?"

"I–I don't know."

Dr. Pearson made another note on his clipboard. "I'll need to find a way to speak with this, um," — he ran his finger down the page — "Kyle Miller."

As he said the name, *Mamm* drew in a breath and squeezed her eyes shut. *Dat*'s body jerked, but he kept his head down. Lydia's stomach clenched. It was clear they all needed to work on forgiving Kyle.

The psychiatrist continued. "You said your sister was heading home, but she was unsure of her reception?"

Mamm's voice came, soft and hesitant, from across the room. "Emma would know we'd forgive *her.*"

Dat started violently. He lifted his head and shot *Mamm* a warning glance. She shrank back in her chair.

The psychiatrist steepled his fingers. "It seems, though, that Emma was not certain of her family's reaction. Is that so?" He directed his question to Lydia.

Lydia squirmed. She could not meet his eyes, nor those of her parents. Head bowed, she murmured, "Yes."

Placing his hands on his knees, Dr. Pearson leaned forward and in a soft, syrupy voice said, "I intend to check with the boyfriend, of course, to see if they had any issues. In cases like this, though, we often find that reassuring the patient that she is loved and accepted helps. It sounds as if Emma worried she would not be accepted or forgiven. If each of you offers your forgiveness, it may overcome the fear and hysteria keeping her in the coma."

Dat's chair scraped across the floor as he jumped to his feet. "This is foolishness." He strode to the door and yanked it open. When it banged shut behind him, some of the tension in the room leaked away.

Mamm wrung her hands. "Please forgive Reuben. He doesn't believe in this emotional . . ." She waved a hand vaguely.

"Neither do I." *Mammi*'s tartness left no doubt of her disdain. "But I see no reason why we shouldn't assure Emma of our forgiveness."

Dr. Pearson nodded. "That would be wise. And if you can convince Mr. Esh as

221

well . . ." He stroked his goatee. "It seems as if he holds a great deal of pent-up anger toward his daughter. Forgiveness might be good for both of them."

Mamm's gaze strayed toward the door. "I'm not sure . . ."

"Perhaps in time," Dr. Pearson murmured.

"Perhaps," *Mamm* echoed, but her words carried little assurance.

Lydia vowed to talk to *Dat,* to convince him Emma wanted his forgiveness most of all. *Dat* had always been the one Emma looked to for approval. The others would help, but *Dat* was key.

CHAPTER SEVENTEEN

Dr. Pearson stood and shook the creases from his crisply pressed pants. "We'll be monitoring the patient, um, Emily, until she's transferred to the rehabilitation center to see how she responds."

Emily? Lydia hid her grimace. He hadn't even gotten the name right. Could they trust him to get the diagnosis correct? Good thing *Dat* wasn't here, or he'd never let any of them try what the psychiatrist had suggested. He'd be even more convinced the man didn't know what he was talking about.

Mammi's pinched lips revealed her struggle not to correct him. Her grandmother didn't usually swallow down her words, so why now? *Mammi* caught Lydia's eye and warned her with a glance to keep silent. Not that Lydia had planned to say anything. She'd never correct an elder. Certainly *Mammi* knew that.

"Yes, well . . ." Dr. Pearson tucked his

clipboard under his arm and nodded toward *Mamm.* "I have another appointment. I hope you'll all seriously consider what I said. And encourage your husband to do so as well."

"We will," *Mamm* said to his retreating back.

After the door closed behind him, *Mammi*'s breath whooshed out. Holding her tongue must have been extremely difficult. "That —"

Mamm's frown silenced *Mammi.* "We should not judge him." Her eyes flickered toward Abe and Zeke.

Mammi nodded briefly. "I'm sorry. I let my temper get away with me. Please forgive me." She turned to the boys. "I hope you will not be so quick to criticize as your grandmother." Then she rose. "We should at least see if the doctor is right. If he is, maybe Emma will return home soon. And even if he's wrong, offering someone forgiveness is something God would have us do. Let's go."

Mamm cast one last desperate glance toward the hallway.

Mammi grasped *Mamm*'s arm. "I feel the need for some assistance. My legs are still a bit wobbly." She gave *Mamm* a stern look. "Surely Reuben wouldn't want you to deny his mother the help she needs?"

Lydia's heart went out to her mother. Poor *Mamm*. Caught between *Dat*'s ultimatum and *Mammi*'s determination.

Reluctance in every line of her face, *Mamm* complied. The boys clung close to *Mamm* as if someone might snatch them away. Sarah followed, casting nervous glances over her shoulder.

When they got to the door of Emma's room, *Mammi* halted and freed her arm from *Mamm*'s. "If you wish to obey your husband's orders, you can stay here."

But *Mamm* wasn't listening to *Mammi*'s words. Her gaze was locked on Emma's face. "Emma," she breathed. Her arms dropped to her sides, and her face moved rapidly through a gamut of emotions — shock, pain, fear, and then longing. She took one step into the room and held out her hands imploringly. "Emma," she begged.

Everyone stood still as *Mamm* moved toward Emma as if drawn by a force beyond her control. When she reached the bed, she placed a hand on Emma's shoulder. She closed her eyes for a second as if regaining her balance. Then she opened them and gazed hungrily at Emma's face. "She's breathing." A tear trickled down *Mamm*'s cheek. "She looks well. Like she's sleeping."

Sarah and the boys edged into the room as *Mammi* lowered herself into a chair beside Emma. They too seemed to be mesmerized by the still figure on the bed.

"Is she sleeping?" Zeke whispered. Then in a louder voice asked, "Why doesn't she wake up?"

"Just shake her." Abe danced impatiently on one foot. "Come on, Emma. Time to get up."

Sarah leaned over and put an arm around Abe. "Hush. We want her to get well."

"Is she still sick? She doesn't look sick."

Lydia moved closer to Zeke and laid a hand on his shoulder. He was staring at Emma with a puzzled frown. "If she's just sleeping, why can't she do that in her own bed instead of here?" His last words came out wobbly.

Mammi sniffed. "If I had my way, that's where she'd be right now, but let's do what the doctor suggested. Who wants to start?"

The burdens on Lydia's heart were so heavy, she couldn't put them into words. And she certainly couldn't say some of the things she wanted to say in front of everyone else. She looked at *Mammi*. "Do you think it might be best if each of us has some private time with her?"

Mammi pulled herself shakily to her feet.

226

"Why don't we go from youngest to oldest?"

Abe backed away. "Can Sarah stay with me?"

"Of course." Lydia moved closer to Sarah, her arm around Zeke's shoulders. "Maybe the three of you could stay together. I'll stay here too, if you'd like."

Sarah flashed her a grateful glance.

"I'll stay too," *Mamm* said hurriedly.

"Pff." *Mammi* plunked back down in the chair. "Guess we'll all stay together. But you young ones can go first."

Abe tiptoed to the bed. "Emma, I hope you get well."

Zeke moved closer and elbowed him. "You're supposed say you forgive her."

"Oh." Abe stood silent for a moment. "I forgive you for jumping out and scaring me. And for that time you got me to jump down from the haymow and I broke my arm and . . ." He took a deep breath.

Zeke sighed. "We don't have to say every single thing she ever did." He looked up at Sarah. "Do we?"

Sarah smiled. "No, I don't think that's necessary."

Lydia leaned closer to both boys and whispered, "Pretend she's just asked you to forgive her. What would you say?"

"I don't know." Abe shuffled from foot to foot. "Depends on what she done to me."

Lydia hid a smile. "Just saying 'I forgive you' will be enough."

Abe looked relieved. "Emma, I forgive you for every bad thing you done." He breathed a sigh of relief and stepped back.

Zeke stepped toward the bed, but Abe muscled in front of him. "I forgot to say something important."

Zeke shoved him. "You had your turn. Now it's mine."

Mamm, who hadn't torn her gaze from Emma's face until now, frowned at both boys.

Sarah intervened. "Let's not upset Emma with fighting. Zekey, could you let Abe finish what he wants to say?"

Zeke thrust out his lower lip. "I guess so."

Abe moved right up to the rails of the bed and set his chin on them. He peered at Emma for a moment. "I think you're just faking. And you're waiting until I come close. Then you'll jump up and say 'boo.' But you're not going to trick me this time."

Sarah brushed away a tear, but Zeke pushed Abe again. "She's not faking. She's hurt and sick."

Abe crossed his arms. "She might be. She's a good faker. Remember that time when —"

Lydia said softly, "Abe, why don't you let Zeke have his turn to talk to Emma."

Zeke pressed his lips together and took Abe's place. "Emma, don't listen to Abe. He don't know what he's talking about. I know you're not faking." He sucked in a deep breath. "I forgive you for everything." His words came out in such a rush that they were barely distinguishable. "And . . ." He gripped the rail until his knuckles turned white. "We want you to come home. Now. So please get better."

He stepped back and squinched his eyes.

Sarah put a hand on his head and swallowed hard. She turned imploring eyes to Lydia. But all the words Lydia wanted to say had clogged in her throat.

The silence grew. Then *Mamm* picked up Emma's hand. "Please come home to us, baby girl. We all forgive you and we love you." She leaned back and nibbled at her lower lip. Then she took a deep breath and continued, "And your *dat,* he's upset about all this. Too upset to come in here and talk to you. But I'm sure he'd forgive you too." She gulped and mouthed, "I hope."

Mammi interrupted. "Of course he would. Don't you worry. We all love you and forgive you. It sure would make it easier on me if you'd come home. These old bones aren't much for sitting in hospital chairs." She sighed. "Not that I'm complaining about visiting you. I'm just wishing you were home with your family." She looked over at Sarah and Lydia. "You two have anything to say?"

Sarah cleared her throat. "Oh, Em, we miss you so. Won't you please come home? Whatever you've done, we forgive you, and it will never change our love for you. Please just get well." Sarah turned her back to the bed and covered her face with her hands.

Lydia was so choked up she could barely speak. "Would it be all right if I speak to her alone?"

Mamm gave her a puzzled glance, but *Mammi* stood. "That's a fine idea." She turned toward Emma. "We'll be headed home now, Emma, but don't ever forget we forgive you, and so does God."

Sarah ushered the boys to the door, and they all exited the room, leaving Lydia alone with Emma.

Lydia moved to the bed. "Emma, I wish I knew what you need forgiveness for, but whatever it is, we *all* still love you and forgive you. We'll welcome you home with open arms." Lydia's voice wobbled a bit. Was that a lie? Would *Dat* forgive Emma?

She swallowed hard. "I need you to forgive

me as well. I'm sorry for everything I did. You were right about my pride. It got in the way of being a good sister, but if you'll forgive me and come back home to us, I'll try to do better." Lydia's throat closed up. But she had something more she wanted to, needed to say.

Brushing the hair back from her sister's forehead, she forced out the tear-choked words. "And Em, if you need me there when you confess, I'll be right beside you. I promise."

Eyes blinded by tears, head down, she stumbled from the room, and blundered into something solid. Arms closed around her, holding her tight.

"Lydia?" Caleb's breath tickled her cheek. "Is everything all right?"

Now it was, here in his arms. Lydia sighed and moved closer. *Wait. What was she doing?* She forced herself to break the embrace, to push away. "I–I'm sorry. I shouldn't have — I didn't mean to —"

"Hey." Caleb reached out and tilted her chin up so he could look into her eyes. "You needed comfort, and I was here. There's nothing wrong with that."

There was if you were planning to marry another man. And if you yearned for more than friendly comfort. Lydia's cheeks burned, and she lowered her lids to hide those longings from Caleb.

"But you didn't answer my question. Did you have bad news about Emma?"

Too choked up to speak, Lydia only shook her head and took another step back.

Caleb's hands dropped to his sides. "Are you coming or going?"

Lydia's mind and emotions were in such a whirl that she almost answered, *I'm staying. Staying here with you.* The thought of *Dat* freezing outside brought reality crashing back. "I–I have to go."

"I'll walk you down to be sure you don't walk into anyone else." Caleb's teasing smile brought a teary one of her own.

He put a gentle arm around her shoulders and guided her to the elevator. Lydia trembled at his touch. Her conscience warned her to move away, far away. But her bruised and aching heart begged her to move closer to Caleb's comfort.

Before the elevator reached the lobby, Lydia turned so they were no longer touching. "My family may be out there," she whispered.

With an understanding nod Caleb put some distance between them and melted into the crowd exiting the elevator, but when he reached the clinic hallway, he gave her a brief wave.

Lydia kept her gaze fixed on his retreating back until he disappeared into a cubicle.

CHAPTER EIGHTEEN

Friday evening at dinner the family had barely gotten seated before *Mammi* leaned toward *Dat*. "The hospital says Emma is ready to be moved to a rehabilitation center." *Mammi*'s accusing glare made it clear that she blamed *Dat* for Emma not recovering.

Dat glowered at his plate and picked at his pot pie, but said nothing.

Mammi huffed out an impatient breath. "Emma should be here with us. I'll ask about having her discharged into our care."

"No," *Dat* snapped, his voice low and flat.

"She should be here where she can be cared for. By family." *Mammi*'s voice brooked no argument.

The thundercloud that was Dad's brow lowered, threatening a major storm. "Absolutely not."

"Reuben, whatever has gotten into you? This is your daughter we're talking about."

"She is no longer my daughter." Each word dropped like a boulder into a pond, sloshing waves of anger, splattering it around the room.

Mammi sat, her mouth forming words that did not emerge.

Mamm gave a strangled cry. Her hands twisted her apron into a knot.

"Whatever do you mean by that?" *Mammi* glared at *Dat* over the top of her glasses.

Dat drew himself up. "I do not have to explain my decisions. I will say it only one more time. I will not bring her into this house. And furthermore, I will no longer transport any of you to the hospital or to the rehabilitation center." He spun on his heel and banged out of the kitchen.

They all stared after him in stunned silence.

Lydia's brain could not make sense of it. Was it grief that had so twisted his soul into this unrecognizable shape? Or perhaps fear — or certainty — that Emma would die? Did he not realize how far she had come already? She had improved rapidly and no longer needed the ventilator. And she responded to commands. That was a good sign.

Mammi cleared her throat. "If your father does not want Emma in his house, then we shall respect his wishes."

"But . . ." Lydia couldn't bear to see Emma in a rehabilitation center. How could they visit her? All this traveling was already hard on *Mammi*. She'd never be able to make the trip in the buggy. And *Dat* would not pay Andy for such long trips.

One corner of *Mammi*'s mouth turned up in a wry smile. She turned to *Mamm*. "Ruth, when they're ready to release Emma, I want you to give permission for the discharge."

"What?" Lydia stared at her grandmother. "You said we would respect *Dat*'s wishes."

"So we will." *Mammi* paused to draw in a breath, and Lydia's heart rate spiked. "Your *dat* said Emma was forbidden to enter the doors of his house. He did not say she could not enter the doors of the *daadi haus*."

Mamm's eyes widened. "I'm sure Reuben meant . . ."

"I know perfectly well what he meant. But I will not stand by and see my grand-daughter moved to a rehabilitation center."

Mammi looked at Lydia. "Perhaps your Caleb could help us when they transfer Emma? He seems to know a lot about medical care."

Shock filled *Mamm*'s eyes. And Lydia's heart squeezed so tightly she could barely breathe. What must her mother think? It would be rude to say he was not "her" Caleb. But that wasn't the only reason she was reluctant to say it. She couldn't trust *Mammi* not to bring up some evidence to prove it.

When *Mamm* turned questioning eyes toward her, Lydia hurried to explain. "Caleb's a hospital worker who's helped with Emma." Although her conscience bothered her, she omitted the fact that he was Kyle's brother, and *Mammi* didn't correct her. "I'm sure Caleb would be glad to help. He seems to have taken quite a shine to *Mammi*."

"The admiration is mutual. He's been a tremendous help to us so far. I'm sure he can be persuaded to continue his assistance. He seems to enjoy spending time around you."

"Mammi!" Lydia's shock sharpened her words.

Mammi waved away her protests. "I cannot endure any more bickering tonight. This traveling back and forth to the hospital has exhausted me. I'm heading to bed."

"Do you need any help?" Lydia started to follow.

"No, stay here with your *mamm*. She needs you. I'll be fine."

Lydia hesitated, her gaze ping-ponging back and forth between *Mammi*'s shuffling form and *Mamm,* who had collapsed onto the bench, her elbows propped on the table, her shaking hands covering her face.

Lydia rounded the table and set a hand on her mother's shoulder. *"Mamm?"*

"I'm not sure what to do. I don't want to go against your *dat*'s wishes. But his *mamm . . ."*

Lydia too was torn. As much as she wanted Emma home, she did not want an explosion. A dropped spark would set the kindling ablaze. And poor *Mamm* would be caught in the middle of the flames.

Mamm looked up, eyes bright with unshed tears. "And what your grandmother said earlier." Her gaze seared Lydia's soul. "You are not falling for an *Englischer* too, are you?"

Lydia could not lie. She didn't answer the question directly, but spoke to her mother's underlying fears. "You needn't worry. I have no intention of leaving the faith. Ever. Not for any reason." With Emma's current situation, she had no reason not to join the church. "With spring soon here, baptismal classes will be starting. I'll tell the bishop I'm joining the church."

Mamm's shining eyes warmed Lydia's heart, but she still hadn't answered the question of whether or not she was falling for an *Englischer.* No matter how much being around Caleb tempted her, though, Lydia determined to remain true to her faith.

And once Emma came home, she would no longer face the temptation of being around Caleb. Part of her was filled with relief to have that issue resolved. So why then did she ache with a deep sadness?

For the next few days silence hung heavy in the air, dragging down everyone's spirits like heavy winter blankets sagging on a clothesline. The only one unaffected by the tension was *Mammi*. She whirled through the many chores that needed to be done that Lydia was exhausted just watching her.

Mammi borrowed a cell phone from Andy's teenage son to make calls. He showed her how to use it, and her first call was to an *Englisch* neighbor near the bishop's home.

Within an hour the bishop came calling. He and *Mammi* met in the *daadi haus,* and then he knocked at the kitchen door to ask if he could meet with the family after dinner.

Mamm agreed to gather the family for his visit later, but she also invited him to stay for dinner. The pot roast she had just taken from the oven perfumed the air with the tang of onions and carrots.

Bishop Zook inhaled deeply, and his grave expression lightened for a moment. "It smells delicious, but Mary is expecting me home for dinner. And I must meet with the elders to discuss Emma's situation."

"Oh." The paring knife fell from *Mamm*'s hand and clattered onto the cutting board. The potato she'd been peeling landed on the floor by her feet.

The bishop bent and scooped up the potato and held it out. A long curlicue of skin dangled from the partially exposed whiteness. "Don't let me interrupt your dinner preparations."

Mamm still stood in a daze, so Sarah dashed over and took the potato. Then she handed the bishop a dish towel. He wiped his fingers and wished them a good evening before he exited. After the door closed behind him, *Mamm* picked up the knife again, but her nervous fingers dropped it twice.

Lydia moved her aside and offered to finish peeling the potatoes. She motioned to the rocker in the corner of the kitchen and attempted to get *Mamm* to sit for a while, but her mother shook her head, a glazed look in her eyes.

She muttered, "I must tell Reuben that

240

his mother asked the bishop about electricity." She squared her chin and marched toward the kitchen doorway. "What must be done, must be done."

Their parent's bedroom shared one wall with the kitchen, so a short while later *Mamm*'s apologetic tones and *Dat*'s irritated ones filtered into the kitchen. Sarah clutched Lydia's arm, dread in her eyes.

Although Lydia couldn't make out the words, the argument was unmistakable. "He'll calm down," she hastened to assure Sarah. "He always does."

Sometimes their *dat* blustered, but he turned reasonable fairly quickly. The worst fights were when *Mamm* and *Dat* didn't speak to each other for hours, the icy stillness hanging in the air until bedtime. They both took seriously the admonition to never let the sun set on their anger. But until then . . .

An ache started deep in Lydia's chest. Dinner would be uncomfortable, but if the bishop and elders supported *Mammi*'s plan, *Dat* would be livid. Lydia worried that sunset might not be enough to cool his rage.

When Lydia went to call *Mammi* for dinner, her grandmother was chattering into the cell phone as if she were an *Englischer* or one of the *youngie.* After an order to see that the bed was delivered tomorrow, she clicked a button and accompanied Lydia to the kitchen.

All through the meal *Dat* appeared to be dry tinder waiting for the least spark to explode. Lydia felt as if she were stomping out sparks continually or batting them away with bare hands covered with singe marks. She sent warning frowns to the boys for the slightest mealtime infractions.

Sensing *Dat*'s anger, they ate quietly, heads bent over their plates, but it didn't save them from his wrath. Sarah too did her part to keep peace when *Dat* thundered, but tears welled in her eyes, and her voice grew more and more timid as the meal progressed.

Dat picked at his meal, and before dessert he shoved back his chair. "I find I am no longer hungry. Please excuse me." He hurried from the room.

A collective exhale released some of the anxiety, but everyone stared at each other with fear-filled eyes when someone rapped on the front door.

Lydia hurried to answer it, but *Gut-n-Owed* died on her lips at the sight of Jakob standing on the doorstep behind his father. She had dreaded the bishop seeing her father's orneriness, but having Jakob witness it seemed even worse. And if the bishop refused *Mammi*'s request, the heartache would be too great to bear. She did not want Jakob to witness her breakdown.

Her reluctance must have shown on her face because Jakob's grave smile, fitting for the seriousness of the occasion, wavered, then drooped into sadness.

Lydia hurried to make amends. "*Ach,* I am so sorry to keep you waiting like this. What must you be thinking of me?" She pulled the door open wide and motioned for them to enter. "Come in. Please. It is only that we are all so upset about Emma and . . ."

Her words trailed off as the bishop patted her shoulder. "It is a troubling situation, one I hope we will resolve tonight."

Lydia took their coats and led them down the hall to the kitchen. A warm cinnamon aroma greeted them and spoke of comfort and hominess, but it played a counterpoint to the anxiety boiling underneath.

Mamm wiped her hands on her apron and greeted the bishop. She gestured toward *Dat*'s chair at the head of the table. "Please sit. The streusel cake will be out of the oven in a few minutes." She smiled at Jakob, but strain showed in the lines around her eyes. "Why don't you sit in your usual place?"

As Jakob rounded the table to the boys' bench, *Mamm* and the bishop shared a knowing look, and the churning in Lydia's stomach increased. She rushed to the oven to remove the streusel cake, keeping her back to the room while she struggled to control all of the anxieties and fears whirling through her brain and battering her stomach. *Please, God, make me willing to accept whatever decision the bishop has made. And give me an obedient heart about my future.*

Perhaps she should have asked God to clear her mind of Caleb. But once the hospital discharged Emma — either to *Mammi*'s or to the rehabilitation center — Lydia would never see him again. Maybe when Caleb faded to a distant memory, she would be ready to give her heart to Jakob the way she should. After all, *Mammi* had managed to forget her *Englisch* boyfriend to marry *Daadi,* and that had turned out well.

Once everyone had been seated, the bishop addressed *Dat.* "I have met with the ministers, and we have prayerfully considered Esther's request to have electricity installed." His sorrow-filled eyes moved from *Dat* to *Mammi.* "It goes against everything we believe in. We are to be in the world, not of it."

244

"But what about Emma?" *Mammi* burst out.

"*Jah,* it is a grave situation. It pains me to think of one of our own taken so far from the community to live among *Englischers.* I do not want to see her separated from her family, but . . ."

Mammi's breath hissed out between her teeth, but she remained silent.

Dat's hunched shoulders straightened. He sat up taller and trained his gaze on the bishop.

Lydia's stomach twisted, and tears burned behind her eyes. So they planned to refuse *Mammi*'s request. *Oh, Emma.*

The bishop spread his hands as if pleading for understanding. "First, let me tell you what I have done since I talked with Esther earlier today. I spoke with hospital personnel and with John Bieler, one of our own who works for an *Englisch* construction company, to see if other alternatives might be available to power the machinery. They all expressed doubts about the reliability of a generator. When I met with the ministers, we took that into consideration when we prayed over the decision."

The bishop cleared his throat. "Letting one person install electricity could lead to a loosening of standards. Others in the community may feel we have sanctioned it. They may find excuses for why they need electricity."

Dat leaned forward, eagerness in every line of his body.

Mammi too leaned forward, looking ready to jump from her seat and protest. Her tightly pursed lips revealed her battle for control.

Mamm's downcast eyes focused on the edge of the apron she was twisting between her fingers. Sarah had her head bowed and her eyes squeezed shut.

Jakob gave Lydia a sympathetic smile, one Lydia's muscles refused to return. She lowered her gaze and concentrated on stilling the nervous movements of her hands. If only she could clap them over her ears to tune out the bishop's words.

The bishop rubbed his forehead. "I never thought I would ever say this, but despite our concerns, in this case, electricity seems to be the lesser of two evils."

"What?" *Dat* leaped from his chair, fists clenched.

Mamm tugged at the back of his vest, and *Dat* deflated. He sank back in his chair and buried his head in his hands.

Bishop Zook's voice grew low, soothing, and conciliatory. "Emma belongs at home.

She should not be living among strangers. Among *Englischers*. And as much as we dislike going against the *Ordnung,* we deem Emma's need to be among family and community as more important."

Beside him, *Mammi* smiled triumphantly.

Dat held up a hand. "Even if you and the ministers have agreed to this, I have not given my consent. I refuse to allow electricity in my home. If I am forced to, I will sign Emma over as a ward of the state. Then a nursing home will be the only choice."

Mammi's gasp was the only sound in the stillness of the room.

Dat stomped from the room, and the bedroom door slammed behind him.

Bishop Zook bowed his head and murmured quietly.

Lydia too wanted to pray, but her brain had iced over. Her thoughts lay buried under an iceberg. *Dat* couldn't — wouldn't — do that, would he?

Lifting his head, Bishop Zook said in a quiet voice, "It's understandable Reuben feels his role as leader of the family has been usurped." He fixed a stern glance on each of them, ending with *Mammi*. "But he is a reasonable man. I expect he will come around given some time to mull over the matter. I have every confidence in his integrity."

"His integrity is not in question," *Mammi* muttered. "Emma's future is."

"I counsel patience, Esther. All is in God's hands. Allow Him to work in Reuben's heart and trust that His will be done, whatever Reuben decides." The bishop turned to Lydia. "If your father decides to bring Emma home, I believe it would be in your family's best interest if you were here to help. Rebecca can substitute at the schoolhouse for the rest of the school year."

"But —"

"Is Rebecca not doing a satisfactory job?"

"She's doing a wonderful job." Though it pained her to admit it, Lydia added, "I believe she does a better job than I do."

"That's not what Rebecca tells me. But she does find Sarah a highly competent assistant."

A flush swept up Sarah's neck and colored her cheeks, and a slight smile tilted her lips.

"So what is your objection then?"

"It's only that I —" Lydia couldn't put into words the hurt of being displaced by Rebecca, perhaps permanently. She jerked back to the present to hear the end of the bishop's sentence.

". . . give up teaching when you marry."

What? Had they been talking about her marrying Jakob again? From Jakob's scarlet cheeks and satisfied smile, it seemed so. He gave Lydia a shy, apologetic smile. Evidently Jakob had discussed their marriage with everyone but her. Not that he hadn't tried to talk to her, she amended.

The bishop repeated his question. "Isn't that so, Lydia?"

What choice did she have? She had no idea what she was agreeing to, but she couldn't contradict the bishop. "Yes." Her meek reply evidently pleased everyone.

Mamm blew out a small breath and leaned back in her chair. Jakob's smile was so wide, his teeth gleamed. *Mammi* gave a self-satisfied grin. The bishop's tense shoulders relaxed, and he hid his smile by stroking his beard.

The bishop rose. "*Wunderbar.* Then we'll see you at the baptismal classes in May."

With the grin still plastered on his face, Jakob followed his father's lead but stood with evident reluctance. He looked as if he were hoping Lydia would protest his departure, but she sat dazed. Her whole future had been arranged for her. She'd gone from teacher to caretaker (if *Dat* agreed) to baptismal candidate to bride in the space of a few moments. All without saying a word.

The door had no sooner closed behind the bishop than *Mammi* turned to *Mamm.* "I'll make arrangements for Emma's homecoming. Then I'll need you to sign the papers when the hospital is ready to discharge Emma."

Mamm turned wide, frightened eyes toward *Mammi.* "But you heard Reuben."

Mammi stood, a bit unsteadily, and started for the door. "I heard my son, but I refuse to believe he can be that cruel. When he comes to his senses, he will apologize for the way he has been behaving. Meanwhile, the bishop gave his permission, and I will proceed as planned."

Mamm nodded, but her shoulders slumped as she shuffled along the hall to the bedroom. She stood for a long time, one hand on the doorknob, as if reluctant to enter.

Lydia's heart went out to her. She hoped *Mamm* would not bear the brunt of this evening's discussion.

CHAPTER NINETEEN

Friday afternoon Lydia walked through the back door of the house and slumped at the table. *Mamm* hadn't started dinner yet, so at least the kitchen was quiet. The silence was soothing after the busy school day. Lydia dropped her school satchel on the bench beside her, cut a slice of the shoofly pie on the table, and then headed for the stairs. She'd work on some lesson plans before helping with dinner.

Although arrangements were being made to bring Emma home, *Mammi* insisted Lydia continue teaching until her sister's discharge. Rebecca tried not to show it, but it was obvious she was eager to take over the classroom. During Lydia's many absences the students had grown more attached to Rebecca, and they often turned to her rather than Lydia with their questions. If Lydia had thought a day at the hospital was tiring, she'd forgotten how much energy it took to handle a classroom full of lively students.

A knock on the front door had her pausing midstep on her way upstairs. Who would be calling at this time of day?

The boys and Sarah were playing baseball in the backyard. *Dat* was in the barn mending a harness and avoiding the family. *Mamm* was ironing in the basement. All present and accounted for. Lydia breathed in a sigh of relief. How long would it be before she stopped panicking when someone came to the door unexpectedly?

She pulled open the door, and her heart pattered into a drumbeat so rapid blood thumped in her temples. "Caleb?" Seeing him here on the front porch shook her. Memories of being in his arms flooded back, and her cheeks heated.

Caleb was shivering in the chilly spring rain, and she was standing there staring at him. "C–come in." She opened the door wide so he could step into the hall.

He removed his boots as he had done before. Lydia couldn't take her eyes off his broad back and the raindrops glistening in his dark hair. Soft footsteps padded up behind her, and *Mamm*'s hand descended on her shoulder, making Lydia realize how long she'd been staring.

She turned to introduce Caleb to her mother, trying to keep her voice calm and even. She almost said his brother was the one who'd caused Emma's accident, but stopped herself. No point in upsetting *Mamm.*

Caleb inclined his head politely and offered a friendly greeting, but *Mamm* looked him over and then studied Lydia, a question in her eyes, before responding.

"I'll just take Caleb into the parlor," Lydia said, hoping her mother would go back to her ironing.

But *Mamm* stood there, looking from Lydia to Caleb and back again. Lydia motioned for Caleb to have a seat in the parlor, and he took the same chair as before. *Daadi*'s rocking chair. Lydia went to the couch facing him. *Mamm* remained where she was for a while longer.

Then she turned and left, saying sharply over her shoulder, "I can trust you, Lydia." Yet her voice carried more of a question than a tone of assurance.

Caleb cleared his throat. "Perhaps we should have asked your mother to stay?"

Lydia was tempted to call her back. With *Mamm* there, it might slow her heart and breathing to normal levels. At least having her mother around would remind her of proper behavior and keep her from gazing too long at Caleb, the way she was doing now.

Caleb startled her by saying that he had something to ask her parents.

Her parents? That didn't sound good. Maybe she'd better find out what he wanted. *Mamm* did not need any more stress. And *Dat*? Well, that was better left unsaid.

"Lydia?"

Caleb's question jolted her back to the room. What should she say? "Why don't you tell me what you plan to ask them, and I'll let them know? Right now they're busy with chores, so it would be best not to interrupt them."

Although that was the truth, Lydia's heart felt heavy. She was becoming adept at telling partial truths to evade uncomfortable situations. What had happened to her honesty? And what must God think about her conduct?

Once again Caleb interrupted her thoughts. "I've come because your grandmother told me Emma will be coming home rather than going to a rehabilitation center." When Lydia nodded, he continued. "I'd like to help with her care. It's the least I can do, given the circumstances."

Lydia's confusion must have shown on her face, because he gestured toward the road outside the window. "The accident was my brother's fault. I suggested Kyle take his college fund and pay any of Emma's hospital bills that aren't covered by our insurance, but he balked."

"Oh, no, please don't have him do that. Emma's bills will be paid. Our church community will take care of it."

"Nevertheless, I think he needs to make some restitution."

"We do not expect that," Lydia insisted. "He owes us nothing. I'm sure God has a purpose in all this." Though Lydia was hard pressed to see what it was right now, sometime in the future she hoped to understand. Right now all she could do was accept this as God's will.

Caleb waved that away. "I need to atone for my guilt then. Actually what I'm offering to do is rather selfish. I know a lot about caring for patients like Emma. I could help with medical things."

Lydia had been worried about that. Although the hospital had trained them to care for Emma and would send visiting nurses, Lydia had been nervous about the procedures. There would be so much to remember. What if she forgot something or did it wrong when a nurse wasn't around?

Mamm had been too upset to concentrate during the training sessions, and *Mammi* seemed confused by the machinery. *Dat* had absolutely refused to enter the hospital or take any part in it, though he might have been the best one at figuring it all out. He had maintained a tight-lipped silence ever since *Mammi* had informed him of her plans.

"Although I'd be grateful for the help, we can't accept it," Lydia said.

Caleb looked confused. "Why not?"

His question floored Lydia. *If a neighbor offered to help, would you feel so adamant?* Most likely not, but the neighbor wasn't a handsome man who made her insides quiver. "Thank you very much for your kind offer. But we will decline." The sooner she turned her mind toward Jakob and baptismal classes and forgot Caleb, the better.

Caleb leaned forward, disappointment evident in his eyes. "May I speak with your mother and grandmother? Perhaps they would like to be part of the decision."

Mamm would likely agree with Lydia. She preferred not to be beholden to people, and she definitely wouldn't want an *Englischer* around her daughters. But *Mammi*? That was a different story. *Mammi* would welcome Caleb's help.

"I don't think that's necessary." She hoped she didn't sound ungracious. "It's not that we don't appreciate your offer. It's wonderful kind of you, but I think *Mamm* would prefer that we take care of Emma ourselves." And she had her own reasons for refusing.

"Lydia, please? You don't know how burdened I've been because of all of this. It would be a small way of easing my guilt and pain. I can't live with myself if I don't do something — even if it's something small — to make amends. Please let me help."

The pleading in his voice and the earnestness of his expression made it hard for Lydia to refuse. "You aren't responsible for Kyle's actions."

"I certainly am. I'm the one who's raising him, and I'm the one who should have trained him better, checked his misbehavior and rebellion before it got out of hand, taken the car keys until he learned to drive safely." Caleb's voice broke. "I relive this nightmare every day. I ask myself what I could have done to prevent it, and believe me, there was plenty I could have done, if I'd been a more responsible guardian."

"Stop blaming yourself. Kyle is an adult now. He's responsible for his own choices."

"That may be, but it doesn't alleviate my guilt."

Lydia sighed. How could she convince him that his brother's actions weren't his responsibility? "We accept what happened to Emma. It was God's will. And though we don't always understand why things happen the way they do, we know that all things work together for good, for God's purpose."

"Maybe it's God's purpose for me to help care for her. I may not be a full-fledged doctor, but I did have two years of med school. I know what needs to be done. Lydia, please consider my offer."

Oh, she was. And considering how being around him would make her feel. And considering how much she wanted to agree to his offer. She racked her brain for a valid excuse. "But you work full-time."

"I could come after work and watch Emma so your family could have dinner together. But I thought I'd be the biggest help on the weekends. I could free all of you to go to your church services. I don't go to church, so it would fill a gap in a day that's lonely."

Caleb's eyes begged her to understand. "There's another reason why this is so important to me. When my parents —" He choked up and covered his face with his hands. After a few moments he spoke again. "My mom was on life support, and they convinced me to pull the plug. I've always wondered if she might have recovered."

Lydia's heart went out to him. That faraway look was back in his eyes, the look that made her long to reach out to comfort him, but the couch that earlier had been a safe distance from him now seemed far too close. His face held such deep sadness that she gripped the arm of the couch to keep herself in place. If she crossed the gulf between them . . .

Caleb choked out his next words. The endless days while his mother was in the hospital when he stood by helplessly, unable to do anything. The way he'd studied everything he could about caring for patients in comas and on life support. And then the day they announced that his mother was brain dead. The agony of deciding whether or not to pull the plug.

Lydia's heart broke as he recounted his tale. She blinked back tears at the thought of the young medical student face-to-face with deciding his mother's fate. Something a son should never have to do. And the guilt of making that final decision.

Caleb rubbed his forehead, shielding his eyes with his palm, and his voice came out shaky. "After I walked away that day . . ." He stopped and drew in a shuddering breath. "I vowed to help other brain trauma victims recover. I promised myself someday I'd save someone the way I couldn't save my mom."

Compassion clogged Lydia's voice, making it stick in her throat. When she did speak, it came out hoarse. "Oh, Caleb, I'm so sorry."

He turned pleading eyes toward her. "I need to do something to ease this guilt. Not only the guilt over what my brother's done and the pain it's caused your family, but also for the past, for my mom." Each word sounded as if it were torn from the depths of his soul. "Helping Emma might give me some peace. I couldn't believe it when they said she'd survived. I knew then I wanted to do something, anything to help her recover." Caleb's voice held a fierceness, a determination that reminded her of *Mammi.*

"Emma might not recover," Lydia whispered, "though we hold out hope she will. We've seen God work miracles many times."

Caleb tilted the rocking chair forward. "I'd like to be a part of that miracle."

Lydia's heart clenched. She couldn't say no after all he'd said, but saying yes was much too dangerous. It took all her will-power to respond, "This isn't my decision to make. I'll speak to my parents and *Mammi* to see how they feel about this and let you know." Lydia stood abruptly. If she gazed at his bowed head or pleading eyes any longer, she'd be tempted to give in. The sooner she got him out of here, the sooner her heart would return to normal. Caleb also rose. "I've never told anyone about — about my mom. Thank you for listening. It meant a lot to me." He paused. "You don't have a phone, so should I come back another day?"

What had she done? Ensured that he would return? "I guess that would be best."

"Tomorrow?"

She needed time to think straight, to come up with a valid reason for refusing his help. For now, all she could do was hold him off until she did. "It might be a few days until we have a chance to talk about this. We have so much to do to prepare for Emma's homecoming." Which reminded her they did have a phone. At least *Mammi* did. But she didn't know the number and couldn't risk having him call *Mammi*.

"I'm aware there's plenty to do and would be glad to help you with the equipment you'll be using. I've studied so much about it and about brain trauma. If I go back to med school someday, I want to specialize in it. I couldn't save my mother" — he swallowed hard — "but maybe I can help others. Like Emma."

Her heart aching for him, Lydia kept her hands clenched at her side so she didn't reach out to comfort him. The effort made her words come out more stiff and clipped than she intended. "As I said, I will speak to my family about it and let you know." But she already knew the answer she needed to give. No matter how much her heart yearned to do the opposite, she must think about her future. A future that included forgetting she'd ever met Caleb. A future that included joining the church, marrying Jakob, and doing her best to be a good wife. A future that included being true to her faith and following its ordinances.

She left the room, and Caleb followed her into the hallway and bent to pull on his boots. When he stood, their gazes locked. Lydia was near enough that she could reach out and lay a hand on his arm. She clenched fistfuls of her skirt to keep from touching him, from stroking the chin that she'd been imagining with a beard.

Caleb leaned toward her. "Lydia?" he whispered, his breath soft on her face.

Although it was the hardest thing she'd ever done, Lydia rocked back onto her heels instead of moving closer.

Caleb shook his head, and then he turned and reached for the doorknob.

Lydia's heart plummeted.

As soon as the door closed behind him, she collapsed against its chill. For a moment, she'd thought he was going to kiss her. And as much as she'd dreaded it, part of her had longed for that kiss.

CHAPTER TWENTY

In the distance pink dogwood dotted the nearby hills as the boxy white ambulance pulled into the driveway. Along the walkway to the main house, jonquils bobbed in the breeze. Emma was home. Both the flowers and her sister's arrival lifted Lydia's spirits. She whispered a quick prayer that Emma would blossom the way the world around them showed signs of new life.

Mamm stood in the open doorway, her hesitation revealing she was torn between her loyalty to *Dat* and seeing her daughter. Zeke and Abe bounded out of the house, Sarah close behind.

Zeke thrust out his lower lip. "Why don't they have their siren and lights going?"

Lydia laid a hand on his shoulder to restrain him. "They only do that when they're in a hurry. For emergencies. This isn't an emergency."

Zeke's shoulders slumped. "It would have

been more fun."

"For you maybe," Lydia said. "What about for Emma? Or the neighbors? The noise might have startled them."

"Aw." Zeke tucked his hands inside his galluses. "Everyone likes loud noises sometimes."

Sarah came up beside him. "I don't." She set a hand on his shoulder. "Maybe I should take the boys inside. They might be a bit too rambunctious."

Lydia smiled at her sister. "Good idea. Once Emma's settled, they can come in for a brief visit."

As Sarah herded her protesting brothers toward the house, the attendants rolled the stretcher across the newly green grass. Emma lay pale and still, tucked under the white sheet and beige blanket, as if sleeping. Lydia motioned for the EMTs to follow her up the ramp and into the *daadi haus.* When she opened the front door, a black truck pulled into the driveway beside the ambulance.

Caleb? What was he doing here? He got out of the truck, and Lydia's heart, which had been thrumming, beat even faster. It took a few moments before it dawned on her she was still holding the door open, letting in chilly air, although the EMTs had

265

already entered. She closed the glass storm door and waited until he reached the porch to reopen it. "Caleb, what are you doing here?" That didn't sound very welcoming, but fighting his magnetic pull was sapping all her inner strength.

"Your grandmother and I talked at the hospital, and she agreed that I should come today. I'll be over in the evenings and on weekends."

Lydia was confused. "But I never had a chance to ask *Mamm* or —"

Caleb entered the house and filled the hallway with his presence, making Lydia feel closed in and almost claustrophobic. She backed up a bit, but every nerve in her body was aware of his nearness.

He closed the door behind him. "I know." He didn't sound annoyed or upset. "Your grandmother was surprised to find out I'd talked to you about it. But I know you've been busy, so I figured I'd take matters into my own hands." He turned and studied her face. "I get the impression you're upset."

Not exactly. More like fluttery. Overwhelmed. Exhilarated. She had no words to describe the odd sensations quivering through her when she was around him. When she thought she'd seen the last of him the other night, she'd been devastated. But now he was standing in front of her and might be for quite some time.

Lydia froze for a few moments, her gaze on his lips, remembering the almost-kiss, before she realized she'd never denied his statement. "I'm not upset, just surprised." *And conflicted.* Her heart was dancing, but her conscience was issuing dire warnings.

Trying to act calm and casual, she invited him to accompany her, but she had trouble thinking coherently as he followed her down the hallway to the living room, where the hospital bed had been set up in the middle of the room. The couch had been pushed against one wall. The rest of the furniture, with the exception of a few chairs, had been carted upstairs and shoved into the extra bedroom. A few small tables had been placed near the bed to hold paraphernalia.

The EMTs had transferred Emma to the bed and were adjusting the sides and setting up the equipment. A visiting nurse would arrive shortly to help, but between visits Lydia and *Mammi* would have to handle it all. Lydia worried they might forget something important. And with Caleb here, she'd have even more difficulty than usual concentrating.

He laid a gentle hand on her back, and Lydia forced herself not to jump. "It all seems confusing now," he whispered, "but after a few days, everything will become routine. You'll get used to it."

Lydia nodded, grateful for his attempt at comfort, but she doubted caring for Emma would ever become routine when he was around.

Mammi motioned for them to join her. Lydia had been so focused on Emma — and Caleb's touch — that she hadn't noticed her grandmother standing in the corner of the room.

A little of the tenseness in *Mammi*'s face drained away when Caleb joined her. "I've already forgotten what they taught us."

Caleb gave her a reassuring smile. "Don't worry. The EMTs will take care of everything. And the nurse will help you get into a routine. It'll all be written down, and you'll have plenty of assistance."

But the lines on *Mammi*'s forehead deepened, and she pursed her mouth. "They told us that, but now it seems like such a great responsibility we've taken on. I worry we've made a mistake. What if something goes wrong?"

It wasn't like *Mammi* to be so flustered or nervous, but with all the supplies the EMTs were carrying in, Lydia's head was spinning too. Or maybe that was from Caleb's nearness and the thought that he'd be here nearly every day.

Caleb set a hand on *Mammi*'s shoulder. "You have the emergency numbers? Really, nothing should go wrong. Emma's been stable for a while now. She's breathing and even responding at times. All she needs is time to recover. Being here with family, with people who love her, in familiar surroundings should work wonders. You'll see."

Mammi still looked doubtful. "I hope you're right. I've alienated a lot of people by doing this, including my own son." She pressed her lips together and turned away.

Lydia understood *Mammi*'s concerns. Her grandmother had not only had electricity installed, but she'd also refused to give up a cell phone, using a possible emergency as an excuse. *Dat* had retreated into a fury-filled silence. He refused to speak to *Mammi* or even look at her. The tension became unbearable at times as *Dat* went out of his way to avoid *Mammi.* Some of the people in the church sided with *Dat* and were upset with the bishop's decision as well. Lydia's and *Mammi*'s only hope was that Emma would recover and this dissension would be forgotten.

Caleb had gone over to help one of the EMTs and continued to talk to him as he set up equipment. His eagerness to learn all he could showed in the way he shadowed the EMTs, asking questions and suggesting ideas. He stayed until all the paraphernalia was in place and the visiting nurse arrived. After she left, he slowly, patiently went over everything again to be sure they understood it.

When *Mamm* called them for dinner, Caleb motioned for them to go ahead. "I'll stay here with Emma until you return. As it's her first day home, she may appreciate some company."

Mammi nodded. "Yes, I don't want to leave her alone. Lydia, please ask your *mamm* to send us both some dinner."

Caleb waved a hand. "No need to bring me anything. I'll eat when I get home. I didn't mean to intrude on your dinner hour."

But *Mammi* ignored his protests and insisted that Lydia return with an extra plate of food for Caleb as thanks for all the help he'd given them. Lydia scurried to the kitchen, loaded two plates, and rushed back to deliver the meals. Returning to the kitchen, she slid into place on the bench just as *Dat* lumbered in, his steps heavy, his brow glowering.

Mamm hovered over him, serving him, but

he brushed her away. "I'm not hungry. But I will sit here for the prayer."

Though they all bowed their heads, the tension in the room made everyone edgy. When they lifted their heads, *Mamm* dished food onto *Dat*'s plate. But he only sat there stoic, unmoving, staring at the wall just above her head after she took her place. His jaw muscles worked, moving back and forth as everyone around him sat stiff and uncertain.

Sarah cast a nervous glance at Lydia. Abe looked puzzled but leaned over his plate and shoveled food into his mouth. He glanced up twice. Then seeing that no one reprimanded him, he resumed scarfing down his meal.

Dat rose, scraping the chair across the floor in a quick, violent movement, and through clenched teeth, said, "If you'll excuse me?" His tone wavered between angry and apologetic.

"Of course," *Mamm* whispered in a choked voice.

Dat, shoulders hunched as if in pain, rushed from the room. A few seconds later the bedroom door slammed.

Sarah pushed her plate away. *Mamm* picked at her food. The sickish feeling in Lydia's stomach increased. She set down her fork. *Dat* couldn't stay angry forever, could he?

Distressed over *Dat*'s anger, all she wanted do was escape to the *daadi haus,* but there she'd face a different struggle. Would she ever feel at home or at peace anywhere again?

CHAPTER TWENTY-ONE

The next week was busy for Lydia and *Mammi* as they adjusted to caring for Emma and monitoring the equipment. Caleb came to relieve them every afternoon so they could have dinner with the family, although *Mammi* usually preferred to eat with Emma. And Caleb often stayed into the evening. He even showed up on the weekend. Waving away Lydia's protests, he explained that with Kyle working evenings and weekends, he preferred being around people rather than at home alone.

Mammi liked his company, and Lydia tried not to admit how her heart skipped whenever he arrived. The more time she spent with him, the more she found herself attracted to him. She enjoyed his conversation and appreciated his efforts to include Emma in every discussion. Although if she were honest, those were not the only things drawing her to him. Every time he arrived, her whole day became brighter. She had to guard against staring at him longingly across the room.

Often she forced herself to chant *Jakob, Jakob, Jakob,* under her breath to remind herself of her intended, but repeating his name only increased her guilt. Jakob hadn't been able to visit much because of working long hours in the fields and helping in his father's business. Bishop Zook had a stroke a few days after Emma came home, an occurrence *Dat* saw as God's punishment for the bishop going against the *Ordnung.* Though her heart was burdened for both Jakob and his father, Lydia was also relieved. She needed to get her wayward feelings under control before she faced Jakob.

Mammi must have noticed her preoccupation because one morning she handed Lydia a tattered copy of *In Meiner Jugend.* "Perhaps you should study this. Maybe you could read parts of it aloud to Emma, so she'll be prepared for her baptism when the time comes."

Lydia's heartfelt "thank you" was for more than the book, which contained the *Dordrecht Confession,* along with prayers, hymns, baptism and marriage formularies, and other readings. Perhaps this would keep her mind off Caleb. She suspected that had been *Mammi*'s intention.

When Sarah stopped by to bring them lunch, she looked wistfully at the book in Lydia's hands. "I wish I were old enough to join the church and study that too."

"No reason why you can't learn along with Lydia," *Mammi* said. "Why don't you come back when you've finished your afternoon chores?"

"That would be *wunderbar.*" Joy suffused Sarah's face.

Mammi leaned over Emma. "You see how your sister reacts to learning about the faith? I hope you have the same enthusiasm."

Whenever Sarah had time, she stopped by to study the readings in High German. She had a natural gift for it and often surpassed Lydia in her understanding of passages. But as much as she enjoyed learning, Sarah was always eager to flee from the medical equipment, visiting nurse, and feedings.

"How do you stand it?" she whispered to Lydia late one afternoon after the nurse took care of Emma's feeding and catheter. "I can't bear to look, but *Mammi* says you often do that."

Lydia shrugged. "It's not that hard. We do what we have to do."

"I suppose." Sarah squinched up her face. "I could never do it. It's all I can do not to get sick."

"We all have our gifts. Yours is being sensitive to people's feelings. Perhaps that's why this is so upsetting."

Before Sarah could answer, a knock on the door announced Caleb's arrival. Sarah greeted him and then scurried away.

Caleb watched her leave. "I hope I'm not the cause for her hasty retreats."

Lydia shook her head. "Of course not. Sarah has a fear of hospitals, blood, and illness."

Caleb followed Lydia into the room, where they found *Mammi* waiting. He greeted her and then strode over to the bed to talk to Emma. His hair flopped onto his forehead as he bent to take Emma's hand. When he flicked his head to get his bangs out of the way, *Mammi* sucked in a sudden breath.

Lydia turned to her alarmed, but *Mammi* was staring at Caleb.

"Do that again," she commanded. "Brush your bangs forward. Then lift your chin like you did and tilt your head back." *Mammi* demonstrated, and when Caleb obeyed, she ordered him to stay that way for a minute.

Again Caleb did as she asked.

"It's coming back to me. Your profile reminds me of . . ." *Mammi* made a humming noise under her breath. "Yes, yes. I think it is. Eli Miller."

Caleb turned startled eyes to her.

"Now let me see . . ." *Mammi* wrinkled her brow and pursed her lips. "Eli and Martha. Their son married the Yoder girl. What was her name again? Pretty girl. Dark hair and blue eyes. Rather like yours," she said to Caleb.

She frowned at the ceiling for a few minutes. Then a triumphant smile lit her face. "Daniel. Yes, Daniel Miller. He married Hannah Yoder."

Caleb gasped. "Those were my parents' names."

"I knew it would come to me," *Mammi* said, satisfaction in her tone. "You look so like Eli when he was your age. But the dark hair is what mixed me up. Eli was blond." She studied Caleb's face. "So you're Daniel and Hannah's little one."

"But, but . . . how did you know who my parents are? And who is Eli?"

"Eli would be your grandfather."

Caleb shook his head. "No, my parents were orphans. When I did a family tree in third grade, they didn't even know their parents' names."

"They said that?" *Mammi*'s question was gentle.

"I don't remember what they said. All I remember is being the only kid in the class with a blank chart. And they always claimed they had no family."

Mammi's eyes held deep sadness. "I suppose they didn't. With the *meidung.*"

Caleb's eyes held a question, and Lydia hastened to explain that *meidung* meant *shunning.*

Caleb held up a hand. "This is going too fast for me. I understood the word *meidung,* but I'm totally confused. Who was shunned?"

Mammi motioned to the chair beside Emma's bed. "Perhaps you'd better sit. It's a long story."

Caleb sank into the chair, his eyes dazed. Lydia, feeling as confused as he looked, scooted her chair closer to the foot of the bed.

Mammi gazed off into the distance. "I knew your grandparents well. But I was living here by then, raising a family of my own. Elizabeth — your grandmother — and I wrote letters for years. Until she died a few years back."

"But how do you know she was my grandmother? It could be another Daniel and Hannah."

"I suppose," *Mammi* said. "Why don't I

tell you the story, and we can see if there are any similarities?" At Caleb's nod, she continued. "I'll try to remember what Elizabeth wrote. Daniel and Hannah were teenagers. Daniel was born a few years after Reuben, Lydia and Emma's *dat*." *Mammi* nodded toward Lydia.

Emma kicked at her covers, startling them.

"*Dat*'s name seems to bother her," Lydia mouthed.

They all watched Emma for a few moments, but when she remained still, *Mammi* resumed her story.

"I don't remember why, but Hannah's parents forbid her to associate with Daniel. She disobeyed. But what they didn't know was that she was already in the family way. When her father found out, he was furious. He disowned her. Hannah and Daniel ran off together. They got married at a justice of the peace in Ephrata."

Caleb sucked in a breath. "My parents were married in Ephrata." He hesitated. "After they died, I discovered I was born five months after they married."

Lydia tried to make sense of everything. "But why didn't they get married in the church?"

"Elizabeth always wondered that." *Mammi*'s words held a weight of sorrow.

279

"Both Hannah and Daniel had already joined the church, so they could have. When they came back to visit after the baby was born, Hannah's father refused to open the door. He wouldn't let her mother or any of the rest of the family speak to Hannah or Daniel. He insisted that the family shun them. And not only shun them, but break off all relationships with them and their child."

Mammi's voice broke. "Elizabeth always wished they'd come to her and Eli first. Perhaps they planned to repent."

"How could a family turn their backs on one of their own?" Caleb frowned. "I don't understand a faith that would do such a thing."

"Not everyone is that harsh," *Mammi* said, "and shunning isn't intended to break up the family. It's intended to bring the wayward ones back into the fold."

"It didn't work with my parents. They lived their lives lonely and bitter. I was denied my extended family. I never knew my heritage." Caleb clenched his fists and his jaw worked. "It destroys people. And families."

"Not everyone carries it to that extreme. We don't refuse to talk to them or . . ." Lydia's voice trailed off as thoughts of *Dat*'s

280

unbending judgment came to mind.

Caleb stared off into the distance. "I wish I'd learned this while my parents were alive. Do you think I could have convinced them to reconcile? And if they had, would I have grown up Amish?" he asked in a wondering voice.

Mammi leaned toward him. "Elizabeth believed so. She tried to contact them. But her letters went unanswered. She was heartbroken to learn that the bishop had gone to see them, and they refused to have anything to do with the community or the church."

Caleb lowered his head and pressed his fingers to his forehead. "So that's why they wouldn't go to church. Yet they insisted on daily devotions. Dad read from *Our Heritage, Hope, and Faith* every morning. And we prayed the Lord's Prayer at every meal."

"So your parents raised you as they had been raised?" *Mammi* smiled.

Caleb looked from one to the other. "What do you mean?"

Lydia spoke up. "We read from that too. And say the Lord's Prayer silently before meals."

"You do?" At her nod, he pressed a knuckle against his lip, a thoughtful expression on his face. Then his eyes filled with sadness. "I used to criticize my parents because they never voted, refused to have a radio or TV, and wouldn't let us get school pictures taken."

Mammi had tears in her eyes. "Elizabeth would have been happy to know all that."

"And we always spoke German at home. It wasn't uncommon for my friends' grand-parents to speak Pennsylvania Dutch. My parents were much younger, but I never questioned it, never asked them why."

Mammi stared at Caleb. "Elizabeth so wanted to meet you."

"But what if this is coincidence? Yoder and Miller are common names."

"No one could be such an exact replica of Eli and not be related. If it hadn't been nigh on fifty years since I'd seen him, it would have come to me sooner." *Mammi* pursed her lips. "I don't know if Eli is still alive, but some of your aunts and uncles should remember the story."

Caleb had tears in his eyes. "I thought Kyle and I were alone in the world. Do you think they'd speak to me?"

Mammi shrugged. "There's no telling how they might react. It's entirely possible that the children who are your age — your cousins — have never heard of you."

Caleb sat, staring as if in shock. "A whole family I never knew about? Relatives, grand-

282

parents?"

Lydia blinked back tears.

After a few moments Caleb spoke again. "It was hard losing my parents and having no one to turn to, but it would be worse to contact relatives and have them reject us."

Mammi looked thoughtful. "Perhaps I could write to them to see if —"

Eagerness blazed in Caleb's eyes. "Would you?"

"It's the least I can do after all you've done for us." *Mammi*'s look held a warning. "But best not get your hopes up."

Two weeks later Caleb rushed through the door of the *daadi haus,* grinning. "Oh, Mrs. Esh, I can't thank you enough. I've met my grandfather and some aunts, uncles, and cousins."

Lydia's heart swelled at the joy on Caleb's face. There was no doubt the meeting had gone well.

Mammi smiled. "I hope you extended my greetings."

"I certainly did. My grandfather remembered you and appreciated the letter you sent. It's hard to believe I have a family." Caleb swallowed hard. "I've been so alone since my parents died."

Mammi leaned forward. "No one should

have to go through life alone. Family and community are important."

Caleb looked down. "Growing up, I wanted to be like other kids in my classes at school. When they talked about going to see relatives, I was jealous, wishing we had someone, anyone we could visit."

Lydia pictured him as a small boy, and her heart went out to him. She smiled as Caleb launched into a description of meeting his relatives for the first time, how excited and happy they'd been to meet him, an eagerness he attributed to *Mammi*'s introductory letter. They'd already made plans to get together again.

Caleb eyes shone. "After I asked *Daadi* what I could read and study to help me understand the faith better, he recommended this book." He held up the *Dordrecht Confession.* "I started reading it, and do you know what? My father sometimes read us this too for devotions before school. I see now how much of their Amish heritage they kept. Many of the values they insisted on — pacifism, for example — came from their background." When Caleb stopped for breath, his eyes were shining. He shook his head. "*Daadi* got tears in his eyes when I opened the book and started to read the first paragraph. Then I looked up and recited the rest."

Lydia couldn't stop moisture from forming in her own eyes at his excitement.

Caleb rubbed his fingers over the lettering on the book cover and swallowed hard. "When I was young, I rebelled against their old-fashioned ways." The wistfulness on his face made it clear he regretted that decision. "I was embarrassed to bring school friends home. It was hard to fit in at school, and I didn't fit in at home either."

Mammi pinned him with a look that stopped his reminiscing. "And what are your plans now? Do you plan to join the faith? It's not an easy road, you know."

Caleb looked thoughtful. "In some ways I'm drawn to it. But it would mean giving up too many things. Once Kyle graduates, I want to go back to med school." He shook his head. "If I'd grown up Amish, I might not have these dreams, but . . ."

Lydia pictured Caleb in Plain clothes with the beard of a married man. She couldn't catch her breath.

"Now I understand why Kyle was attracted to Emma," Caleb said. "She must have made him feel comfortable and at home, but she wasn't as stuffy as my parents."

Movement on the bed interrupted him.

Lydia leaned closer. "Emma? Did you hear us talking about you?"

Caleb reached out and took Emma's hand. "Emma, thank you for your part in helping me reconnect with my family. If it hadn't been for you and — and the accident." Anguish filled his eyes, and he drew in a shaky breath. "I'm sorry for the pain it brought you."

Lydia moved to the other side of the bed beside *Mammi,* who was watching Emma intently. Lydia took her sister's hand and spoke around the lump in her throat. "Squeeze my hand if you understand what we've been saying, Emma."

Faint pressure on Lydia's fingers made her throat constrict even more. "She does hear us." Lydia's voice came out choked and unsteady.

Caleb's eyes shone with wetness. "You're healing, Emma. You'll soon be well."

"Of course she will." *Mammi*'s tartness was tempered by a slight quaver.

Lydia's gaze locked with Caleb's. His smile showed how much he cared about her sister. But his look revealed deeper feelings that set Lydia's pulse thrumming.

Mammi's sharp "ahem" startled them both. They broke eye contact as *Mammi* shifted in her chair. "Well, Emma, I suggest you keep paying attention while Caleb tells us the rest of the story." Her tone contained both command and censure.

Caleb sat back and focused his attention on *Mammi.* "I have you to thank as well, Mrs. Esh. It's wonderful to know we have family. I wish my brother would come along next time."

Mammi nodded. "That would be good. Family can often keep wayward *youngie* in line. Isn't that so, Emma?"

Caleb's eyes held a hint of sadness. "If only that were true for my brother. *Daadi* invited us both for dinner." He glanced at Emma and lowered his voice until he was practically mouthing the words. "But Kyle's insisting he wants nothing to do with the Amish. Unfortunately I think his guilt is keeping him prisoner."

Lydia sensed the pain behind Caleb's words. "But no one holds him responsible. Please assure him of our forgiveness."

"He's been told that many times over, but it's himself he won't forgive."

"*Ach,* that's pride speaking," *Mammi* said.

"Perhaps so." Caleb leaned back in the chair and closed his eyes. "I never dreamed I'd ever have any other family. It's wonderful, but also scary."

Lydia was surprised. "Scary?"

Caleb's brow wrinkled. "*Daadi* is old and not in the best of health. I'm afraid of getting too attached. What if I do and he dies? I'm not sure I could go through that pain again."

Mammi studied him with compassion in her eyes. "It's not easy losing loved ones. I've been through it many times. And it never gets easier. But one thing I can tell you is that being lonely every day isn't worth it to prevent the future pain." She leaned forward, her face earnest. "Even worse than losing someone you're close to is wishing that you'd spent more time with them, done more for them, showed them how much you loved them. If you love someone, let them know. Spend time together, show your feelings. Don't walk away and regret it."

Lydia hung her head and stared at her hands. If only she could take *Mammi*'s advice. Of course, *Mammi* had meant it for Caleb and his family — not for her and Caleb.

CHAPTER TWENTY-TWO

As spring warmed into summer, Emma lay still and unresponsive, except for occasionally squeezing their hands to answer questions. Caleb read all the latest research and suggested new techniques, but *Mammi*'s frustration mounted at the slow results. She insisted *Dat*'s forgiveness was the key to Emma's healing. And to his own.

One broiling hot afternoon in early July *Mammi* banged into the *daadi haus* after spending several hours closeted with *Dat,* who had stayed home from work. Her face damp with perspiration, she dabbed at her forehead and blew out a frustrated breath. "This whole situation has made your *dat* ill. If only I could convince him to forgive Emma."

Lydia motioned with her head and eyes toward Emma, who had begun tossing restlessly.

Mammi stopped speaking.

"Did you see how sunny it is outside?" Lydia injected a bright, cheery note into her voice.

Caleb's approving smile turned her heart upside down. "I love seeing the fields filled with corn when I'm driving to work." He leaned toward Emma. "Do you have a favorite summer activity, Emma?"

Emma quieted.

Lydia sent Caleb a look of gratitude. "Emma loves to play baseball. Don't you, Em?"

Caleb returned her smile and then turned toward Emma again. "So Emma, what would you think about playing baseball? Wouldn't that be fun?" He shot a questioning glance at Lydia and mouthed, "Do you have a baseball?"

Lydia nodded and rushed to the house to retrieve a baseball. When she returned, Caleb was describing one of his games. Lydia held up the ball and was rewarded with such a heartfelt smile she almost dropped it.

"Guess what, Em! Lydia brought the baseball, so I'm going to challenge you to a game." He took the ball from Lydia, and their hands brushed.

Sparks tingled down her arms, and she closed her eyes to get her feelings under control. When she opened them again, Caleb was staring at her, his eyes telegraphing a message. A message that had nothing to do with Emma. Or with the baseball he clasped in his hand.

Biting her lip, Lydia lowered her gaze, hoping her eyes hadn't reflected the feelings in her heart. Feelings that were more than gratitude for helping Emma. Feelings that were much more than friendship. Feelings that were now swirling out of control.

The front door snicked open. Sarah walked in, followed by Jakob. "Some of Jakob's cousins have arrived from out of town to help with the work." Sarah's smile glowed more brightly than the sun outside. "So he's taken time off to visit."

Shame pooled in Lydia's stomach as Jakob stared from her to Caleb and back again. She hoped her face didn't reveal her inner turmoil. She'd seen little of Jakob since his father's stroke. He usually tried to catch her attention during their baptismal classes, but with him sitting on the men's bench, and her choosing a seat as far away as possible on the girls' bench and concentrating hard on the lessons, she'd managed to avoid revealing her guilt over her secret attraction to Caleb. Jakob often hurried home immediately after baptismal classes to care for his father, and she was busy caring for

Emma, so they hadn't had much time to talk or be together the last few months.

Caleb blinked as if startled awake from a dream and turned toward Emma. He cleared his throat. "Are you ready to play ball, Emma?" He set the ball in Emma's hand and gently closed her fingers around it.

Lydia struggled to calm her racing heart and say something welcoming to Jakob, but her mind and her mouth refused to form words.

Unaware of the undercurrents flowing around her, Sarah continued her cheery patter. "I bet she'd love to play, wouldn't you, Em?"

Jakob's scowl, which had been directed at Caleb, turned into a puzzled frown as he looked first at Emma, then at everyone else as if they were crazy. "But she's —"

Lydia cut him off. "Sarah will beat you at baseball if you don't get out there and practice, Emma."

"I'm not that go —" Sarah cut her protest short at Lydia's frantic signal. "I'm working hard to be a better catcher. But I could use your help."

"You hear that, Emma?" Caleb's words were serious. "You can't let your younger sister beat you." He released the hand he had cupped around her fingers and exhaled in relief when Emma continued to clutch the ball. "Why don't you throw her a pitch?"

Emma's arm moved slightly upward, but she kept her grip on the ball.

Caleb cheered. "That's it. Wow, look at that pitching arm!"

Jakob looked from one to the other as if they were crazy. When he opened his mouth to object, Lydia held back an impatient sigh and motioned for him to follow her to the door. His eyes lit up, and he trailed her down the hall so closely that she was concerned he'd step on her shoe. After they'd stepped out on the porch, she shut both the door and the screen and turned to Jakob.

His broad smile made it obvious he thought she wanted time alone with him. Before he could launch into a discussion about them or their relationship, Lydia asked about his work, his cousins' visit, and then moved to the real reason she'd invited him outside. "Oh, and I want to explain what we're doing with Emma."

"We're?"

The way Jakob said the word revealed his bitterness, and Lydia's guilt increased. She fixed her gaze on the roses blooming near the door, so Jakob couldn't read the shame in her eyes.

Taking a deep breath, she said, "Caleb's been researching different methods for dealing with coma patients. He says some of the best results occur when the patient is included in conversations. And we've also been using a startle method that he read about."

Jakob's brows drew together. "How often is he here? And why is he researching cures for your sister?"

Lydia bit back her annoyance by reminding herself he had every right to be jealous. More so than he knew. "*Mammi* asked him to help with Emma. Her medical needs are overwhelming at times."

"He's not a doctor."

"No," Lydia answered evenly. "But he has some expertise in Emma's condition."

"Expertise he's quite willing to share with *you.*"

Lydia ignored the dig. "Yes, and *we're* all grateful. Emma has made some improvements already since we've started acting as if she can answer us."

"But Emma's in a coma. How likely is it that she can hear you, let alone answer?"

"Caleb says —"

"Caleb says, Caleb says." Jakob's words were high-pitched and mocking, and then he sobered. "And must you do everything

294

Caleb says even if it seems foolish?"

Lydia tamped down the shame that rose in her at Jakob's accusing tone. "We're grateful that he's committed to Emma's recovery, so, yes, we will try whatever he suggests."

Jakob stared at his boots as he scuffed a toe back and forth on the wooden planks of the ramp. His voice, when it came, was hesitant and tinged with hurt. "It's not Emma he's interested in. I've seen how he looks at you."

Lydia shook her head. If anything, it was the other way around. "I don't think you can blame Caleb . . ."

Jakob lifted his head and looked into Lydia's eyes. "I don't blame him. That is" — his cheeks turned scarlet and he gazed off into the distance — "I understand how he feels. I mean . . ."

Lydia gulped back the rush of emotion that tightened her throat. This was as close as Jakob had ever gotten to expressing his feelings for her. But his words stirred up a whirlwind of confusion. Was Caleb really attracted to her? Or was Jakob's view colored by his own feelings?

All these thoughts swirling around made Lydia dizzy. She had no right to think or feel this way about Caleb. Especially not when she was standing here with Jakob. But she wasn't ready to hear Jakob's declaration.

Lydia reached out but stopped short of touching Jakob's sleeve. She let her hand drop to her side. Being around Caleb had made her much freer with physical touch, but it would shock Jakob.

"Jakob," she said in a rush, "I didn't ask how your father's doing. Is he recovering well?" *Please,* she begged silently, *say anything, anything at all that might change the subject.*

"He's doing as well as can be expected." Jakob's voice dropped so low she could barely hear him. "I'd hoped we could spend some time together."

"Oh, Jakob, I wish I'd known you were coming. I'd have planned differently, but I'm eager to see what will happen with Emma and the baseball." *Is that the only thing you're concentrating on?* Lydia's conscience jabbed her, but she forced her attention back to Jakob. "You're welcome to join us."

Jakob shook his head. "No. I will be going. And I hope you will forgive me."

"There is nothing to forgive."

"*Ach,* there is more to forgive than you know."

Jakob's words could have been an echo from her own heart. Lydia could not meet his gaze. She needed a great deal of forgiveness. From Jakob and from God. So much she was not yet ready to confess. She must at least make a start, though. "I'm sorry that my conduct gives you cause for worry."

"Ah, Lydia, it is not so much your conduct as it is my wayward thoughts."

Lydia did not argue, but she was well aware her own wayward thoughts were causing the greatest trouble.

"I can't help being jealous that you're spending a lot of time with another man, but I trust you, and I don't want this to come between us."

It already had, but Lydia knew her duty to God and to her community. She would do what was expected of her, bury her passion for Caleb, and be a good wife to Jakob. As good a wife as she could be when her heart was elsewhere.

The heat of summer had set in, and they kept fans whirring around Emma's hospital bed. *Mammi* jokingly mentioned air conditioning. At least Lydia hoped she was joking. *Mammi* and *Dat* still hadn't reconciled. And bringing in any more electrically powered appliances would only widen the rift between them. Lydia made sure *Dat* understood the fans were battery-powered. Not that it helped.

Trickles of sweat slid down Lydia's back as she cared for Emma during the day. Although Caleb was used to cool air at work and in his truck, he never complained about the heat. They continued the baseball experiment. Emma could make an abbreviated throwing motion now, but had yet to release the ball.

One evening *Mammi* turned to Caleb and suggested he join the family for the meal. When he refused and insisted on staying with Emma so *Mammi* could eat with her family, she frowned. "You've done enough today. And I would like some time alone with Emma."

Caleb hesitated, but at *Mammi*'s stern look, he held up his hands in mock surrender and added that he could tell when he wasn't wanted. He had a twinkle in his eye when he said it, but *Mammi* trained a serious gaze on him.

Looking him in the eye, she said sternly, "We could never have done this without you. You are always wanted here. Is that not so, Lydia?"

Caleb flushed, but like *Mammi*, he turned toward Lydia.

Mammi's words had startled Lydia out of a reverie, one in which she and Caleb were walking hand in hand through fields of wildflowers. With the two of them staring at her, Lydia felt as if a lantern had been trained on her deepest thoughts. Heat rushed through her body, and strange feelings swirled inside her — a mixture of gratitude, longing, and that odd magnetic pull — forming a lump in her throat that words couldn't push past.

"Lydia?" *Mammi*'s tone was a sharp rebuke.

How rude she must seem after all Caleb's kindnesses. Lydia struggled to speak. If she gushed that he was always welcome, more than welcome, and always wanted, she would give away her true feelings. Instead, her slow and measured words were almost a monotone. "We're grateful for all you've done."

Mammi's eyebrows rose, then she squinted and studied Lydia closely.

Lydia squirmed under her grandmother's scrutiny. She stood abruptly and turned to hide her burning cheeks. Her movements to the door were jerky as she struggled to rein in her wayward feelings and return to some semblance of peace.

"Go with Lydia," *Mammi* commanded. In

spite of Caleb's protests, she was not to be deterred. "It's the least we can do for all your help with Emma. Lydia, you could reassure Caleb that the family would love to have him." *Mammi* spoke as if Lydia were a recalcitrant three-year-old.

Her grandmother's comment increased Lydia's inner turmoil. She wanted to add her plea to *Mammi*'s, but feared she couldn't do it without revealing her deepest feelings. In a desperate attempt to sound normal, Lydia said, "Sarah and the boys will be delighted to have a dinner guest." *And so will you,* her conscience jabbed.

"I don't feel right imposing on your family," Caleb mumbled. "If it weren't for my brother —"

Mammi's sharp voice sliced through the room. "You are not responsible for your brother. And you have been around us long enough to know that he has been forgiven. You bear no guilt in this."

"If I'd done what I should have, this never would have happened."

The pain underlying Caleb's words tore at Lydia's heart. She whirled to face him. "Don't blame yourself. You did what you could. It isn't your fault Kyle ignored your guidance."

Emma moaned and thrashed on the bed.

Everyone turned startled eyes toward her.

Mammi reached out and took Emma's hand. "What is it, Emmie? What's wrong?"

Lydia rushed to the other side of the bed. What had they said to cause her distress? Was it mentioning Kyle's name? When she and Caleb had mentioned his name in the hospital, Emma's heart monitor had increased. The one time Caleb mentioned it here, her sister had also reacted.

Emma's other hand clawed at the sheet. Lydia smoothed her sister's hair back from her forehead. Remembering the psychiatrist's instructions, Lydia hastened to reassure her, "We love you, Emma. Everything's all right now. We forgive you."

Lydia's words only increased Emma's agitation. Emma kicked at the sheets. Her free hand clutched a fistful of bedding.

Then *Mammi*'s low croon, light as a breath of air, floated on the air like a balm. A hymn from the *Ausbund.* Her voice barely above a whisper, Lydia joined in. Slowly Emma relaxed. Her hand unclenched, her legs stilled.

"All the more reason for Emma and me to have our little talk." *Mammi* waved a hand toward the door. "You've left your mother alone with the dinner preparations long enough, Lydia."

Lydia should be helping *Mamm,* but she didn't want to leave Emma. Not now when they'd seen her first full body movements, violent and distressed though they might be. And Lydia was reluctant to leave *Mammi* alone in case Emma became restless.

As if sensing Lydia's concern, *Mammi* looked deep into Lydia's eyes. "I can handle her. Never you worry. I soothed her this time, did I not?"

"Yes, but what if . . ."

"Lydia." *Mammi*'s tone held impatience. "You must learn to trust God's timing. He never gives us more than we can handle."

Lydia pondered her grandmother's words. Over the past months she'd been at the breaking point several times.

"You made it through," *Mammi* said. "Is that not so?"

Could *Mammi* read her mind? But *Mammi* was right. In spite of all the stresses, Lydia had survived. That didn't mean she hadn't endured pain, and guilt, and — *face it, Lydia* — temptation. Lydia nibbled at the inside of her lip. She still wrestled with that. And eating dinner with Caleb?

Lydia pushed aside the thoughts that crowded into her mind. *Mamm* and Sarah needed help with the meal. "We'd better hurry so *Mamm* doesn't have to do all the chores." Lydia headed toward the door.

Caleb followed, but hesitated in the doorway of the room. "You look worried. I can stay with your grandmother."

Strains of another hymn, slow and solemn, filled the air. *Mammi* was right. Lydia did need to trust God. Including with temptation. "*Mammi* will be fine until we return."

Outside gray clouds blanketed the sky. Rain fell in torrents, cascading from the roof edges like waterfalls. Lydia had been so engrossed with Emma's movement, she hadn't noticed the weather until now. She reached for *Mammi*'s black umbrella on the wall peg by the front door. Caleb's hand brushed past her arm to open the door, and she shivered. *Relax, Lydia. He's only being polite.* But logic did little to calm her runaway heart.

Before they left the shelter of the porch, Caleb slid the umbrella open and then edged nearer so they could share it. Lydia inched away so they weren't touching, but Caleb slipped an arm around her shoulders and drew her closer.

He smiled down at her. "It's a small umbrella. I don't want you getting soaked."

Would she ever get used to Caleb's courtly gestures? Did *Englisch* girls react like this to each casual touch?

As they hurried across the slick walkway, a streak of lightning flashed across the sky followed by a boom of thunder. Lydia jumped, and Caleb's arm tightened around her. She stiffened and clenched her jaw, fighting the part of her that longed to snuggle closer to Caleb.

Mammi often said lightning was God's way of getting people's attention. Lydia didn't need the lighting's warning. She already knew she was playing with fire.

She had to stop thinking about Caleb's touch. Had Jakob ever touched her like this, even accidentally? Probably not. He always kept a respectful distance between them. She would recall tingling like this if he had, wouldn't she? During the obligatory hand-holding at weddings, Jakob's sweaty palms had never —

"Lydia?"

Caleb's soft question jolted her back to the present. They'd reached the door, but she stood there frozen, never wanting this moment to end. She wrapped her hand around the doorknob, willing her concentration and focus onto the damp, chilly metal. Then she twisted the knob and yanked open the door, hoping the bustle of the kitchen would banish the quivering inside her.

Mamm had her back to them, slicing the

meat loaf. Sarah stood at the sink draining the potatoes.

"Oh, good, Lydia, you're here." Sarah scooted to one side to make room for Lydia. "Could you mash the potatoes while I strain the peas?"

Mamm brushed a wayward strand of hair from her forehead with the back of her hand. "We could have used your help earlier, Lydia."

"I'm sorry." Lydia picked up the hand masher and thumped it down on the potatoes.

"I thought with that *Englischer* your grandmother insisted on having, you'd have more time to help with chores." *Mamm*'s disgruntled tone made it sound as if Caleb were an imposition.

"Umm, *Mamm,* Caleb is . . ." Lydia shot Caleb an apologetic glance and had to force her gaze away.

"Yes, Caleb. All I hear is Caleb this and Caleb that. You'd think the *Englischer* —"

"Mamm," Lydia pleaded, "Caleb is —"

"I know what he is —"

Caleb's deep voice interrupted. "Is there anything I can do to help?"

Mamm jumped. Grease and juices splattered the counter. She turned to face Caleb, her overheated face going an even

305

deeper shade of scarlet. She wiped her hands on her apron. "My apologies. Will you forgive me?"

Caleb inclined his head in her direction. "Of course. I know it's not easy having a stranger and an *Englischer* in the house, especially one who is responsible for your daughter's accident."

"You are not —" Lydia burst out.

But *Mamm* hushed her with a wave of her hand. "We do not hold you responsible. What happened was God's will." Her voice broke slightly, but she continued. "We trust that He has a purpose in this, although we may not yet know what that is. And please assure your brother that we hold no grievances."

Caleb stared at the floor. When he spoke, his voice was husky. "I still don't understand it, but I appreciate the generous and forgiving spirit of your family and community."

"It's what God would have us do," Sarah said softly.

"Yes, well." *Mamm* turned back to the meat loaf. "We'd better get this dinner on the table before it's ice cold."

"I really would be happy to help." Caleb moved toward the counter where Lydia had poured milk into the potatoes and was rapidly mashing them. "I've always mashed potatoes with an electric beater, but I have strong arm muscles. I'm sure I could manage this."

"No, no, you're a guest." *Mamm* brushed past him carrying the meat loaf platter. "Have a seat at the table."

Sarah glanced at him, then her gaze skittered away. "You cook?"

"I've taken care of my brother since our parents died, so cooking was one of the many things I had to learn."

"*Ach,* I'm so sorry. I didn't mean to stir up sad memories."

"You couldn't have known."

"I hope it was not recent." Sarah stood, holding the serving bowl of peas, her eyes sympathetic.

Caleb pursed his lips together for a moment before he spoke. "It's been two years, but I'm not sure it's something you ever get over."

"I imagine not." Sarah set the dish on the table. "I know how awful we all felt when Emma —" She clapped a hand to her mouth, and her cheeks pinkened. "*Ach,* I did not mean to distress you yet again. I meant only to comfort."

"I understand. No worries."

Sarah turned a puzzled gaze toward him. Lydia smiled. "He means do not fret about it." She hadn't realized that spending all this time around *Englischers* had led to being a translator.

Caleb reached for the heavy pot, his hands brushing Lydia's in the process. She jerked back and would have dropped the pot if Caleb hadn't gotten a firm grip on it.

While they were filling the serving bowl, *Dat* stomped his feet on the mat outside the back door. Abe and Zeke pushed past him and tumbled into the kitchen like playful puppies. Spying Caleb placing the dish of mashed potatoes on the table, they stopped and stared. Although Caleb had been helping with Emma for almost three months now and had met the boys on numerous occasions, he had never before joined them for dinner.

"Mind your manners," *Mamm* warned. "And go wash up for dinner."

When the boys returned, they greeted Caleb, but *Dat*'s stiffness put a damper on their usual chatter. Conversation was strained and awkward, and requests were confined to passing items until Caleb broke the silence.

"Mr. Esh, sir?" Caleb cleared his throat. "I'm Caleb Miller. I'm sorry we haven't had a chance to talk before now."

Lydia's cheeks heated. *Dat* had steadfastly

avoided visiting Emma, and because of that he'd never officially been introduced to Caleb either. "I'm sorry. I should have introduced you." She'd been so busy staring at him that she'd forgotten her manners.

Caleb waved a hand. "No worries." He turned his attention back to *Dat.* "Although no apology can make it right, I want you to know how sorry I am about Emma —"

At the sound of her name, *Dat*'s hand froze partway to his mouth, and his lips twisted.

"My brother was responsible for that accident."

Dat's fork clattered to his plate, splattering gravy, and he squeezed his eyes shut.

Caleb's Adam's apple bobbed up and down. "I don't blame you for being angry, sir."

"*Dat*'s not angry." Sarah's sympathetic glance moved from one to the other. Then she said hesitantly, "Are you, *Dat*?"

Mamm laid a restraining hand on Sarah's arm. "Hush."

Dat scraped back his chair. "I'm not feeling well. Please excuse me." He rose and hurried toward the doorway.

"But *Dat* . . ." Sarah's gentle words stopped him. "You haven't told Caleb you forgive him and Kyle."

His back rigid, *Dat* stood in the doorway, and without turning, he said in a monotone voice, "God commands us to forgive so we, in turn, will be forgiven." His voice broke. "Tell your brother he is forgiven." He rushed from the room.

Caleb pushed back his own chair. "I should go. I don't feel right eating here when . . ." He gestured in the direction of the *daadi haus.*

Sarah's eyes brimmed with tears. "*Ach,* no. It's not you *Dat*'s upset about. He's been, um" — she stumbled to a stop, then finished in a rush — "not himself lately." She glanced around the table as if for confirmation.

Lydia nodded. "It's true."

"He's been *grexy,* for sure," Abe said then hung his head when *Mamm* frowned at him.

"I can't say I blame him. It's hard not to feel helpless when someone you love is suffering." Caleb swallowed hard.

"*Ach,* we've done nothing but bring you sorrow tonight." Sarah held out an imploring hand. "Please forgive us."

"There's nothing to forgive." Caleb set his napkin beside his plate. "I should get back to help with Emma."

"At least have a piece of pie first."

Lydia stood. "Maybe we could take some

with us. Emma was restless when we left. And *Mammi* hasn't eaten yet."

Sarah jumped up from the table and scurried to pack the food for them. As she handed Caleb the basket, she said, "I hope your brother has recovered well and doesn't blame himself for the accident."

Sadness filled Caleb's eyes. "I think he's still struggling with guilt."

"Please assure him of our forgiveness." Sarah eyes mirrored his pain. "And we'll be praying that God will work in his heart."

"Thank you. My family's also praying."

"That's wonderful *gut.* God can work miracles."

Lydia needed one of those miracles to calm her wildly beating heart. If only she could be like Sarah, concerned only that God's forgiving love would prevail in the hearts of Kyle, Caleb, and *Dat.* But she felt far removed from that kind of spiritual strength and certainty.

Although the rain had slowed to a drizzle, she took an extra umbrella from the wall peg and handed it to Caleb. Best to avoid temptation. Kyle wasn't the only one struggling with guilt.

CHAPTER TWENTY-THREE

The next morning Zeke raced into the house holding the stack of mail. He skidded to a stop by the kitchen table and gazed hungrily at the stack of pancakes on the serving platter. Keeping one eye on the pancakes, he set a small pink envelope beside *Mammi*'s place and deposited the rest of the mail and the newspaper by *Dat*'s plate. Then he slid into his place at the table and *rutsched* in his seat.

Everyone sat waiting for *Dat.* Abe and Zeke both sat, their forks ready, glancing between the door and the steam rising from the plate in the center of the table. *Dat* was never late for meals. If he took much longer, breakfast would be cold.

While they waited, *Mammi* slit open the envelope and pulled out a small flowered card. As she read, a small *oh* escaped from her lips. They all turned toward her expectantly, but then *Dat* entered the kitchen and lowered himself into his chair at the head of the table. All heads bowed for silent prayer.

The minute the prayer was over, *Mamm* began serving the meal. Zeke licked his lips as she piled pancakes on each plate. The minute Zeke had his, he drowned them in syrup and stabbed his fork into the stack in front of him.

Mamm's lips quirked, but her smile seemed to be contained between tight lips. "Wait until everyone is served." Her words sounded rote rather than animated.

Dat shifted in his chair. He looked haggard. Deep lines slashed from nose to mouth. Bags under his eyes revealed a sleepless night. Last night he had paced the downstairs rooms for hours. Lydia had awakened in the middle of the night to his measured footsteps, moving back and forth in rapid rhythm.

But this morning, rather than looking angry, *Dat* appeared haggard, depressed, and — Lydia couldn't quite identify it — worried? No. Fearful? Not exactly. Defeated? A bit. Uncertain? Maybe. His bluster and temper of the past several months had drained from him, leaving him smaller, deflated.

Sarah turned to *Mammi*. "Can you tell us who the card is from? Or is it private?"

Mammi smiled. "It's only a note from the ladies who work with me on the charity auction telling me how much they've been missing me. They wish I could come to the quilting bee today and bring you girls. But they know I need to take care of Emma."

Lydia hated to see *Mammi* miss a chance to visit with her friends. "It's been ages since you've done anything outside the house, *Mammi*. Why don't the three of you go? I can look after Emma."

"No need." *Dat* stood and brushed some nonexistent crumbs from the table into his callused hand. "I will sit with her until you all return."

Every sound in the kitchen stilled.

Even Zeke, who had been gobbling his food, froze with his fork in midair. *Mamm*, bent over the sink, rinsing dishes, stiffened, but didn't turn. Lydia's mouth flopped open and closed, but no words came.

Dat moved stiffly to the trash can. He lifted the lid and scraped the crumbs from his hands into the bin with care, his back to them. He harrumphed, then said, "I'll give you money to pay Andy. What time will you be leaving?" His words sounded casual, almost too casual. As if he had practiced making them come out smoothly. This was the first time he had spoken directly to

314

Mammi since the night of the bishop's visit.

"We should leave in an hour," *Mammi* answered in an even tone. "That should give us enough time to get there." Although her face registered the same astonishment as everyone else's, her words sounded as casual and matter-of-fact as *Dat*'s had.

"I'll be over in half an hour then, so you can show me what to do." *Dat* strode out of the kitchen.

Abe opened his mouth to speak, but Lydia hushed him with a warning glance and a shake of her head. His shoulders slumped, but he nodded. Then he returned to his third helping.

Sarah and Lydia glanced at *Mamm*'s rigid back and exchanged puzzled looks. *Mamm*'s unusual silence indicated something was wrong. And what had prompted *Dat* to offer to sit with Emma? Had it been Caleb's apology last night?

Lydia started to clear the table, but Sarah shooed her away. "Why don't you and *Mammi* get Emma ready? I'll help *Mamm* with the dishes."

Lydia put the syrup and sugar in the pantry and then hurried to the *daadi haus*. She was still in shock, but *Mammi* seemed unperturbed.

"I'm glad he's finally come to his senses."

Mammi said as she opened the door. "Perhaps you should get your sister ready, so your father doesn't have to do it. I'll call Andy to see if he's available. And it'll take me a while to get dressed."

"Of course." Lydia prepared Emma's feeding, but her mind raced. *Dat*'s switch from grumpiness to agreeing to care for Emma was so unexpected, she was still trying to process it, when *Mammi* came downstairs ready to go.

Just then the door banged open, and *Dat* entered.

"It's about time, Reuben." *Mammi*'s words sounded like a tongue lashing. It was evident she wasn't referring to his present arrival time but was chiding him for not visiting his daughter sooner.

Dat did not reply, only gazed at his boots. His bowed head gave the appearance of humility, but the set of shoulders spoke of determination and his jutting chin of stubbornness. He didn't even look in Emma's direction, only said gruffly, "Show me what I need to do."

Mammi ordered Lydia to go get ready, and she bustled around showing *Dat* the equipment. By the time Lydia returned, *Dat* was sitting in the chair near Emma's bed, looking everywhere except at the still form lying in the bed.

A frown creased *Mammi*'s brow. "Are you sure you'll be all right, Reuben?"

"I'll be fine." The hoarseness of *Dat*'s voice did not sound convincing.

A horn honked outside. *Mammi* hesitated a moment, then motioned for Lydia to precede her. "I'll be praying for both of you."

Lydia too murmured a quick prayer for *Dat* and for Emma. As they walked to the car, she ran over a mental checklist for Emma's care, hoping *Mammi* hadn't forgotten to tell *Dat* anything important. Lydia had laid everything out on the table, but she hadn't been there to hear *Mammi*'s explanations. When they got to the car, she assisted *Mammi* into the front seat. But when she opened the back passenger door where *Mamm* and Sarah were already sitting, her mother was a bundle of tension.

Worry lines creased her face. "I'm nervous about leaving Reuben alone with Emma. I know how confusing all the feeding and equipment is. What if something goes wrong while we're gone?"

Mammi sighed. "You're right. I remember how hard it was the first few days, trying to remember the routine. I'll go in and keep an eye on him."

Lydia shook her head. "No, you're going. I can stay here and help *Dat*. All of you do a better job at quilting than I do."

The relief on *Mamm*'s face made Lydia glad she had volunteered. To stop Sarah or *Mammi* from protesting, she said, "I don't mind staying if you'll bring me back one of those delicious strawberry tarts your friend Martha makes, along with a piece of shoo-fly pie."

Sarah promised to fill a napkin with goodies, and Lydia waved until the car was out of sight. She was so glad *Mammi* was finally having an outing. Her grandmother had given up all her social life to care for Emma. Lydia too had spent more time at the *daadi haus* than anywhere else. Of course Emma needed care, but if she was honest, spending time with Caleb was an even greater incentive.

Her mind on Caleb, she drifted toward the door. She turned the knob slowly, a bit worried whether *Dat* would welcome her company. Perhaps she should just let him know she'd stayed home and she'd be in the house if he needed her. She eased open the door to hear the low murmur of *Dat*'s voice.

"I don't hold with all this foolishness of talking to people who don't respond." *Dat*

318

sounded stern. "If you really can hear the way the doctor said, why don't you answer? Why don't you wake up?"

Lydia paused in the entryway. Should she let *Dat* know she was here? Or should she slip out quietly? One hand on the doorknob, Lydia halted. If *Dat* heard the snick of the door, it might interrupt his conversation with Emma.

"I needed this time alone with you today. I can't go on carrying this burden of guilt. The rest of the family has paid. I can't say a civil word to anyone."

Lydia shouldn't be standing here eavesdropping, but she couldn't leave without alerting *Dat* to her presence.

"Oh, Emmie, what have I done? I'm a foolish, prideful old man who will regret his actions the rest of his life. You shamed our family. But I did something much, much worse."

Dat's chair creaked. When his voice came again, it was heavy with tears. "The doctors said we should assure you we forgive you. But I'm the one who needs forgiveness. If you can hear me, will you forgive me?" He gulped in a breath.

Dat's quiet sobs tore at Lydia's heart. She shouldn't be listening to this private conversation. What *Dat* was saying was for her sister's ears alone.

Curiosity warred with guilt, but Lydia plugged her ears with her fingertips. She had no idea how long she stood there, focusing on mentally singing hymns from the *Ausbund* to drown out the buzz of Dad's words. When she uncovered her ears, she heard nothing but silence.

Then *Dat* began to weep.

His sobs were so loud and heart-wrenching Lydia longed to rush into the room to comfort him. But instead she turned the doorknob as quietly as she could and let herself out of the *daadi haus*. She eased the door shut and fled to the kitchen.

Hearing *Dat* cry tore at Lydia's heart, but what worried her even more was that he was burdened with so much.

Lydia hurried upstairs and threw herself into her chores. But her thoughts swished around faster than the dust mop. Why had she covered her ears instead of listening? *You did the right thing, the honorable thing,* her conscience assured her. But being upright meant living with all these questions about what *Dat* needed to confess. Was he feeling guilty for forbidding *Mamm* from visiting Emma in the hospital and avoiding her himself, or for expecting — maybe even hoping — she would die when they pulled the plug, or for threatening to turn her over as a ward of the state and refusing to allow electricity? She too understood the pain of needing forgiveness from someone who couldn't respond.

By lunchtime Lydia had worked herself into a state of nerves. She had to let *Dat* know she was here in case Emma needed something, but she couldn't break into their private time together. She fixed ham and cheese sandwiches for *Dat* and her brothers. Then she placed two of the sandwiches on a tray with chips, homemade applesauce, broccoli slaw, and a glass of milk. Zeke and Abe had been playing football in the backyard, grateful to be free from their usual chores. She called them in for lunch before she took the tray to *Dat.*

When she reached the *daadi haus,* she banged the front door open. *"Dat,"* she called out, "I brought you some lunch, and I can help with Emma if you need me to." She hoped she'd given *Dat* sufficient warning.

The chair in the other room creaked. *Dat* peered around the door jamb, and his face relaxed momentarily at the sight of her and the tray. Then he stepped into the hallway and frowned. "You made more noise than a two-year-old. If the doctors are right and

321

your sister can hear, did you not think about how you might have startled her?" He placed a hand over his heart. "And me."

"I'm sorry, *Dat.*" Lydia tried to sound contrite, but she couldn't keep the relief from her voice.

Her father took the tray from her. "I could use a break, and I have some work I need to do at the shop if you can stay with your sister. But why didn't you go with the others?"

"We were afraid we might have forgotten to tell you something important. And I knew *Mamm* was worried about leaving the household chores undone. I did them so she can relax when she gets home." Although it was all true, Lydia couldn't help but feel guilty for not telling the whole truth.

"That was thoughtful of you." *Dat*'s words were kinder than they had been in a long time. Perhaps his time with Emma had helped heal some of the hurt within, but he still avoided looking directly at her. "If you don't mind staying with her, I'll take my lunch with me to the shop." *Dat* sounded eager to escape. "The boys can go with me to help."

Lydia settled into the chair *Dat* had vacated. Her brothers wouldn't be thrilled to be taken from their football game to *Dat*'s shop to sweep up wood shavings and saw-dust, but Lydia only smiled at *Dat.*

He didn't smile in return, but he held up his tray. "Thank you for that — and for this."

Tears pricked at Lydia's eyes, and she blinked rapidly to control them. For the first time since Emma's accident, she and *Dat* had engaged in a normal conversation, one without anger and biting comments. After the door shut behind *Dat,* Lydia relaxed back into the chair. She was happy to see *Dat* more at peace with himself, but she wished she knew what he had said to Emma.

For most of the afternoon Lydia talked to Emma, but her thoughts kept straying to Caleb. He'd picked up a Saturday shift for a coworker who was attending a wedding. Lydia couldn't help hoping he'd stop by after work, but after a six-day work week, most likely he'd be too exhausted. Knowing that everyone was gone and she had the house to herself, with only Emma for com-pany, Lydia let her imagination drift into daydreams about Caleb, an indulgence she rarely allowed herself. Usually she kept a tight rein on her thoughts and forced them back to the present and to reality, ever mindful of her future and her duty to Jakob and the church.

The day passed quickly, and *Dat* arrived back at the *daadi haus* about ten minutes before Andy's car pulled into the drive. *Mammi* rushed through the door and skewered *Dat* with her gaze. "I hope you made peace with your daughter, Reuben. What did you say to her?"

A crimson flush spread up *Dat*'s cheeks. "What I said to her is between me and God."

"Did you tell her you forgive her?" *Mammi* barked the question.

Dat lowered his head. "Not in those words."

"Why are you being so stiff-necked about this? Surely you would not put your pride before your daughter's well-being?"

"You think not?" The bitterness in *Dat*'s words deepened *Mammi*'s frown. *Dat* spun on his heel and left *Mammi* with her mouth open.

Mammi's face caved inward. "I do not understand what is going on with Reuben. He hasn't been himself since Emma's accident."

Lydia wasn't sure if *Mammi* was talking to herself or if she expected an answer, so Lydia kept quiet.

Emma rolled from side to side.

Lydia leaned toward the bed. "Is everything all right, Em?" She wondered if *Dat*'s sharp words had made Emma restless. Lydia repeated the words the psychiatrist had suggested. "We love you and forgive you. *Dat* forgives you too, even if he hasn't said so."

Her words only increased Emma's thrashing. Was that a good thing? Or should they try to calm her down? Lydia wished Caleb were here so she could ask him. Maybe she should change the subject.

Emma moaned.

Lydia met *Mammi*'s startled glance. They both leaned close to the bed. Lydia reached for her sister's hand, but Emma jerked away. Emma moaned a few more times, then lay quiet.

Lydia rested a hand on her sister's forehead. "Emma?"

No response.

The light disappeared from *Mammi*'s eyes, and she slumped into the chair.

Her grandmother might be discouraged, but Lydia held out hope. Perhaps *Dat*'s talk with Emma would bring results.

A short while later *Mammi* admitted that the outing had tired her out more than expected. She went upstairs to take a nap before dinner. Lydia, her heart still filled with gratitude at the change in *Dat* and

Emma's responses, looked up to see Caleb standing in the doorway, and her heart expanded even more. His eyes lit up when he saw her, and Lydia had trouble remembering why she'd been waiting for him and what she'd wanted to tell him. She stammered out her concerns about Emma's reaction following *Dat*'s second visit, but Caleb's smile grew even broader.

"Her restlessness and movement sound like a great sign." Caleb opened his arms in an expansive gesture that reminded Lydia of being enclosed in them, and she longed to walk into his embrace.

Caleb glanced around and, seeing that they were alone, said, "I'd love to whirl you around in a happy dance right now."

His smile lit a flame in Lydia's heart, but she shook her head.

He sighed. "Yeah, I guess that wouldn't be appropriate."

Inside Lydia was already dancing. Being in his arms would be *verboten,* but that didn't stop her from wishing he'd try.

That night at dinner Lydia was savoring her last bite of shoofly pie, courtesy of the quilting bee, when *Dat* cleared his throat. They all looked up.

"I need to say something." *Dat*'s voice

sounded strained as if his throat had closed too tightly around the words to let them out. "I owe you all an apology. I have been snapping at all of you. I have asked God's forgiveness, and now I ask it of you."

Murmurs of assent flowed around the table.

"I will try to do better in the future." *Dat*'s voice was gruff. Or was it thick with tears? He kept his gaze on his hands and pushed back from the table. "Come, boys. There's still work to be done tonight."

Lydia stared after *Dat* as he led Zeke and Abe out to the barn. *Dat* wasn't quite back to his old self, but he was much closer than he had been. Perhaps the talk with Emma had done him good.

Later that evening after the dishes were done and her parents were in bed, Lydia returned to the *daadi haus* to prepare Emma for bed.

"Mmm . . ."

Lydia looked around. *Mammi*'s eyes were closed, and her breathing had turned to light snores.

But the low humming sound came again. Barely more than a whisper. Lighter than a breath.

Emma? Lydia leaned closer to the bed. A spark of electricity shot through her. She

327

placed her head near Emma's mouth.

"Mmma . . ."

It was Emma. Tears of joy flooded Lydia's eyes.

She reached out and held Emma's hand. "It's me, Lydia."

Emma jerked back.

Lydia's heart sank. Of course. Emma wouldn't want to speak to her. They hadn't been on the best of terms before the accident.

"Do you want me to get *Mamm*? Or *Mammi*'s here too."

The mumbled *mmm* came again.

Lydia squeezed Emma's hand. "I'll go get *Mamm*. I'll be right back."

First Lydia tiptoed over to *Mammi* and shook her shoulder gently.

Mammi opened her eyes, but looked dazed. "What?"

"I think Emma woke. She seems to be saying '*Mamm*' or '*Mammi*.' I'm going to get *Mamm*, but I thought you'd want to see if she'll say anything more."

Mammi rose and tottered over to the bed. She leaned over and took Emma's hand in her wrinkled one.

Lydia patted *Mammi*'s shoulder. "I'll go get *Mamm*."

Once again Emma flinched at the sound

of Lydia's voice. Lydia's heartache grew. Emma must not remember their reconciliation.

Lydia ran into the house and knocked on her parent's door.

Dat's gruff "who is it?" sounded heavy with sleep.

"I think Emma's coming to, and she's calling for *Mamm.*" At least Lydia hoped that was true.

Mamm shuffled to the door and gazed at Lydia with sleep-blurred eyes. When Lydia begged her to hurry, *Mamm* wrapped a shawl around her shoulders, slid her feet into slippers, and shuffled to the door, her braid flopping down her back.

When they entered the *daadi haus,* a smile wreathed *Mammi*'s tired face. "Emma's struggling to speak, but I think she wants her mother."

Grasping the bedrail for balance, *Mammi* shifted sideways, so *Mamm* could approach the bed.

"Emmy?" *Mamm* laid her hand over the restless fingers gripping the sheet. "Did you call for me?"

Emma flicked from side to side and gurgled out, "Ssorree."

Mamm looked to Lydia. "What do you think she's saying?"

"Did she say *sorry*?" Lydia asked.

"My old ears aren't what they used to be, but it sounded that way to me." *Mammi* nudged *Mamm* over a bit and bent close to Emma. "We all forgive you."

The tense hands clutching the bedsheet relaxed. Emma went quiet. They all stood for what seemed hours, bent over the bed, hoping for another word, another sign, another movement. But nothing came.

The next few days were disappointing, but Caleb was excited when he heard what had happened. "That's terrific. It sounds like she not only tried to talk, but she responded to what you said. It may seem like this is slow, but keep doing what you're doing and talking to her. I have a strong belief she's going to recover fully."

Mammi looked at him askance. "Of course she is. There's never been any doubt about that. Emma's needed in this family."

"And you are too, *Mammi,*" Lydia added.

"*Hmph.* If God thinks so, He'll let me know."

Lydia's lips stretched into a smile. "I think He already did. He knew we couldn't do this without you."

"*Pah.* You would have figured out how to handle things."

Lydia shook her head. "I would never have

pursued electricity after *Dat* forbid it." Then she looked at Caleb. "And we couldn't have done it without you either." She held his gaze a second too long.

Caleb gave her a look so intimate, so intense, that Lydia's hands shook and her legs trembled.

Mammi cleared her throat, and the two of them jumped. *Mammi*'s raised eyebrows and disapproving glare pierced Lydia's heart. Her conscience clamored even more loudly.

She turned away and pressed her hands to her hot cheeks. She had to keep her feelings under control. Caleb was off limits. He'd made it clear that he'd never be joining the faith. She mustn't fall for an *Englischer,* but a small voice inside warned that she already had — and hard.

CHAPTER TWENTY-FOUR

The next evening Emma's eyes flickered open and closed. It happened so quickly Lydia wondered if she'd imagined it. Across the room Caleb leaned forward in his chair, his gaze riveted on Emma's face.

They both sat motionless, staring at Emma, willing her to open her eyes again. Her lashes fluttered once more, and Lydia blew out a silent, frustrated breath as Emma's eyes stayed shut. Seconds ticked by, then minutes. Lydia was about to give up, when Emma's lids lifted again, and this time they stayed open.

Lydia longed to rush to her sister's bedside, but she clenched the chair arms to hold herself in place, hardly daring to breathe, unsure if even the slightest movement might startle her sister. Caleb stayed motionless as well, but every line of his body revealed his tension.

Emma, a slight frown on her forehead,

stared at the ceiling, looking puzzled. Next her gaze strayed to the nearby wall. Then she glanced around the room, staring at each object as if nothing were familiar. She studied Lydia and Caleb as if they were part of the furniture, with no sign of recognition on her face. After examining everything in the room multiple times, she focused on Caleb. Her brows drew together. "Whooo you?" she murmured.

Lydia sucked in a breath.

Caleb caught Lydia's eye and shot her an excited glance. Then he turned to Emma. "I'm Caleb Miller. A friend of the family." He added, "I hope."

"Of course you are," Lydia said.

Emma whispered only, "Ohh," and sank back against her pillow. Her eyes closed, and within seconds, her chest rose and fell in a slow, even rhythm.

Caleb motioned with his head toward the doorway. Lydia slipped into the front hall, and he followed. He laid a hand on her arm, but at her involuntary jerk, he withdrew it. He whispered *sorry* but didn't look repentant. His hand lingered in the air as if he still intended to touch her. Lydia forced herself to move out of temptation's way.

Hurt flared briefly in Caleb's eyes but was quickly replaced by resignation. "You looked upset in there."

"She doesn't seem to recognize me."

"Temporary memory loss is common after a head injury. She may have trouble remembering new things as well. And most people recall nothing about the accident itself."

"That would be a blessing."

"Yes, it is. Our brains block out traumatic events to protect us. No telling how far back her memory loss will extend. She may not even remember Kyle."

"I pray that'll be the case." The less Emma remembered about her time and experiences in the *Englisch* world, the better.

A few mornings later when Lydia arrived at the *daadi haus,* Emma's eyes were open, and they stayed open all day. Emma's gaze roved the room, and surprise lit her features as she studied each detail of the furniture, curtains, and quilt again and again. Lydia tried to imagine what it would be like to wake and not recognize people or your surroundings. How disorienting that would be.

Then Emma turned toward Lydia, studying every detail of Lydia's face and clothing with an almost clinical detachment. "Where . . . man . . . ?"

"Man?" Did she mean Caleb? Or was she trying to say another word?

Emma lifted her arm and pointed to the chair where Caleb usually sat.

"He's at work."

"Wurrk?"

Was she questioning where Caleb worked, or did she not remember the word *work*? "He works at the hospital during the day. Do you remember the hospital?" Maybe she shouldn't bring up that subject.

Emma made a strange humming under her breath and then a soft whooshing sound that resembled the sounds of the machinery in the hospital room.

Lydia smiled at her. "That's right. Those were the sounds you heard every day while you were there."

Emma tried to smile back, but her lips barely lifted.

Lydia was overjoyed. This was Emma's first attempt at a smile.

Now that Emma was conscious, the visiting nurse started her on a liquid diet, which was soon followed by soft foods. Once Emma was eating regular meals, the feeding tube could be removed.

The physical therapist added new routines. Emma sat for longer periods each day and gained more mobility each week. For the first time Lydia allowed herself to hope that her sister might recover.

When, in late July, Emma stood for the first time, Caleb cheered. It had been five long months since the accident, and three since she'd returned home. Lydia swallowed back her own cheers because *Mammi* would frown on praising Emma, but inside Lydia was singing hallelujah and thanking God. *Mammi* ducked her head, but not before Lydia noticed the tears and pride shining her eyes.

Mammi cleared her throat and, in a voice choked with tears, said, "Now that you're on your feet, young lady, you can soon help your *mamm* with chores."

The physical therapist turned shocked eyes toward *Mammi*. "It will take a while for her to build up her muscles. We've been working them so they didn't atrophy, but this is only a first step in a long process."

"I'm only reminding her of her duties so she works hard on her exercises."

The therapist's eyebrows rose at *Mammi*'s tart reply. "One thing at a time. Let's encourage her to get steady on her feet first."

After brief sessions with a gait belt and a walker, the therapist helped Emma into bed. Emma exhaled loudly, collapsed back on the pillow with sweat beading her brow, and drifted off to sleep. Slowly she built her stamina so she could walk on her own with the walker.

Emma's speech also began returning. In the mornings *Mammi* greeted Emma. "How are you this fine day, young lady?"

"*Gut,*" Emma gurgled.

"Try again and speak more clearly this time. And I expect politeness. You should always reply, 'And how are you?' Do you understand?"

"*Mammi?*" Lydia said. "I don't think Emma —"

"Hush, Lydia." *Mammi* waved an arm in Lydia's direction. "I'm speaking to Emma, and I expect her to respond. Please don't interrupt." She leaned a little closer to the bed. "Now, Emma, look at my lips. Here's what I want you to say: '*Gut mariye, Mammi.* How are you?' Now let me hear you say that." *Mammi* repeated it one more time, enunciating each word clearly.

"*Gut . . . mar . . . yaa.*" Emma squeezed her eyes shut.

"I know it isn't easy, girl. But keep trying." *Mammi* reached out and stroked Emma's hand. "You'll get it, Emmie. You will."

The uncharacteristic tenderness in *Mammi*'s voice brought a lump to Lydia's throat. She cleared her throat quietly so she didn't disturb *Mammi*'s conversation with Emma, but *Mammi* started.

"Are you still here, Lydia? I thought you'd gone to get us breakfast." The sharp edge was back in her voice. "Get moving. Both of us are hungry."

Lydia hurried to the door, but she marveled at seeing another side of *Mammi*. That must be how *Mammi* talked to Emma when no one was around. Lydia had no doubt that under *Mammi*'s crusty, no-nonsense exterior she loved each of them deeply, but Lydia had rarely seen her grandmother let her guard down and expose her tenderness.

By the time Lydia returned with apea cake, scrambled eggs, and scrapple, *Mammi* had Emma repeating the greeting. It wasn't quite clear yet, but it had improved from the garbled sounds she'd made earlier.

"Isn't Emma doing well?" *Mammi* asked, when Lydia walked into the room with the wicker tray.

"She's doing a fabulous job. We're all very proud of you, Emma."

Mammi frowned. "No *hochmut* here. She's only doing what she should be doing."

"Of course, *Mammi*." Lydia tried to sound suitably chastened, but she hid the smile that tugged at her lips. *Mammi* had certainly sounded proud of Emma a few seconds ago.

But Lydia wouldn't mention that.

Lydia helped Emma to a sitting position and held out her sister's tray. "Here's your breakfast, Emma." Lydia pointed to each item on the plate and named it. She waited until Emma repeated it.

Mammi rutsched in her chair. "At this rate breakfast will be cold before I get my first bite."

"Oh, I'm sorry, *Mammi*. I should have served you first." Lydia set Emma's tray on the bedside table and handed her grandmother a plate she'd covered with a cloth to keep it warm.

Mammi harrumphed. "About time." She tucked into her meal with gusto.

Lydia sat beside Emma and forked small bites of scrambled egg into her sister's mouth. Emma's teeth moved slowly, methodically, as if she needed to remind herself how to chew. After a few bites, she clamped her lips shut and turned her head away.

"You need to eat more than that, Emmie. Please take another bite."

Emma shook her head and leaned back against the pillows with her eyes closed.

"Emma Esh," *Mammi* barked.

Emma's eyes popped open.

"Ha. That's better." *Mammi* gave her a stern look. "Finish every bite on that plate.

We do not waste food. And you need to eat everything you're served if you want to get rid of the feeding tube."

"Tie . . . rrd."

"You may be tired, but the rest of us are too. And your *Mamm* slaved over a hot stove to make that apea cake. And Lydia probably fried the scrapple and eggs. You will show your gratitude and clean your plate."

Emma's *yes, ma'am* came out more like a hiss, but she opened her mouth and let Lydia feed her the rest of the meal.

"That's much better." *Mammi* glanced approvingly at the empty plate. "You'll never gain your strength back if you don't eat properly. You've come a long way, Emmie girl, and" — she bent her head and fumbled for the hankie she kept tucked in her sleeve — "we want you to get back to your old self."

Lydia thought *Mammi* sniffled a little behind the handkerchief.

But her grandmother cleared her throat and continued. "Maybe not completely your old self. You could do with a bit more decorum and a little less high spirits." The usual sternness had reentered her voice.

Lydia marveled. Despite the brusqueness, *Mammi* seemed to be dissolving into tenderness more and more often.

Mammi stood and dusted off her hands. "While I dress, Lydia will clean up the breakfast things. A job you" — she pointed at Emma — "should be doing. You'd better hurry up and get out of that bed so you can be a help to your *mamm.* Lydia is waiting to get married. She can't stick around here forever taking care of invalids."

"So . . . rree."

"No need to be sorry. Just get yourself out of bed and get moving."

"Mammi," Lydia interrupted. "Emma needs time to heal." She turned toward her sister. "Take all the time you need."

Mammi planted her hands on her hips. "Are you contradicting me, girl?"

Lydia did not give in. "I suppose I am."

Beside her, Emma gasped.

They both turned toward the bed. Emma glanced first at one and then the other. Then she giggled.

"Emma?" they said in unison.

Emma's face remained stiff and immobile, but there was no doubt that it was a laugh issuing from her mouth.

"What's so funny?" *Mammi* demanded, although it was obvious she was close to tears.

Lydia blinked back the wetness in her own eyes. Emma laughing. She'd understood enough of their conversation to know it was funny.

Emma's eyes closed, and she leaned back on her pillow with a sigh. But this time her lips curved into a slight smile.

Caleb would be thrilled when he heard. Lydia wished he could have been there. She went through the rest of the day with a song in her heart.

CHAPTER TWENTY-FIVE

Lydia, late for helping *Mamm* with dinner the following Monday, rushed from Emma's bedside. In the front hall she collided with Caleb, who was entering the door. Caleb clasped her arms to steady her, his face inches from hers. Her apology died on her lips at the tenderness in his gaze.

"Lydia?" Caleb's voice came out breathy, soft, and gentle. His eyes probed hers as if searching for the secrets of her heart.

Her breathing stopped. Every muscle in her body stilled. She became lost, entangled in the messages Caleb's eyes were conveying. When his palms slid down her forearms to her hands, she didn't resist. The caress of his fingers on hers stirred a yearning to be loved, cherished.

Caleb lifted a fingertip and trailed it along the side of her face. Lydia leaned toward him as if drawn by an invisible force toward his descending lips. She turned aside at the last minute, and his lips grazed her cheek. Her free hand reached up and cupped the spot he'd touched. But she took a step back.

Caleb closed the distance between them. He drew her into his arms, cradling her close. Lydia rested her head against his chest, feeling safe and warm. The steady thumping of Caleb's heart soothed her, lulled her, melted her. She wanted to stay here forever.

"You want this as much as I do, don't you, Lydia?"

Lydia couldn't lie, she couldn't say no. But she had to get away. Now. She forced herself to break free of his arms.

He reached for her again.

"Don't," she burst out, her words sharp and desperate. If he touched her, she'd give in. She'd already gone beyond what she should have. Lydia held up a hand as if to ward off evil and stumbled backward until she was out of touching distance. "I mustn't do this. It's wrong. Very wrong." But why did something this wrong feel so good, so natural, and so desirable? Because the devil made temptation attractive.

Lydia squeezed her eyes shut and tried to pray, but no words came. Only one thought burned in her mind. *Go.* She had to get out, get away now. Flee temptation.

Lord, give me strength.

Lydia opened her eyes and met Caleb's, willing herself not to get sucked into their depths. "Please, will you let me get by?"

"Lydia, what's wrong?"

"I've done something wrong. Something I never should have done." Though her heart yearned for Caleb, her spirit longed for God. "We appreciate all you've done for Emma, but it would be best if we never saw each other again. Jakob and I —" Her steely resolve cracked. She didn't want to say the words. Though they'd never made a formal commitment, Lydia knew Jakob's intentions.

The pain in Caleb's eyes and the slump of his shoulders showed how great a blow she'd dealt him. He stood silent for a minute, gazing at her. Then he set his jaw, but each word he spoke seemed a great effort. "I understand. Deep down I've always known you were spoken for. I can't compete with Jakob for your heart. He's a good man and will give you the life you deserve. What can I offer you that can compare with that?"

Words burbled up inside Lydia, but she choked back the stream that threatened to rush from her lips. She couldn't, wouldn't tell him of her attraction to him. She forced her thoughts away from the curve of Caleb's lips, the message of love in his eyes. *Jakob.* She must keep her mind on her future. On her faith.

"Jakob," she choked out the name. She muttered it again like a talisman to ward off evil. "Jakob."

Each time she said the word, Caleb winced. She hadn't been trying to hurt him, only to remind herself of her duty. A vivid image of Jakob standing behind Caleb, frowning, accusing, shocked, gave her the courage to resist Caleb's outstretched arms.

Temptation whispered to her, begging her to close the gap between them, but Lydia kept her gaze fixed on the image of Jakob's disapproving face. "I'm sorry," she whispered, not sure which man the words were intended for. "I shouldn't have done this."

The tightness of Caleb's jaw and his fists clenched at his sides revealed his struggle to control his emotions. "I'm the one who's sorry."

Lydia's heart ached for him. And for herself. If she'd been different, she could have given in, discovered what it felt like to be kissed. For a fleeting moment she even wondered if she could give up her faith for Caleb. The longing to be encircled in his arms again overwhelmed her.

You still haven't joined the church. You could try it.

As tempting as it was, Lydia couldn't do that to Caleb. She loved him too much to toy with his affections. *Loved him? No.* She couldn't love an *Englischer.* When? How had it happened?

Caleb turned away, but not before she caught a glimpse of the pain etched into his face. "I'm sorry, Lydia."

Lydia kept her gaze fixed on the floor to prevent him from seeing the desire she was fighting. She gripped the sides of her apron to avoid reaching out to him. "Caleb —"

His eager *yes* made it hard for her to continue.

"I–I can't. We shouldn't."

His words came out stiff as if each were a pebble he was spitting out. "I should not have overstepped my bounds. Once I wouldn't have known what all this meant to you. But now —" His voice broke. He drew in an unsteady breath. "Now that I know . . . being around you, your family, your community. Meeting my relatives. I've come to understand and respect your way of life. One of the reasons I was attracted to you is because of your firm convictions, your unwavering faith. It's an integral part of you. It makes you who you are. It's why I fell in love with you."

Love? He loved her?

Caleb stepped closer and pressed his lips to her forehead. Lydia trembled. She wanted to melt against him. To be in his arms again. But she must remember Jakob. She had to be strong, yet her voice wavered as she begged, "Please don't do that. I belong to another man."

"And a lucky man he is. The luckiest man on earth."

"We don't believe in luck."

"I know, but I can't help wishing I'd met you first." He stopped and cleared his throat. "Would I have had a chance with you if I had?"

Her eyes swimming with tears, Lydia could not respond. She had to get out of here before the tears cascaded down her cheeks. But Caleb was blocking the door.

"Please . . ." Lydia began, but couldn't force out the words, *please let me pass,* when her heart was crying, *please take me in your arms again.*

Caleb kept his face averted as he pushed the door open. "I know you're spoken for. I never meant to let you know how I felt about you. Now that Emma's recovering, you don't need me anymore. It would be best if I stopped coming."

The deep sadness behind each word tore at Lydia's heart. Longing, shame, and regret swirled through her. She clamped her lips together to stop herself from begging him to stay.

After the door shut behind him, Lydia buried her face in her hands. The finality of the crunch of gravel under his truck wheels left a huge hollow inside. A cavern that nothing could ever fill. An emptiness that she'd carry forever.

Oh, Mammi, you were right. This cart not only careened out of control, it overturned.

Lydia spent the night on her knees, agonizing in prayer, although she already knew God's answer to the question. Could she accept His will for her life? When she rose from her knees at dawn to help with the chores, her mind and heart were as one, but a heaviness lay in her stomach as if she'd downed the cast iron skillet along with the griddle cakes. To succumb to her feelings for Caleb meant giving up something she had longed for from the time she was a child.

Her sacrifice was nothing like Christ's when He went to the cross and bore the world's sin. But she must obey her conscience, her church, her family. To stay true to her faith meant joining the church, and that meant forgetting Caleb. Why did doing what was right break your heart?

But now she knew how Emma felt, what had drawn her sister away from her faith. When Lydia had chided Emma, she had no idea how powerful the attraction to another person could be.

Lydia had always felt safe and secure around Jakob. His steadiness reassured her, and they had a wonderful friendship, but this . . . this . . . Lydia had no words for the magnetic pull that drew her to Caleb. The irresistible force that made her long to be with him. She only prayed it would fade in time.

"Mammi?" Lydia hesitated. She was unsure about asking her grandmother such a personal question. The busyness of the day was over, and having just settled Emma down for the night, they sat beside her bed.

"What is on your mind, Lydia? You've been moping around for days now since . . ." Her gaze bored into Lydia's. "Hmm . . . seems to me it's since Caleb stopped coming by to care for Emma. Am I right?"

"You could say that," Lydia mumbled the words and studied the pattern of the rag rug beside the bed. She should have prepared her words, her questions. Instead she took a deep breath and blurted out, "You said once that you were in love with an *Englischer.*"

Mammi's eyebrows raised. "I said that?"

Her grandmother's tart reply made Lydia doubt what she'd heard, but she pressed on. "At the hospital when you were admitted for appendicitis."

"Hmph." *Mammi* fixed her gaze on her hands, which were clasped in her lap. "I must have been in too much pain to watch my tongue."

"Anyway, I wondered how you dealt with giving him up," Lydia mumbled. "And how you forgot him and did your duty."

Mammi glanced off into the distance and sighed. "It was long ago. They say time heals all wounds, but some stay buried deep." *Mammi* leaned forward like a crow, her eyes bright and intent. "You didn't take my advice, did you? I rather suspected as much with the way you two kept eyeing each other."

Lydia hung her head. "I wish I had listened. Will it always hurt this much?"

Mammi released a slow breath through her teeth. "You decided to do the right thing?"

"I asked Caleb not to come back."

"Well, that's a step in the right direction."

"I know I did the right thing. My spirit is at peace, but my heart . . ." No words could describe the agony that kept her awake at night.

"It may feel that way for a long time. I tried to warn you. But God blesses those who obey His will."

Lydia bit her lip. Knowing that didn't take away the sleepless nights, the ache of loss. "Does anything get rid of the pain?"

Mammi gave her a sympathetic glance. "Hard work and setting your mind on a new course is the best antidote. It doesn't eliminate suffering, but it keeps you from dwelling on it."

Lydia had already tried that, but helping with the housework wasn't enough. Neither was assisting Emma, who needed less and less care each day. "I wish I had teaching to distract me. Emma will soon be up and around by herself. Then what will I do with my time?"

Mammi laid a hand on the book she always kept on the bedside table. "Study the *Dordrecht Confession*. Prepare with all your heart and soul and mind for each class. By the time you're baptized, you will find that it's become easier."

A distraction to fill the hours would help. She and Sarah were already reading each week's lessons, but she'd spend every spare minute on them. Studying would keep her mind occupied and maybe, just maybe, it would help to push the memories of Caleb away.

"There's one other thing you can do." *Mammi*'s tone was tender, a soothing balm to Lydia's agitated heart.

"What?" Anything that would ease this misery she would gladly do.

"Think of the future. Your young man" — she hesitated, then stressed the next word — "Jakob. Dream about your future together. Birthing children is one of the greatest blessings a woman can have. Think of those little ones and all the joy they'll bring to you. Thoughts of the *Englischer* will pale in comparison to that."

Lydia wished that were so, but thoughts of Jakob only filled her with shame and guilt. The bleak darkness of endless night engulfed her whenever she thought of a future with him.

Mammi must have sensed her hesitation, because she said, "It may not feel like you can do that right now. But give it time. The feelings will come."

Lydia remembered *Mammi*'s warning in the hospital. "But you never got over Myron Landis, did you?"

Mammi averted her eyes. Her arthritic fingers rubbed pleats into her skirt. It was awhile before she spoke. "No, not completely. It will always hurt. And the guilt came back to haunt me for years." She cleared her throat. "But it lessened over time. And now I can work with Myron on the quilt auction and know that we both chose the right path. God has blessed me many times over for obeying His will."

If only Lydia could be assured of the same thing — future peace to replace her present pain and turmoil.

In a voice heavy with tears, *Mammi* said, "I would have missed the joys of having all my children and the even greater joy of grandchildren." She met Lydia's eyes, and her own were wet with tears. "Every day I count my blessings when I look at you children. God has given me health and a wonderful family. What more can I ask?"

Tears slid down Lydia's cheeks. She had always known *Mammi* loved them, but her grandmother had never expressed that in words. Lydia had just been given a precious gift. She had a wonderful heritage. Family, community, and faith were the most important things a person could have. Lydia had chosen her faith. She'd made the right decision. The only decision. If only it didn't hurt so.

Sacrificing the things of the world was part of joining the church. Some gave up cars or cell phones. Others gave up partying. Yet others came with clear consciences. She had sacrificed a relationship that meant the world to her.

CHAPTER TWENTY-SIX

Lydia lay curled on her bed early Saturday morning. Later that day the youth planned to get together to play volleyball, and she would see Jakob for the first time since she'd sent Caleb away. Thinking of it, Lydia couldn't gather the strength to get up and get dressed.

Sarah bent over her. "What's wrong, Lyddie?"

"I'm feeling overtired and a bit sickish. Perhaps I'm coming down with something."

"Oh, no. I hope you don't have the flu." Sarah laid a hand on Lydia's forehead. "You don't feel warm, but if you're truly not feeling well, why don't you stay in bed? Extra sleep might help." Sarah patted Lydia's shoulder, making her feel even guiltier. She wasn't physically sick. Just mentally and emotionally drained.

Sarah looked at her sympathetically. "I'd be glad to give Jakob a message from you. I

356

know he'll be extremely disappointed not to see you."

For once Lydia wished Sarah weren't unfailingly kind and thoughtful. If only she were more like Emma, who'd always been so caught up in her own plans and actions that she rarely spared a thought for others. Lydia's uncharitable thoughts added to her already unbearable burden of guilt. And when she thought about Jakob . . .

Sarah pinned on her *kapp*. "I'll tell him you're very sorry you couldn't come and that you're missing him greatly, shall I?"

Though Lydia didn't really want that message conveyed to Jakob, she didn't trust herself to speak.

"Oh, Lydia." A worried frown crossed Sarah's brow. "You must be feeling awful if you can't even come up with a message for Jakob. Do you want me to get you anything?"

Lydia groaned, lay back, and closed her eyes. She couldn't let Sarah see the truth in her eyes. "I'll be fine. I just need some time . . ." Time to recover. Time to get over the pain. Time to adjust to the future. A future without Caleb.

"Let me get you some water, some aspirin. Is there anything else you need?"

"I'll be fine, Sarah. You should go. I don't

want you to be late."

But Sarah bustled around, gathering supplies and seeing that Lydia was tucked into bed. Sarah's ministrations made Lydia feel even worse. When her sister scurried downstairs to leave for the volleyball game, a great sense of relief washed over Lydia. She'd avoided facing Jakob today, but she couldn't keep it up forever. Sooner or later she'd have to talk to him. She just prayed that he wouldn't bring up marriage. She wasn't ready to deal with that yet.

Lydia was grateful for the day of respite. Other than bringing her lunch and dinner, her family left her alone so she was free to pray, to think, and even to sleep a little. Mainly she tossed and turned, trying to get comfortable — in her bed as well as with her conscience.

The following Sunday morning, though she longed to feign illness again, she had baptismal classes at Jakob's Aunt Miriam's house. She had to attend. Slowly, reluctantly, she dressed, had breakfast, and trailed her family out to the buggy.

On the way to the service Sarah reached over and patted Lydia's restless hands. "I know it's not right to say this, but I wish I could trade places with you."

"What?" Lydia dragged her mind from the

thoughts tumbling through her brain —
replays of her last conversation with Caleb
interspersed with dread of facing Jakob and
accepting what the future held. Why would
Sarah want to go through this pain?

Sarah's voice turned wistful. "If only I
were old enough to attend classes."

"Classes?" Lydia had trouble wrapping
her mind around the word when her mus-
ing had been so far afield. *Oh, classes.*
Sarah meant the baptismal classes. The
topic that should be foremost in Lydia's
mind. With effort Lydia jerked her attention
back to the present, but she couldn't stop
memories of Caleb from coloring her mood
the somber gray of the clouds that scuttled
across the sky.

"Oh, Lydia, how exciting it will be for you
to finally join the church. You've waited so
long."

Lydia squeezed Sarah's hand. "You're
right. I have waited a long time. A very long
time." But what had once been a fervent
dream now appeared more like a dreary
prison, locked away from love, living a lie,
doomed to lifelong loneliness.

While the rest of the congregation sang
hymns, Lydia and several other *youngie* followed the ministers into the basement. As

everyone settled onto the benches that had been set up, Jakob tried to catch Lydia's eye. She pretended to fasten her gaze on her hands, which she was twisting in her lap, but her peripheral vision registered Jakob's every move.

When she didn't look at him, Jakob slumped back on the far end of the boys' bench. His defeated posture changed, though, as soon as the ministers stood before them. Jakob snapped to attention, his gaze avid.

Lydia's thoughts drifted back to the first class, when she too had been eager to join the church. The opening question had been directed to Jakob because he was the first applicant on the bench. "Do you have anything to say? What is your desire?"

Jakob answered as he'd been taught, "My desire is to renounce the devil and all the world, accept Jesus Christ and this church, and this church to pray for me."

One by one, they each answered in turn, "That is my desire too."

And as Lydia replayed the scene in her mind, she repeated the words and clung to that avowal. This was her desire, her deepest desire. Amid all the grief, this one truth remained. She would dedicate herself to God, to her faith. She pushed all memories of Caleb from her mind and concentrated on the teachings. But no matter how well she schooled her thoughts, her heart flared with pain as if it had been seared by fire.

After class was over, they all filed back into the service. Lydia scurried to her place and sank onto the women's bench, relieved. She'd avoided Jakob's glances, but he'd most likely try to corner her after the service.

The minute the service ended, Lydia fled to the kitchen. She worked steadily filling bowls and platters for others but avoided taking out any food trays herself until Mary Zook barreled through the doorway and grabbed her arm.

"Lydia, what are you doing back here?" She picked up the tray of ham and cheese slices Lydia was arranging and thrust it into her hands. "Here, take this out to the men."

When Lydia emerged from the kitchen, Jakob was leaning against the wall near the serving table, beaming. He waited until she'd set the platter on the table to move closer. In a low voice he said, "Lydia, I'm glad we're both joining the church. I can't tell you how happy that makes me." The gleam in his eyes added another meaning to his words.

Lydia swallowed hard and tried to match

his cheerful demeanor. But her joy over doing God's will was accompanied by a depth of despair, knowing she'd never see Caleb again.

She tuned back into Jakob's whispered words in time to hear, "And I'm sure you know" — he cleared his throat — "how I feel."

Actually Lydia didn't know. She could guess, of course. But unlike Caleb, who had been free with his expressions of love, Jakob stuttered and stammered.

"I wanted to be sure of your feelings, though."

How could she convince him of her feelings when she wasn't even sure of them herself? The churning mass of guilt, regret, sorrow, anguish, duty made her feel ill. The concern in Jakob's eyes added to her queasiness.

He reached for a chair. "Do you need to sit down? You look faint."

"I–I'll be fine." *I hope.* "I need to get back to the kitchen." Lydia whirled around and, in her panic to escape, collided with Rebecca.

Pickled beet juice splattered Lydia's face and dress. Purplish liquid from the red beet eggs soaked into her apron.

"*Ach,* I'm very sorry." Rebecca set the

half-empty dish on the nearest table. She grabbed Lydia's arm. "Let me help you clean up."

"No, no. I'll be fine." Lydia rushed past Rebecca into the kitchen.

Sarah, busy arranging bread slices in a wicker basket, glanced up, and her mouth formed an *O.* "Are you all right, Lyddie? What happened?" She dropped the slices and hurried over.

"I bumped into Rebecca. She'll need help cleaning the floor."

Sarah's eyes filled with concern. "Oh, no. You stay here and get cleaned up. I'll get a mop."

Lydia shook her head. "I made the mess. I should clean it." *Ach,* she'd made more than a mess on the floor. She'd made a mess of her life — and Jakob's life too.

Sarah waved away her protests. "You can't go out there looking like that." She giggled. "You look worse than Zach when he had the chicken pox."

Lydia clapped her hands to her face. She'd forgotten the splashes.

Mary Zook brushed past, then stopped and stared. "Oh, my goodness, what happened?"

Sarah rushed to explain. "Lydia and Rebecca had a collision. I'm going to help Rebecca."

Mary set down the bowls she was carrying and set a hand on Lydia's arm. "You should soak your dress and apron right away. Those stains will set if you don't." She turned to her sister, standing at the sink. "Miriam, I'm going to take Lydia upstairs to clean up. Can someone take those bowls out to the table?"

"You don't have to —"

Mary ignored Lydia's protest and, wrapping a protective arm around her shoulders, led Lydia up the back staircase. Lydia's sickness increased with each step. Fleeing from Jakob, she'd bumped into his sister, and now she was in his mother's embrace. Kindness she didn't deserve because the stains on her heart were greater than those on her dress.

Mary's gentle and calming touch increased Lydia's guilt as her future mother-in-law gave her a clean dress of her niece's to wear and insisted on soaking Lydia's soiled garments.

Lydia tried to respond to the cheerful patter, but the words stuck in her throat.

But when Mary brought a pitcher and wash bowl of warm water to wipe Lydia's face, Lydia protested. "You've done so much for me. I can do this myself."

"You can't see your face, dear one." Mary swabbed Lydia's forehead with a cloth.

The gentle touch, so undeserved, brought tears to Lydia's eyes. She blinked, trying to clear them away, but they spilled down her cheeks and dripped onto the bodice of the borrowed dress.

Mary pulled back to look at her. "Did some of the juice get in your eyes? That can sting."

Lydia wished she could blame it on the juice. A simple nod would be all it took. But Lydia couldn't lie to this caring woman. To Jakob's mother. To her future mother-in-law. "No, it's —"

"We all need a good cry now and again." Mary dipped the cloth in the bowl and wrung it out. "You've been carrying some heavy burdens."

If only she knew, she wouldn't be so loving, so kind. The soft words only made Lydia's guilt greater. How could she betray Jakob and his family?

Several evenings later as Lydia and Sarah were baking caramel pies, someone knocked at the door. Sarah dusted off her hands and hurried to answer it.

"Oh, Jakob, welcome. Come in, come in."

Lydia's stomach clenched. She couldn't face him yet. She stood to one side of the kitchen doorway so he couldn't see her while he hung his hat on a peg and slid off his coat.

Sarah hurried to take the coat from him. She shook it out and hung it up. Her voice floated down the hall. "Lydia will be glad you're here. She's been rather low lately. I expect she's been missing you."

Oh, Sarah, if only you knew. Lydia wished she could sneak upstairs, but she'd have to pass Jakob in the hall. Sooner or later she had to face Jakob. She may as well do it now.

Her sister led Jakob down the hall to the kitchen.

Lydia hoped her smile wasn't too wobbly. Jakob's beaming one in return indicated that her inner turmoil didn't show.

"Have a seat. Sarah has caramel pies in the oven." Lydia motioned to the bench on the other side of the table. "We always make an extra for the family, but if you don't mind it hot and runny, I'm sure she'll cut you a piece after it cools for a bit."

Her nervousness had transformed her usual quietness into talkativeness. "Actually, I'm glad you're here. Perhaps you can help me with something I'm having trouble with. In fact, why don't you sit here with Sarah while I go to get it?"

Jakob looked at her a bit oddly as she rambled on. His look also contained disappointment. He had wanted time alone with her, as she'd suspected.

"I'll be right back." Lydia rushed from the kitchen and to her bedroom.

Wringing her hands, she sank onto the bed and tried to calm her thumping pulse. She forced herself to take several deep breaths. If only hiding out in her room all night were an option. She stilled her hands and whispered, "Help me to accept Your will for me, Lord. Give me an obedient heart."

Peace descended over her. And deep down inside she had a reassurance that God understood she needed time to heal, to adjust.

He would hold Jakob's declaration until she was ready to hear it.

Although she still wasn't sure she'd ever be ready to accept it. But she would follow God's leading.

She needed to head back to the kitchen. They'd be wondering what was keeping her. Lydia snatched up the *Dordrecht Confession*. This might keep the conversation from straying where she didn't want it to go.

When she returned to the kitchen, Sarah,

her cheeks pink, was bent over at the oven. "These look done."

Lydia set the *Dordrecht Confession* on the table and hurried over to remove the pies and set them on the wide windowsill to cool.

Flushed, Lydia sat across the table from Jakob. She pulled the book toward her. "I've been trying to read this, but I'm slow at translating it. I thought maybe you could help."

Sarah watched with wistful eyes. "I can't wait until I'm sixteen and can join the church."

Jakob flashed her a smile. "It won't be long."

Sarah wiped off the already clean counters and rechecked the stove. "It seems like forever. Lydia's letting me study with her, though, so I'll be ready." She moved one of the pies on the windowsill over an inch. "Well, I guess I'll leave you two alone." Her reluctance to go was obvious.

"No, no, Sarah. Please stay. I know how interested you are in learning this." Lydia slid over and patted the bench beside her.

Jakob's frown changed into a semi-smile as Lydia continued, "I'm sure Jakob can explain this much better than I can repeat it to you."

Sarah stood twisting her hands together.

"If you're sure? I don't want to interrupt anything."

"We'd love to have you join us, wouldn't we, Jakob?" Lydia turned a genuine smile to him.

Jakob shifted on the bench and didn't meet her eyes as he said, "Of course, you're welcome to study with us, Sarah. I've never known anyone as young as you who took an interest in this."

Sarah looked a bit crestfallen at his reference to her age. "Weren't you eager to join the church when you were my age?"

Jakob hemmed and hawed a bit. "I'm sure I was. I suppose it didn't occur to me to start studying ahead of time." His cheeks reddened a bit. "I think I had other things on my mind." He stole a quick look at Lydia, but she glanced away before their eyes met. He cleared his throat. "What were you struggling with, Lydia?"

She pointed to a passage and slid the book toward him. "I wish I understood this German more." The everyday German they spoke at home was different from the High German of the Confession. She could have read a translation, but she was determined to teach herself to read it in the original. Being fluent in High German was one of the many tasks she'd set for herself to help her forget Caleb.

The thought of Caleb brought a swift, sharp pain to her heart. She sucked in a breath to gain control of the flood of feelings his name stirred up inside.

Lydia peeked at Jakob to see if he'd noticed, but he was studying the passage with a wrinkled brow. He might have no more understanding of the original language than she did, but he was determined to try. She'd always admired his strong will to do what needed to be done.

In her mind she listed Jakob's strengths, overlaying them on the mental picture of Caleb taking her hand. She clenched her fists in her lap and willed her mind to concentrate on the man sitting across from her, the man she must marry. *Not right away,* she begged God. *Please give me more time.*

Jakob began a halting explanation. He stumbled in the same places she had. After he had struggled for some time, Sarah asked hesitantly if she might suggest a translation.

Lydia and Jakob both stared at her.

With scarlet cheeks she ducked her head and stared at her lap.

"You know how to read this?" Jakob's tone was incredulous.

The look Sarah gave Jakob held a plea for forgiveness as if she were worried she might be stepping on his pride. "I'm–I'm not positive, but I think I might be able to help."

Lydia gave Sarah a questioning look.

Sarah ducked her head. "While you were busy, I took it to *Mammi* and asked her for help. I thought perhaps I could assist you the next time we studied together."

Why hadn't Lydia thought of that? *Mammi* had been a bishop's daughter. And maybe she too had done what Lydia was doing now — immersed herself in learning to heal her broken heart. Perhaps that's why she had suggested it. Thoughts of Caleb intruded, but Lydia pushed them away and forced her attention back to the passage.

She smiled at her sister. "That was a wise idea. And did *Mammi* help you?"

Relief spread across Sarah's face. "I thought you might not like me knowing more than you."

"Why would you think that?" But as she asked the question, Emma's words about Lydia's pridefulness in her spirituality came rushing back and made her wonder if everyone viewed her that way.

"You're the oldest. And it's your class not mine. I wasn't trying to show you up or —"

"Sarah, Sarah, stop," Lydia said. "It's all right. I'm not at all upset. I'm thrilled that you cared enough to find out the translation."

"You are? Really, truly?"

"Of course. I wouldn't say that if I weren't."

Jakob cleared his throat.

Sarah turned guilty eyes toward him. "I hope I didn't offend you."

Lydia brushed aside Sarah's worries. "You didn't offend either of us." She didn't look at Jakob as she said it, but if he was upset, she hoped he'd have the sense not to say so. "Please tell us what you learned."

As Jakob's attention was diverted to Sarah, Lydia's tense muscles relaxed one by one. She listened in amazement as her sister not only translated the words but also explained their meaning.

If women could be bishops, Sarah would be a perfect one. She was humble, had a deep desire to learn the faith, and had a gentle way about her when offering reproof. Lydia smiled. Sarah wouldn't appreciate the joke. Neither would Jakob, so she kept the thought to herself. Perhaps someday Sarah would be a bishop's wife. She would make a wonderful helpmeet.

When Sarah finished, Jakob stared at her with wonder.

Lydia smiled. "That was a wonderful *gut*

explanation."

Sarah hung her head, her cheeks flushed. "*Ach,* they weren't my ideas, but *Mammi*'s."

Lydia was amazed at her sister's grasp of the difficult words. "You made everything quite clear. Perhaps we should both spend time studying with *Mammi.*"

"May I join you?" Jakob asked.

"Of course." Sarah's face glowed. "That would be wonderful. I mean, I'm sure Lydia would love to have your company."

Lydia nodded, not trusting her voice. She didn't want to hurt Jakob by betraying her disappointment. She'd been planning to use her studies as an excuse not to see Jakob. But at least if they were with *Mammi* and Sarah, they wouldn't be alone. She rose from the table. "That pie should be cool enough now."

Sarah sidled up beside her. "I can cut the pie." She leaned close and whispered, "Jakob will want to spend some time with you."

Lydia brushed aside Sarah's last comment. "It's all right. We'll have plenty of time together," she mouthed. Then a bit more loudly she said, "I'm glad you joined us tonight, Sarah. I learned a lot."

"I did as well," Jakob added.

Lydia carefully cut the pie and carried two

pieces to the table. She set the largest slice in front of Jakob. "It's a blessing that Sarah thought about asking *Mammi* for help."

"It certainly is." Jakob took a large bite of pie. "Umm, this is delicious," he said a few moments later.

"Sarah's a wonderful baker." Lydia let the caramel melt on her tongue. One nice thing about caramel pie was that it was a pie to savor, which made it difficult to talk.

"Lydia did as much work as I did," Sarah protested.

Although she knew Sarah didn't like being in the spotlight, Lydia wanted to keep the conversation on neutral topics. She smiled at her sister. "I made the crust, but you made the filling. And that's the most important part."

"They're both excellent." Jakob forked the last bite into his mouth.

"Would you like some more?" Sarah stood and headed across the kitchen.

"No, no." Jakob patted his stomach. "It's getting late." He looked across the table at Lydia with pleading eyes.

Lydia jumped up. "Oh, we didn't mean to keep you this long. Sarah and I will walk you to the door."

"We will?" Sarah's voice sounded squeaky, and behind Jakob's back she gave Lydia a puzzled look.

Jakob pushed back the bench and stood. The look he gave Lydia — a mixture of disappointment and hurt — made her feel small and petty. But she hooked her arm through Sarah's and headed for the door, Jakob trailing behind.

After he had donned his coat, Jakob tried to catch Lydia's eye, but she wished him a brief good night. Relief coursed through her as the door shut behind him.

As they *redded* up the kitchen, Sarah asked, "You don't think Jakob thought I was too forward tonight?"

"Certainly not." Lydia, overjoyed at avoiding time alone with Jakob, leaned over and hugged her sister.

Sarah eyes widened at the unusual embrace.

Lydia looked away quickly and, before Sarah could question her, said, "I can't wait for the three of us to study with *Mammi.*"

Sarah looked excited but hesitant. "Do you really think I should join you?"

"I'd be delighted to have you. I'm glad you're interested in learning more about the faith." Lydia smiled at Sarah, hoping her sister wouldn't question the *I'd* rather than *we'd.*

Sarah's face and eyes held a dreamy

expression. "It will be wonderful."

Ah, if only Lydia felt the same. Perhaps in time she too would have a similar expression.

CHAPTER TWENTY-SEVEN

Long, hot days of end-of-summer canning were replaced by crisp mornings and cool nights. Outside the window scarlet and amber tipped the leaves, a promise of chillier weather and the coming harvest. Inside applesauce and apple butter bubbled on the stove.

In spite of long hours farming and helping in his father's shop, Jakob arrived every Thursday evening to study with *Mammi*. They worked in the *daadi haus* living room, surrounding Emma's bed. Emma's gaze flitted from one to the other. She sometimes engaged in brief conversations, but her concentration soon drifted off.

School resumed, but Rebecca took over the classroom, and Sarah, soon to turn fifteen, became her assistant. Emma continued to recover, as did Jakob's father. Bishop Zook now had only a slight hesitation in his speech and walk, and a smile that tilted a bit higher on one side. For her part, Emma could shuffle around the room with the walker, and a few times she'd practiced with only a cane. Each time Emma crossed another milestone, Lydia longed to share the triumphs with Caleb. Thanks to him, her sister had come a long way.

Studying the *Dordrecht Confession* by Emma's bed made it difficult for Lydia to forget Caleb. Often she'd look up, expecting to see him across from her, and meet Jakob's eyes instead.

Several times after the lessons Jakob hinted about staying later. Sarah, rather than Lydia, usually invited him to the kitchen for a late-night snack. Sarah always baked Jakob's favorite treats every Wednesday evening. And once they all reached the kitchen, Lydia invented excuses to keep Sarah with them the whole time. But inside, Lydia squirmed at Jakob's sorrowful eyes.

One Wednesday night Jakob showed up unexpectedly. Lydia opened the door and hoped her face didn't reveal her dismay.

He removed his hat and twisted it in his hands. "I would like to have some time alone with you."

Lydia tried hard to infuse enthusiasm into her words. "Why not come into the kitchen then? *Mamm* and *Dat* have gone to bed, and

Sarah is almost done baking."

The scent of tart apples and cinnamon welcomed them into the kitchen. If only Lydia's heart held the same welcome. Instead, dread pooled in the pit of her stomach, an acid eating away at her insides.

"Jakob! *Gut-n-Owed.* Are you well?" Sarah's smile exuded the warmth that Lydia's had lacked. "Here, let me take your hat before you bend it all out of shape." She scurried over, rescued the hat that Jakob was wringing, and hung it on a peg. "I've just put apple strudel in the oven. If you'd like a piece when it's done, I'll —"

"Thank you, but I've come to talk to Lydia. Alone."

Sarah's face flushed. "I'm sorry," she gasped out. "I didn't mean to intrude."

Lydia smiled at her sister. "You aren't intruding at all. Is she, Jakob?"

At the sound of his name, Jakob's head snapped up. "What?" The distracted look on his face made it clear he hadn't been paying attention.

"I said that Sarah's not intruding, is she?"

"Oh. Oh, no. Not at all." A look of desperation entered his eyes. "It's just that I'd hoped to — I mean, I wanted to —"

Sarah's blush deepened. "I'll leave you two alone. But you'll need to take the

379

strudel out in twenty minutes." She scurried from the room.

"I'll take care of it," Lydia called after her as she escorted Jakob to the table, ignoring the pained look on his face at her response.

She motioned for Jakob to sit in *Dat*'s chair, but when she started to scoot around to *Mamm*'s chair at the opposite end of the table, Jakob patted the bench beside his chair.

"Sit here, please." Rather than a command, his tone held a note of pleading. "I have a question to ask you."

No, please, no. Not tonight. Not so soon.

But once Lydia had seated herself on the bench, Jakob launched into a speech that sounded memorized.

"We have been courting a long time now, Lydia. And we have both made the decision to join the church. I think it's time we, um —" Jakob's next words tumbled out so quickly that they all blurred together. "Will you marry me?"

Thoughts raced through Lydia's mind like barn cats after mice. She and Jakob had courted no one else the past two years. Saying no would likely mean that she would never marry. If she said no, who would Jakob find to marry? Everyone their age had already paired off. Lydia shook her head, trying to dislodge the swirling thoughts, the fears.

Jakob sucked in a breath, his eyes wide, wary.

"Oh, Jakob, I'm sorry. I wasn't shaking my head in answer to your question. I mean —" What did she mean? Her heart knew the answer, though her head and her conscience disagreed. How could she hurt him so? "It's just that —" *I'm in love with another man.* She couldn't say that. Neither could she lie. She didn't want to give Jakob false hope. Would her heart ever be free of her attachment to Caleb?

To soften the blow, Lydia laid a hand on Jakob's arm. He recoiled as if bitten by a snake. Swiftly she clasped her hands in her lap. Being around Caleb had made her freer with her gestures, her touches, and her affection.

Every line of Jakob's body revealed his shock at her forwardness, even though he'd just asked her to marry him. The difference between this proposal and Caleb's . . . Lydia blocked off those memories. It wasn't fair to Jakob to compare the two. Nor was it fair to consider Jakob's proposal when her heart was still entangled.

Jakob shifted on the bench. She had to give him an answer, but what could she say?

She cared about him deeply, but did not love him the way she did Caleb. Lydia squeezed her eyes shut. Jakob didn't deserve the pain she was about to inflict.

"Lydia?" Jakob's voice sounded unsure.

She swallowed down the lump of grief blocking her breathing, choking her. "I care for you too much to accept your proposal. You deserve a woman whose whole heart is free to give you the love you deserve." Shame coursed through her. She ducked her head to hide the heat stealing up her neck and splashing across her cheeks. Her voice came out as barely a whisper. "I am not that woman."

Jakob's head jerked back as if she'd slapped him. "What? What are you saying?"

Lydia kept her head bowed and concentrated on her damp fingers, pleating and unpleating the folds of her skirt. "I cannot be your wife." Bitterness crept into his tone. "It's him, isn't it?"

Lydia couldn't deny it, but her muscles were so tense she couldn't nod. She couldn't respond. She couldn't, she wouldn't, confirm Jakob's worst fears. She could spare him that at least.

"Oh, Lydia." The words were dragged out of his mouth as if torn from the depths of his pain. "I should have —" His voice broke.

Jakob clenched his fists at his side. "Tell me you don't mean it. That it's all a mistake."

"I–I'm sorry." Lydia's voice trembled, and she couldn't meet his eyes, couldn't bear to see the pain she'd caused.

Jakob fell silent, but his breath came and went in quick gasps.

Lydia kept her head bowed and squeezed her eyes shut to block the tears pooling in them. "Please forgive me."

Jakob did not respond. He stood so abruptly his chair overturned. He and Lydia bent to right it at the same time, and their foreheads bumped. They were so close that the tears glistening in Jakob's eyes reflected all the colors of the rainbow.

The ache in Lydia's heart expanded until it squeezed against her ribs. How could she have hurt him so?

Jakob stormed to the wall peg, snatched his hat, and rushed from the kitchen.

"Is everything all right?" Sarah yelled from the hallway. "What crashed?" She rushed into the kitchen.

Jakob brushed by her, mashing his hat on his head.

Sarah called after him, "Jakob, Jakob, whatever is the matter?"

Jakob didn't answer. He wrenched the front door open.

Sarah's peacemaking voice floated out to him. "The apple strudel is almost ready. Wouldn't you like a piece before you go?"

"Not tonight." Jakob stormed out into the night, slamming the door behind him.

The harshness of Jakob's tone made Sarah's face crumple from eagerness to disappointment. "Did I say something to offend him?" Her voice wavered.

Lydia sank into the chair and covered her face with her hands. "No. I did."

"What happened, Lyddie? Are you crying? Did you two have a fight?"

Lydia waved one hand to signal that she couldn't talk. Not now. Maybe not ever. What happened here tonight was between her and Jakob alone. He deserved that much. Whatever he chose to tell others, she would bear it. It was the least she could do.

Decisions to marry were usually done in secret and not announced until a few weeks before the wedding. Once the congregation knew of an upcoming wedding, they scrutinized the couple's actions and relationship to be sure the two were compatible. Most couples preferred to avoid that by waiting until two weeks before the wedding to share the news. Lydia was grateful that Jakob would be spared the embarrassment of others knowing she'd rejected him.

And maybe he would find another girl to court, though all the girls her age were already married or dating. Perhaps one of the younger girls would make him a suitable wife, perhaps even Sarah. How it would pain her to watch Jakob with someone else, knowing she would never marry, never have children. But she had done the right thing. Her conscience was clear. At least about this. Yes, at least about this.

On Monday evening when they were alone in their room, Sarah faced Lydia, a puzzled frown on her face. "What happened between you and Jakob? He looked so upset at church yesterday. And the two of you went out of your way to avoid each other."

Should she tell Sarah? It was no one's business but hers and Jakob's. Better for his pride if no one knew she had turned him down. However, Sarah was her sister, and she could count on Sarah's discretion.

"Well?" Sarah stood with a hand on her hip and a stern look on her face. The posture was so unlike Sarah that Lydia almost smiled, but remembering Jakob's sorrowful look, she checked the impulse.

"Are you bossing me around, Miss Sarah?" Lydia adopted a saucy attitude not only to counteract her pain but to distract her sister. "Would you say you're guilty of *hochmut*?"

"Oh, Lydia." Sarah clapped her hand over her mouth. "I am sorry. Please forgive me. I did not mean —"

Lydia smiled. "I know you didn't. I was only teasing."

Sarah studied Lydia closely. "Are you changing the subject?"

Leave it to Sarah. She always got to the heart of the matter. "Yes, I am." Lydia pursed her lips. "Sarah, what happened between Jakob and me is a private matter. Less discussed, sooner forgotten."

Sarah studied the wooden floorboards. "I understand. But Jakob was like a brother to me. And now —" She gulped hard and clenched her fists. "He doesn't even speak to me. He turned the other way when he saw me."

"Oh, Sarah, I'm sorry. I had no idea he would treat you differently because of this."

"I just want to know what happened, so I don't say anything wrong, anything to offend or upset him."

You won't. You never do. Lydia pursed her lips. "If I tell you, will you promise never to tell anyone?"

"Lydia." Sarah gasped. "Do you think I would gossip?"

"No, of course not." Not Sarah. She did the right thing no matter what the circumstances. "Why don't we start the pies for dinner? And I can tell you as we work." Maybe making pies would help. At least it would give her something to do with her hands, and she wouldn't have to see her sister's reactions.

Downstairs, Lydia set to work on the crust, rolling it out with more force than was necessary. Sarah stood nearby at the stove, stirring the rhubarb. "When are you going to tell me, Lyddie?"

Lydia used the back of her floured hand to push a stray wisp of hair from her eyes. "When Jakob came over the other night — the night he asked you to leave the kitchen — he wanted to talk about getting married."

The wooden spoon slipped from Sarah's grasp, splattering red juice on the stove and the floor.

"I'm sorry to be such a *dummkopf*." Tears spurted from Sarah's eyes. "I've made such a mess." She moved the pot from the heat, then snatched a cloth and wiped the stovetop, but the smell of charred fruit lingered in the air.

Lydia grabbed the mop to clean the floor.

"And now I've gone and messed up the rhubarb too," Sarah said in a choked voice.

"I think the rhubarb's fine. Just put it back on the burner and keep cooking it. It wasn't off the heat that long."

Sarah clenched her teeth and moved the pot back into place. Her voice sounded sad when she said, "You told Jakob *yes,* of course."

"Actually I told him no."

"No?" Sarah's voice was practically a screech. "But you've been dating forever. Two years and three months to be exact."

"You know how many months we've been together?" Even Lydia hadn't kept that careful a count.

Sarah's cheeks turned the same shade as the rhubarb. "It happened right after my birthday," Sarah mumbled. "Otherwise I probably wouldn't have remembered."

After a few moments Sarah said, "Why, why, why would you turn Jakob down? He's a good man. Handsome. Strong. And a very hard worker."

Lydia sighed. "I know."

"He'd make a perfect husband."

"Yes, yes, he would. Only not for me." This time it was Lydia who turned away. "I don't love him the way a woman should love the man she wants to marry."

"How could you not love Jakob? How could anyone not love him?" Sarah's indignation had her hands on her hips again.

"I just don't." Lydia's voice broke. She'd shared what happened with Jakob, but she could never share what had happened with Caleb. That was a secret that would go with her to her grave. A secret that she tried to push out of her mind. Out of her heart. Out of her . . .

Sarah's eyes shone with compassion. "But who will you marry then? Everyone else has already paired up."

Lydia shook her head. She would rather be an old maid. Perhaps she could return to teaching. She would miss having children of her own, but she could spend time with her nieces and nephews. And as a teacher, she'd have plenty of children to care for. No babies, though, which was heartbreaking.

Maybe she should have told Jakob yes. Not all couples who married were in love. Love could grow in time if the spouses worked together, had children, and served God. With Jakob she would have all of the things she'd dreamed of — a home, a family, a faithful man to provide for her, one she could cook for and help, one who followed the teachings of the church and did the right thing.

She was silent so long she was startled when Sarah broke into her thoughts. "You really turned Jakob down?"

At Lydia's nod Sarah shook her head. "Lyddie, how could you hurt him that way? Poor Jakob."

Now it sounded as if Sarah were more concerned with Jakob than with Lydia's feelings or reasons.

"I had to," Lydia said simply. "It wouldn't be fair to Jakob to saddle him with a wife who doesn't love him. He deserves better than that."

"He certainly does," Sarah burst out. "But what will he do now? All the girls his age are already spoken for or are courting."

"Perhaps he'll have to wait for some of the younger girls to grow up."

Sarah sucked in a breath. "Wait for a younger girl? You think he might do that?"

Lydia didn't want her sister to pin her hopes on Jakob. He'd likely find it too painful to spend time with their family. So she deflected the question. "I have no idea what Jakob plans to do. Perhaps he'll go to visit his cousins in another district."

"Oh, no, I hope not. I mean, it would be hard not to have him around."

Lydia put the pies in the oven, and Sarah plopped onto the bench, her elbows on the table and chin propped in her hands. "I guess that means he won't come over in the evenings to have dessert or play baseball in the backyard with us. I'm going to miss him."

"You can still play baseball with him after church, you know."

Sarah gazed out the window at the dark fields beyond the glass. "I guess, but it's more fun when we play here. That way we get more turns at bat." She sighed. "Now I wonder if he'll ever talk to me again. At first I thought it was because he was upset with me about something I'd done. Then I saw him avoiding you too, which made me wonder if you two had a fight."

In a way, Lydia supposed they had. They certainly hadn't seen eye to eye. "Give him some time to heal. Right now his pride is hurt."

"It's more than his pride, Lydia. He's probably devastated. How would you feel if someone you loved turned you down?" Sarah's indignation bubbled and boiled over the way the rhubarb had.

Lydia didn't know how she'd feel. Probably the same way she felt right now after losing Caleb. Hollow, like her insides had been cored out, leaving her with no heart, just emptiness and the pain of raw exposed skin. And the knowledge that life would never be the same.

She and Sarah, each lost in thought, sat in silence while the pies baked. When the pies were done, Lydia set them out to cool.

Sarah took one look at the pies and burst into tears. "Rhubarb is Jakob's favorite, but he'll never eat pie here again. Ever. Oh, Lydia, I'm going to miss him."

"So am I," Lydia admitted, but she missed Caleb much, much more.

CHAPTER TWENTY-EIGHT

As days grew shorter and leaves began to fall, Lydia concentrated on encouraging Emma's progress. Her sister now took short walks using a cane, but she tired easily. Although Emma sometimes hesitated, searching for words or trying to understand ideas, her sense of humor had returned, and she enjoyed jokes. Only her memory remained elusive. Emma didn't recall Kyle or the animosity she'd expressed at the apartment, which Lydia considered a blessing.

The day of her baptism, Lydia hurried to the *daadi haus* to help Emma dress. The autumn leaves made brilliant displays of red, yellow, and gold, but the bright splashes of color pained Lydia's eyes and heart. The beauty of nature seemed at odds with the barrenness of her heart.

Her mood didn't seem to be catching. *Mamm* was already dressed and waiting, joy shining in her eyes. "Today is the day. I'm so glad the service is at our house, so Emma can attend."

Lydia tried to match her happiness to *Mamm*'s. Obedience to God's will had brought a deep sense of peace. But the emptiness inside sucked away any accompanying gladness. If only she'd followed *Mamm*'s advice that long ago day and not given away her heart. Seeing Jakob today would open fresh wounds. For both of them.

Lydia focused her attention on each small detail of pinning Emma's dress, brushing her sister's hair until it was silky, pinning it back into a bun, and setting her *kapp* in place. Emma smiled throughout these ministrations, but her eyes held a look of puzzlement.

Mammi noticed Emma's disorientation and launched into an explanation of church and baptism that Lydia tuned out.

Once again Lydia's thoughts turned to Jakob. She regretted the pain she'd caused him. Perhaps she'd been too hasty in turning him down. Suppose he was God's will for her? Maybe if she went into marriage with a submissive heart, over time her feelings would change. But would that be fair to Jakob? He deserved a wife who loved him.

No, she had made the right decision, the only decision.

Long, lonely years stretched ahead, but her heart and soul belonged to God. And she would trust Him for her future.

After seating *Mammi* and Emma beside Sarah, Lydia hurried to the front row reserved for the baptismal applicants, keeping her eyes averted from the men's side of the room. She couldn't bear to see Jakob. For years she'd thought joining the church meant their future was settled. Now she had torn apart that happiness for both of them by allowing her thoughts to stray where they shouldn't, by getting involved with an *Englischer.* Not just any *Englischer.* One specific *Englischer.* Caleb. She and Jakob were both paying for her foolishness.

Soon after the service began, Lydia slipped out with the other applicants for a final meeting. She flashed a quick smile at Emma and *Mammi* as she passed, and then her gaze strayed across the aisle. Caleb! Here at church? Her breath hitched. She stumbled but quickly bowed her head and concentrated on shuffling one foot in front of the other. No matter how hard she tried, though, she couldn't erase the picture etched into her mind.

That mesmerizing smile. Crinkle lines surrounding blue eyes. Eyes that drew her into their depths. Eyes that kept her awake at night. Eyes that haunted her dreams.

Lydia prayed her momentary hesitation hadn't been noticeable. She clasped her hands together prayerfully in front of her, wishing she could wring them to relieve the waves of pain and heartache.

What was Caleb doing here at church? Was God sending her this one final test to see if she would stay true to her faith?

She blindly followed the other applicants into the room, where Bishop Zook, his face solemn, reminded them they were making a promise for life.

"If anyone is uncertain about this decision," he continued, his gaze boring into each one of them, "now is the time to reconsider and turn back."

Lydia couldn't meet his eyes. Seeing Caleb again had ripped open her still-raw heart, exposing feelings she'd wrestled with for months now. Her hand twitched as she debated whether or not to raise it. For years she had only one desire — to join the church. That day was here now, and she was conflicted. Perhaps she did not have the wholehearted commitment she needed if she could so easily be distracted by a look, a smile.

If she didn't speak up now, she'd be making an irrevocable decision. The future stretched before her — a desolate landscape filled with loneliness and regret. If she walked away from the church now, she'd be giving up family, community, and God.

Could she do that for one *Englischer*? And if she did, what example would she be for Emma? Sarah? The boys?

In the silence around her, the steady inhales and exhales contrasted with her ragged breathing. She unclenched her fists, which were knotted at her sides, and tried to match the others' calm and measured breaths. As she did, peace descended on her spirit, settling as softly as a dove. She had made the right choice, the only choice.

The other applicants filed from the room, and Lydia took her place in line. When they returned to their seats at the front of the room, many candidates shielded the sides of their faces with their hands to show their humility, but Lydia did it to prevent herself from being distracted. Though she longed for one glimpse of Caleb's face, she had made her decision. Her life belonged to God.

As the service went on, Lydia struggled to keep her full attention on the story of Philip and the Ethiopian that Bishop Zook was recounting. She jumped when the bishop emphasized the Ethiopian's words, "What doth hinder me to be baptized?"

Her anguished heart cried out, "Nothing." She had given up Caleb for her faith, and today she'd make that faith public. This was the moment she'd been waiting for, hoping for, since she was young, but her heart was numb.

As Philip's answer, "If thou believest with all thine heart, thou mayest," rang in her ears, Lydia swallowed hard and silently repeated the Ethiopian's reply. "I believe that Jesus Christ is the Son of God."

Then Bishop Zook said, "Now, if you are still willing, and it is still your desire, you may go down on your knees."

Lydia knelt with the others and bowed her head. She pushed all thoughts of Caleb, Jakob, and her future from her mind, and concentrated solely on the questions the bishop was asking.

Her *yes* joined the others each time the bishop paused. Lydia centered all her thoughts on the moment, on the commitment she was making.

Then the bishop moved down the line, baptizing each person in the name of the Father, Son, and Holy Spirit. When he stood over her, his hands cupped over her head, Lydia's heart expanded until her chest ached. Deacon Lapp poured water into the bishop's outstretched hands. Water trickled through his fingers and onto Lydia's head, and the sense of peace that had filled her earlier increased. She had made the right choice.

Bishop Zook returned to the beginning of the line. He reached down and grasped Jakob's hand. "In the name of the Lord our Father, rise up and I'll greet you as a brother." Though his words were solemn, he beamed at his son and pulled him to his feet to greet him with a holy kiss. Then he moved down the line to greet the other boys.

Mary Zook did the same with the girls. When she reached Lydia, she hesitated. For a brief instant, sadness flickered in her eyes. It disappeared so quickly that Lydia wondered if she'd imagined it. Then Mary's eyes brimmed with forgiveness. She reached for Lydia's hand, assisted her to her feet, and gave her a tender kiss.

Lydia choked back tears. Though Jakob had yet to forgive her, his mother had made her peace. Now Lydia must do the same. She would trust God for whatever the future held.

When the service ended, women and girls swarmed around Emma, fussing over her and asking questions. Lydia slipped through the crowd and into the kitchen. *Mamm,* her back to Lydia, was already busy arranging trays.

Her mother needed help, but first Lydia needed some time alone to get her emotions under control and prepare herself to meet Caleb. She escaped out the side door and headed for the *daadi haus.*

Behind her the wooden boards vibrated with heavy footsteps. Lydia couldn't face anyone just now. She opened the *daadi haus* door and ducked inside, but before she could close it, someone called out.

"Lydia?"

The familiar voice froze her in place. No, it couldn't be. "Caleb?" His name came out soft, breathless. Keeping her back to him, Lydia gulped in air to calm her racing pulse. She pinched her lips together to prevent an overeager greeting from tumbling out.

"I wanted to be here for your baptism."

Lydia kept her gaze fastened on the floor to avoid temptation. "I–I'm glad you were."

"May I come in?"

Why was he torturing her this way? Why was God testing her so soon after she'd joined the church?

When Caleb stepped inside, his shadow crossed the floor, mingling with hers, and his presence filled the entryway. Lydia forced herself to count each whorl in the wood and curled her hands into fists to prevent them from reaching out for him.

"I saw Emma at the service." Caleb's words were light, casual. "How's she doing?"

"Much better. She's standing by herself now and walking with support." Lydia tried to make her tone as matter-of-fact as his, but the agony of being close to him stole her breath. She struggled to form words into sentences. "Emma still tires easily, but they've assured us she'll make a full physical and mental recovery. Well, except for the gap in her memory. They say sometimes the memory comes back spontaneously, but it's also possible she may never remember much of the past year or so."

Caleb cleared his throat. "Might be for the best."

"How true." Lydia wished she had that same memory loss.

Caleb shuffled. "I'd better go. We probably shouldn't be alone like this. No sense in stirring up gossip. I just wanted to —"

Lydia made the mistake of glancing up. Caleb's smile brightened the fall sunshine and dazzled Lydia so much she couldn't look away. It took her a few moments to realize that Caleb looked different. He must have borrowed clothes from one of his relatives. In them, he appeared even more handsome than she'd imagined in her daydreams, except he didn't have a beard. "You're wearing Plain clothes?"

"After —" Caleb swallowed hard. "After leaving you that day, I couldn't help wondering about a faith that meant so much to you. I started attending church with *Daadi.*"

"How wonderful. And you borrowed clothes?"

Caleb nodded. "My cousins were happy to lend me some. I didn't want to offend anyone."

Of course. Caleb had always been thoughtful that way. But Lydia wished he didn't look so handsome in them. She forced her thoughts back to neutral ground. "And what about Kyle?"

Caleb's face darkened for a moment. "He still doesn't want to meet the family. But we're all praying for him. And *Daadi* surprised me the other night by saying that perhaps God wanted an Amish doctor in the family."

"So you're planning to join the church after medical school?" Lydia asked eagerly, but Caleb's forceful "No" sent her hopes into a downward spiral.

"No," he repeated. "One Amish doctor in

the family will be enough. *Daadi* hopes in time — perhaps after medical school — Kyle will come around. After all, if God can change my heart, he can surely change Kyle's." When Lydia raised puzzled eyebrows, he explained, "I've committed to joining the church. I'll be starting baptismal classes in the spring."

"Y–you're joining the church?" *Stop stuttering, Lydia.* She might control her mouth, but she had no control over the stuttering of her heart. "You're joining the Amish?"

Caleb eyes softened, and he nodded. "My family is pleased I made the decision. And so am I. But it was watching your family that convinced me."

"But how? I mean . . ."

Caleb's light laugh tickled places deep inside her soul. Lydia squeezed her hands together and lowered her eyes to hide her reaction.

"I wanted the deep faith I saw in you and your grandmother. *Daadi* was happy to help by providing books to read. I already sold my truck. A coworker drives me to the hospital, but I'm looking for a house near *Daadi* so I can help him on the farm."

Lydia gazed at him in wonder, hoping he wouldn't read any other emotions in her eyes.

But Caleb wasn't looking at her. His eyes had a faraway look. "Finding my faith has brought me such joy, I wish I could convince Kyle to join too." He blew out a breath. "Then again, I'm glad he's still on track to become a doctor."

"That's wonderful. About Kyle continuing his schooling, I mean. And about your joining the church." Lydia worried her stumbling words would reveal all the feelings for Caleb that she'd tucked away in her heart. Feelings that wanted to trip off her tongue.

"It's wonderful that you joined too." Caleb's smile faltered. "I guess that means you'll be getting married soon." His tone mirrored the sadness reflected in his eyes.

Lydia's thoughts were so jumbled she couldn't find the starting place for unraveling them. Caleb joining the church? Somehow it didn't seem real. Yet it must be. He'd decided after that heartrending day. So his commitment must be real. And to sell his truck? "Lydia?" Caleb's voice interrupted her struggle to make sense of everything. "I just came to say good-bye and let you know that you started me on my own journey of faith."

Good-bye? He'd come to say good-bye. Hurt welled up inside and squashed hopes that had begun to blossom. "Good-bye," she echoed.

"Yes, well, I'll be going. I shouldn't have kept you here so long. I'm sure you're eager to get back to your intended."

"You mean Jakob?"

Caleb winced as he had that day she'd invoked Jakob's name to ward off temptation. "Yes. Unless there's someone else?"

Lydia couldn't look at him. She wished there were someone else, but she couldn't say that. How could she answer his question honestly? "Jakob and I . . . we decided . . . well, actually, it was me . . . I decided . . ."

"Decided what?"

Lydia fixed her gaze on a cardinal sitting on the wooden fence post near the barn. "I couldn't marry him."

"You turned him down?" Caleb's tone was incredulous.

Lydia hung her head to keep him from seeing the shame in her eyes. "I had to."

"You had to? But why?"

"I couldn't marry him when . . ." Her face burned.

Every muscle in Caleb's body tensed, and he rocked forward on the balls on his feet.

Lydia wasn't sure how he felt about her now, and she could barely finish her sentence. But she had to tell him the truth. "I was in love with someone else."

"Someone else?" Caleb prompted.

"With you," Lydia confessed.

Caleb stepped closer. With one finger, he tilted her chin up, and their gazes met, his so filled with hurt and hope and longing, Lydia's pulse raced, and her mouth went dry. For a long moment they stared deeply into each other's eyes, the world around them fading into the background.

Caleb cupped her face in his hands. "When I left here that day, I thought I'd lost you forever." The huskiness of his voice conveyed his anguish. "The vision of you with . . . with Jakob —" He sucked in a breath. "It's tortured me ever since."

He slid his hands to her shoulders and enfolded her in his arms, cradling her close to his chest. "Even though I'd lost you, I wanted what I'd seen in you and your family — the caring, the closeness, the faith, the love."

Love. The one thing Lydia thought she'd sacrificed.

"Now I not only have a family and a church community, but I have you."

The ardent timbre of Caleb's voice made Lydia look up. His eyes met hers with eagerness. Then his head descended until their lips met. For the two of them, lost in the kiss, the world around disappeared until all that mattered was their love.

"Ahem."

Lydia and Caleb jumped apart.

Mammi, one arm around Emma, barged into the *daadi haus.* "Your sister's tired. She's had more excitement than she's used to." Frowning at Lydia, she muttered, "And she's not the only one." She steered Emma past them and into the living room.

A few seconds later loud banging in the other room startled them. Caleb smiled and shook his head. "Do you think your grandmother has appointed herself our chaperone?"

"Most likely." Lydia smiled up at him shyly.

Caleb leaned over to whisper in her ear, "I can't wait until we can post our banns."

"Aren't you forgetting something?"

At Caleb's puzzled frown, Lydia couldn't resist teasing him. "You never asked if I would marry you."

"And if I did, what would you answer?"

Lydia pulled back slightly and pretended to tap a finger on her chin. "It's been so sudden. I'll need some time to think about it." Seeing the anxiety in Caleb's eyes — those eyes that had haunted her dreams for so long — she couldn't, wouldn't put him through one second more of misery. "I've had plenty of time to think now. My answer is yes, yes, yes, oh, yes." She nestled against him and sighed as he drew her nearer.

"Perfect answer." Caleb claimed her lips again.

Lydia melted into his kiss, her joy overflowing. God had restored all she thought she'd lost — Emma's health, Caleb, and a future filled with love.

A gleam entered Caleb's eye when the kiss ended. "Should I thank your grandmother for bringing us together? If it weren't for her, I'd never have met my Amish family. And we wouldn't be standing here today."

Lydia tipped her head up to gaze into his eyes and spied *Mammi* in the living room doorway. Taking his hand and locking eyes with *Mammi,* Lydia murmured, "Umm, I think she already knows."

Mammi's knowing smile and nod made it clear they had her blessing.

AMISH GLOSSARY

ach — oh
Ausbund — Amish hymnal
daadi — grandfather
daadi haus — small house attached to the main dwelling
danke — thank you
dat — dad
dummkopf — dummy
Englisch — non-Amish people
Englischer — a non-Amish person
grexy — whiny, out-of-sorts
grosdaadi — grandfather
gude mariye — good morning
gut — good
Gut-n-Owed — good evening
hochmut — pride
jah — yes
kapp — prayer bonnet
mamm — mom
mammi — grandmother
Ordnung — unwritten rules that govern the

409

church district

redded — straightened up, cleaned

Rumschpringe — "running around time"; the period before Amish teens join the church; some experiment with *Englisch* ways

rutsched — wriggled

strubbly — disheveled, messy

U bent welkom — you're welcome

verboten — forbidden

Wie gehts? — How are you?

wunderbar — wonderful

youngie — youth

AMISH RECIPES

BY MARIA LEBO

June's Cracker Pudding

2 eggs, separated
2 cups whole milk
1/2 cup sugar
Pinch salt
1 tsp. vanilla
1 cup saltine crackers, crushed
1/2 cup shredded coconut

In a saucepan whisk the egg yolks. Gradually whisk in the milk. Add 1/4 cup sugar and the salt. Cook and stir over medium-low heat with a wooden spoon, until the mixture is thickened and bubbly. Remove from the heat. Stir in the vanilla, crushed crackers, and the coconut. Pour into a glass or ceramic 1-quart casserole dish and set aside.

Preheat the oven to 350 degrees. In a separate bowl beat the egg whites until soft peaks form. Slowly add remaining sugar

411

(1/4 cup) and beat on high speed until stiff and glossy. Spoon over the hot pudding, covering to the edges. Bake for 12–15 minutes. Let rest 10 minutes before serving.

Sweet and Sour Chow-Chow

1 15-oz. can navy beans, drained and rinsed
1 15-oz. can red kidney beans, drained and rinsed
1 lb. frozen lima beans, prepared according to directions
1 large red pepper, diced in large pieces
1 large green pepper, diced in large pieces
1/2 lb. carrots, peeled and sliced
1 lb. frozen string beans, yellow and green mixed, prepared according to directions
4 cups water
1 small head cauliflower, cut in florets
1/2 small bunch celery, sliced
1 red onion, diced in large pieces
1 cucumber, chopped
5 whole cloves
1 star anise
4 cups cider vinegar
1 1/2 cups sugar
2 Tbsp. kosher salt

Drain and rinse the canned beans. Prepare the frozen beans according to the package directions. In a saucepan bring 4 cups of water to a boil. Flash cook all fresh vegetables (except the cucumber) for 30 seconds, then plunge in a bowl of ice water to halt cooking. Drain. Combine all vegetables and beans in a bowl. Add the cloves and star anise.

In a saucepan combine the cider vinegar, sugar, and salt. Bring to a boil, making sure the salt and sugar are dissolved. Pour hot vinegar over vegetable/bean mixture. Make sure vegetables are submerged; cover and keep in the refrigerator. Let marinate for at least 1 week for best flavor.

Can be made in larger quantities and canned for longer out-of-the-refrigerator storage.

Whoopee Pies

Cookie Ingredients
2 cups flour
1 cup granulated sugar
1/2 cup unsweetened cocoa
1 tsp. baking soda
1/2 tsp. baking powder
1/4 tsp. salt
1/2 cup buttermilk
1/2 cup water
1/2 cup vegetable shortening

1 egg
1 egg yolk

Filling Ingredients
1/2 cup vegetable shortening
2 Tbsp. flour
1 Tbsp. granulated sugar
2 tsp. vanilla
2 1/2 cups powdered sugar
3 Tbsp. milk

Preheat oven to 400 degrees. In medium bowl stir together flour, sugar, cocoa, baking powder, baking soda, and salt. Add the buttermilk, water, and shortening. Beat with an electric mixer on low speed until combined. Turn up to medium speed, and beat for 2 more minutes. Add the whole egg and yolk, and beat on medium for 2 additional minutes.

Drop by rounded teaspoons on an ungreased cookie sheet, lined with parchment paper, about 2 inches apart. Bake in the oven for 6 minutes or until the top springs back lightly when touched in the center. Remove from the oven and cool on a wire rack.

To make the filling, combine shortening, flour, granulated sugar, and vanilla. Beat on medium speed for 30 seconds. Slowly add 1

1/4 cups of powdered sugar and beat well. Add the milk. Gradually add the remaining powdered sugar. Beat well, until light and fluffy.

To assemble, spoon about 2 teaspoons of the filling onto half the cookies. Top with the remaining cookies and sandwich together.

The employees of Thorndike Press hope you have enjoyed this Large Print book. All our Thorndike, Wheeler, and Kennebec Large Print titles are designed for easy reading, and all our books are made to last. Other Thorndike Press Large Print books are available at your library, through selected bookstores, or directly from us.

For information about titles, please call:
(800) 223-1244

or visit our website at:
gale.com/thorndike

To share your comments, please write:
Publisher
Thorndike Press
10 Water St., Suite 310
Waterville, ME 04901